THE DEAD
MAN SAYS

DON THOMPSON

CONTENTS

BEWARE!

FROM HERE ON INDECENCIES ABOUND

1 BUMPER LOHMAN

Let me tell you about Bumper Lohman. Bumper was a nobody. A nothing. He looked like it. He acted like it. At least so most people who came across him thought. They were not aware that they had met him - had dealt with him - that he existed. He was not the kind of guy most people would pick for anything. How can you pick someone you don't know is there?

It may surprise you to know that Bumper was a lawyer. A nobody, yet he was the managing partner of a large Chicago law firm. Why? Because once Lohman worked with you things started going the way you wished they would in your dreams.

Of course you would take the credit for it, but even so you never wanted Bumper to leave you. Ever. You got things done when he was working for you. You got what you wanted when he was around. You thought he was kind of dull though.

Bumper Lohman did not waste words. He was brief, to the point and without pretense. Like all people who know what they are talking about he could describe his subject matter quickly and clearly with simple words of definite meaning. He didn't use a lot of fancy adjectives and

1

adverbs and did not talk a lot. He did not use the popular new words and phrases. He was done speaking before many people realized he had started. He said what he had to say before anyone knew he was speaking. It was one of his biggest defects. Most people do not listen very well. Especially lawyers. They talk. If you want to tell them something you have to get their attention first. Then you have to tell them you are going to tell them something. Then you have to tell them what you are going to tell them. Then you have to tell it to them. Then you have to tell them you told them something. Then you have to tell them what you told them. Then - they still don't get it. As a result of not doing all these "telling thems" Lohman often found himself trying to communicate with people who seemed unable to hear him.

He had started his own practice soon after graduating from law school and he had spent some years at the lower levels of practice like many other solo and small firm lawyers. One of his first cases was a default divorce. Uncontested with no appearance by the defendant spouse. These cases still have to be proven though, so the plaintiff spouse's lawyer goes through a quick presentation of proof. Without any small talk or introductory chatting, Bumper proved up the case. Quickly. Then he rested. The judge then looked up from papers on the bench and said, "You can begin now counsel."

Bumper had a lot of other defects in addition to concision and brevity. Defects that are really attributes. But defects in that they made it difficult to deal with many people. For one thing he refused to tell clients and other partners dates when something would be done when he did not know when things would be done. Universally in law practice lawyers give dates when they say things will be done. They give these dates to clients, other lawyers and judges. Almost always the dates are wrong. Why shouldn't they be? The lawyers make up the dates.

The Dead Man Says

Tomorrow sells better than next week. It sells better than "I don't know" or "as soon as possible". Lohman doesn't give the dates. He just gets the job done as quickly as possible.

Bumper was a worker bee. A cast member. Never a star. He remembered his father saying to him once, "Whenever I think I've finally hit the big time then I know I'm in trouble." For some reason this thought had been prominent in his mind ever since.

Bumper's father was a dentist with a modest practice. The family lived in a well to do middle class neighborhood of Chicago near the lake called South Shore. They lived away from the lake in a modest house. Bumper went to public schools and worked his way through college and law school. With the help of scholarships he managed to go to Northwestern for college and The University of Chicago Law School.

Most University of Chicago Law School graduates do not practice on their own. But Bumper wanted to try it. He had gone to work for a large law firm right out of school and he found it very difficult to work for the fools who populated the place. So he decided to try it on his own. As with most things, he had made a success of it and built up a fairly large firm on his own. Eventually he merged his firm into a larger firm and that firm, in turn, was merged into an even larger firm.

He was hard working and honest and knew right from wrong and he knew a bad guy when he saw one. Trouble makers are often found in law offices. On both sides of the desk. So he often had to get along with people he didn't want to get along with at all. His mother had told him that you get more flies with honey than with vinegar and he kept trying to apply that principle. Who wants flies to begin with? Well, if you have to get them, use honey. Lohman tried to and as a result he got along with

3

almost everyone.

Lohman was married to Gloria Lohman who basically kept house. They had two children, both of whom were grown and had families of their own. Bumper and Gloria had a big huge Great Dane named Louie to substitute for their missing children. Louie loved everything and everybody and one of Bumper's favorite activities was taking Louie out for a walk. Louie was so friendly that Bumper got to meet and chat with almost everyone they came across. Even the people out walking little fluff buckets who kind of confused Louie. It was one of the few times that Bumper got to practice his small talk, something he knew after all these years that he needed practice at.

2 FENTON, PETTIGREW and COHENSTEIN

Now Bumper was the Managing Partner of Fenton, Pettigrew and Cohenstein. It had about 360 lawyers in offices in Chicago, New York, Los Angeles and Shanghai. Most of the lawyers were in the Chicago office. The firm also had a small office in Highland Park, a North Shore suburb of Chicago. It was a general business firm, meaning it offered most of the legal services that larger businesses required. As you may know, Chicago is a parochial place of little significance, but in that context the firm was of the highest repute.

There were about 50 real partners who were the people who owned the firm's assets and voted as owners of the firm. They were called equity partners. There were also about 100 other lawyers who were called partners, but they were partners in name only. They were lawyers who had advanced within the firm and whose compensation depended in large part on shares of the profits they were assigned. They did not have any right to the profits, but part of their compensation was determined by the profits. They did not vote and did not have a right to any of the assets of the firm if it were liquidated. The rest of the 200 or so lawyers were called associates and were the younger lawyers who were employees. The firm also employed contract lawyers who were paid considerably less than the associates and were assigned to wading through the mounds of documents that are involved in legal matters these days. Mostly documents produced in litigation. They were called contract lawyers because the firm arranged things so they were legally identified as independent contractors rather than employees. The result was that they did not get any benefits, besides being paid a lot less. The partners did not count the contract lawyers in their head count. Most large firms did not. F, P & C didn't even consider them lawyers anyway.

The firm also employed a large number of paralegals, who did the menial tasks that lawyers used to do, and a crew of secretaries and clerks. There were receptionists on each floor who also acted as phone operators. There was a crew of waitresses who tended to the refreshment needs of people using the conference rooms. The lawyers were also backed up by a business office handling the non-legal aspects of running the firm, a copy center staff and an IT department which handled the firm's software and computer systems.

Like most large general business firms, Fenton, Pettigrew tried to hire the top graduates of the top law schools. There were so many large firms around that they did not always get the best graduates, but they got a lot of them. The contract lawyers were generally graduates of the lesser law schools. The associates could look forward to becoming partners someday. The contract lawyers couldn't even look forward to meeting a partner. The partners and associates all referred to the firm as Fenton, Pettigrew. The contract lawyers called the firm F, P & C and sometimes Fart, Pee and Crap.

The firm generally billed its clients for the hours spent by its lawyers on the clients' matters. The main job of everyone in the firm was to produce billable hours. The more hours a lawyer billed, the more money brought in for the partners. You kept your job by producing hours. You did not get to be a partner by doing that though. You got to be a partner by bringing in clients who could pay for all those hours. It was a lot easier to bill hours than it was to find clients to pay for them.

The equity partners as a group theoretically ran the firm. They voted in proportion to their ownership of the firm. A handful of the equity partners had over 50% of the ownership. There were nine of them and they were the members of the Management Committee. The Management Committee in practice ran the firm. Needless to say these nine lawyers were the highest paid in the firm and generally generated the most business. Lohman was an equity partner and part of the Management Committee. He was the one with the lowest ownership percentage. He handled the day to day business of the firm and had all the problems delegated to him.

The head of the Committee and Chairman of the firm was Graybourne St. Charles. He was a snob's snob. His childhood nickname was Graybee. Few people called him that, although everyone knew it was his childhood nickname. His partners mostly called him Grabby, at least behind his back. His arrogance was matched only by his ignorance. He was a pompous idiot given to quoting himself for authority. He started many of his sentences with, "As I have often said," or "As I have said many times... ." Curiously enough this works with many people.

St. Charles represented the firm's largest and oldest client group. This was the Swifton family and all their varied interests, including Swifton Corporation, a large international conglomerate. The group had many businesses and multitudes of legal entities to deal with. The Swifton Corporation started out making farm machinery and by early in the 20th Century was the largest company in the world. It branched out into meat packing and the allied businesses. While all this was going on the family members invested in banks, oil and gas, mining and farming. Now its biggest single business was one of the largest banks in the world. Other large businesses the family controlled were engaged in making trucks, selling packaged foods and household products, oil and gas exploration and owning and managing shopping centers and other real estate. There were numerous other smaller businesses. So many that the family members were continually being surprised by what they found out they owned.

The Swifton family and the Swifton Corporation were headed by Arthur Swifton, known as Swifty to those of his friends who knew he liked the implication of cleverness he thought that nickname carried. Those who did not know him so well used Arty. He liked that name too, since he prided himself on being a patron of the arts. Swifty loved large parties and he held them frequently and invited all the important contacts of the Swifton businesses. The family and Corporation used these affairs to network. Some of the top Fenton, Pettigrew lawyers were usually in attendance and they used the events the same way, as did everyone else there.

Fenton, Pettigrew also had a Vice Chairman. This was Zenon Cohenstein. Cohenstein had built up a large firm on his own and was a hard charging aggressive business getter. He represented a large stable of medium sized businesses and one very large client too. His firm had merged with Fenton, Pettigrew about twenty years ago. At that time Fenton, Pettigrew was an old line firm going nowhere and Cohenstein's firm was on the way up. He wanted to cash in with the higher income that goes with larger firms and they wanted to stay alive.

St. Charles went back to the old days when large firms were either not Jewish or were Jewish. None were mixed. The very old days. In time this had changed, especially when Jewish and non-Jewish firms realized that more money could be made by merging. In the past, before the merger, the firm had been called Fenton, Pettigrew, Sidley and Lord and held itself out as being populated by lawyers of superior social standing and lineage. They were old line, waspy and anti-Semitic. They were the world's biggest snobs with the world's least reason to be so. If you had told them they were snobs, they would have thanked you for noticing. Cohenstein was a first generation American whose immigrant parents had started out with a push cart in the Ghetto. He used bad language, had an accent and went to a night law school of little repute. The lawyers in his firm were known as money grubbers. The St. Charles faction were money grubbers too, but did not admit to it and managed to avoid being labeled as such. The two firms merged for money, not compatibility. The St. Charles faction still called the Cohenstein faction new arrivals with much sniffery and ruffling of feathers.

The St. Charles faction was not happy that Cohenstein was added to the firm name. Firm names are fertile grounds for argument amongst partners. They would all like the firm name to contain their name, preferably first. If not first, at least their name should be part of the firm name. But firms with hundreds of lawyers cannot put every partner's name on the marquee. The matter is often settled by using the names of long gone partners. Fenton and Pettigrew were the lawyers who started the firm in the 1880's. They had both died by 1930. Fenton, Pettigrew was an old and venerable name and the firm kept it. A few other names were added over the years, but eventually all had died and no more were added. Sidley and Lord had both died by 1970. After that only dead names were on the marquee. So it had been for years. Each and every partner could imply that he alone was the leading light of the firm that way. And then came Cohenstein.

Technically his name was part of the firm name, but in reality no one was going to actually say it out loud. Just Fenton, Pettigrew.

St. Charles looked the part he acted. He was distinguished looking, dressed expensively and spoke with a slightly upper class English accent. His family, to hear him tell it, had been at the top of the social ladder for years. He pretended to be of ancient English heritage and hinted at noble ancestry, but he never gave specifics. His father had run the firm and was the lead lawyer for the Swiftons and Graybourne essentially inherited the client. He was somewhat of an old boy fraternity brother type and had barely scraped through a minimally respectable law school. At least he did not hold himself out as being the best of lawyers. Most of the dumb ones do. He, however, was not even aware that there were differences in legal abilities. He was very aware of the differences in social rank though and at his level that is what counted.

St. Charles restricted his attention to his share of the profits. Everything else he delegated, which was a good thing since he could screw up anything. He was like a successful politician. Many people think politicians are incompetent. They are not. They are eminently competent at getting elected and staying in office. That was St. Charles' job and he did it well. He was also adept at bringing in new business. Part of his abilities in this regard depended on his complete legal incompetence. He would tell prospective clients whatever they wanted to hear, largely because he was unmindful of that fact that it was neither true nor likely to happen.

Lohman was part of the firm because he had built up his own firm that merged into Fenton, Pettigrew. He was known to have a knack for managing a law firm, so he was made the Managing Partner, reporting to the Management Committee. He was adept at handling the problems that arose in a law firm and with a lot of lawyers you get a lot of problems. He handled the day to day management, like a chief operating officer in a corporation. On top of this he also maintained his own practice.

Lohman's clients were mostly medium sized businesses. Most

large law firms depended for most of their money on very large businesses that required hordes of lawyers to work on their matters. These companies had their own legal departments, but sent matters requiring special talent or more lawyers than they had to outside firms where they thought those talents or lawyers were to be found. Lohman had some of this business, but most of his billings came from medium sized businesses where he had personal relationships with the owners rather than just the heads of the legal department. They sent business to him because they thought he was a good lawyer period, not because they thought he was the world's greatest expert in a specific area. They knew he could always find specific expertise from other lawyers in his firm.

The firm also had someone called a Business Manager who was not a lawyer. This was Geeley McDade who was an experienced executive. He handled a lot of the administrative and housekeeping issues and directly managed the non-legal staff. He handled many issues relating to the lawyers too, such as getting them paid, among other things. He also devoted time to the general marketing of the firm. After all, law is a business, not a profession and the only thing that counts is how much money you bring in.

Fenton, Pettigrew was located in the Swifton building at One Swifton Plaza. The family's bank, The Swifton Bank, was located there. One Swifton Plaza was a large building occupying a whole block in the middle of downtown Chicago. It was katty corner from the Federal court house and near other federal buildings. It was two blocks from the county court house. The building occupied the south half of the block and a plaza occupied the north half. This plaza was across the street from another half block plaza belonging to another large bank that occupied the north half of that lot. One Swifton Plaza was taller and newer.

That other bank was a branch of a large New York bank. Its building had originally been built by one of the largest Chicago banks, but the large Chicago banks had all been acquired by out of state banks. In the past Illinois prohibited branch banking so its banks could not expand like the out of state banks did. Eventually Illinois allowed branch banking, but by that time the large out of state banks were much larger and they acquired all the large Illinois banks. The Swiftons, however, had been expanding outside of Illinois. They had interests in a mid-sized Chicago bank and a whole lot of small Illinois banks too. When the time came they put all these together into a bank as huge as all the others and called it the Swifton Bank. They owned a minority interest, but a big enough one to give them effective control.

The only occupants of Swifton Plaza were the bank and some of its allied entities, the family offices and Fenton, Pettigrew. Other Swifton entities were scattered around Chicago and its suburbs and elsewhere in the world. The building was 85 stories tall. The bank was on the lower floors. The law firm occupied 15 floors in the middle of the building. Above that were the family offices and more bank offices - the ones where the view counted. On top was the Bank's private dining club where it entertained its customers. Certain partners of the law firm and senior executives of allied Swifton entities also used it.

The firm's offices used the building elevators, but there was a private elevator connecting all the firm's floors for those with privileges to use it and three of the floors were connected by a grand staircase rising up from the firm's reception area. The reception area was much larger that it needed to be and served as a showcase for the firm's art collection. The collection was selected from among artists the firm's clients would know were expensive. This was backed up with books and pamphlets distributed around the area which described the artists and their work and described auction and other prices for the artists' works.

The reception room was three stores high. At each level a walkway surrounded it. These walkways led to the staircase. Meeting rooms were arranged around the walkways. Law firms need a lot of rooms larger than the individual offices for groups of various sizes to meet. In a lot of firms this area was called a conference center or something equally pretentious. The firm had refreshments and other services provided to the conference rooms. A crew of waitresses and clerks staffed the conference rooms to see to the needs of the users.

In recent times lawyers had started conducting meetings of only two people in the conference rooms. Lawyers offices are very often piled high with papers and do not always give a good impression, or so the lawyers think. You would not expect the Nizam of Hyderabad to meet people in such a place so why should a lawyer who thinks of himself as being on the same level, higher really, meet people in such a hovel? One might think the answer is that they want a lawyer, not the Nizam. However, the people who run things and decide what lawyer is going to be hired are generally not aware that lawyers work and certainly do not think a lawyer's work involves papers all over the place. After all, those who run things have people to do that sort of thing for them and expect the people they deal with to have similar aides at their disposal. They certainly don't meet with the aides in their office hovels, or anywhere unless absolutely necessary.

The partners' offices were distributed throughout the firm. An effort was made to locate people who often worked together with each other, but this was not always possible since the most important thing was giving the people with more clout the offices they wanted. (Clout is a Chicago term meaning not quite kosher influence). The equity and other higher ranking partners generally got the corner offices. St. Charles and Cohenstein were on the highest of the firm's floors. There was a reception area near the elevators on their floor. At opposite ends of the floor each had his suite. Each suite had a reception area where there was a secretary. There were separate doors from this area to the partner's office and to his own conference room. The office and conference room both had separate doors to the hallway. The two top partners' offices were at corners of the building and were rather large compared to other partners' offices. Most of the other Management Committee partners also had offices on the top floor.

Lohman had an office on the fourth floor of the firm. He wanted to be more in the middle of things. Lohman's office had 25 feet of windows. It was about 15 feet deep. It was unusually large because of his duties. It had lots of shelves and table space. There was a small conference table at one end. His desk was at the other end. Most surfaces in it were piled with papers and files. The art work on the walls was selected by the interior decorators who the firm hired and was not particularly to his taste. However, he did not care to spend his time on interior decoration and he had got used to the art. For the same reason he used the standard firm furniture, although members of the Management Committee got decorating allowances and were permitted to arrange for furnishing their offices to their own taste. The only thing that might distinguish his office from another lawyer's junior to him was its size and a television set. His windows looked north over the Swifton plaza and that of the adjoining bank. Beyond that, other skyscrapers blocked much of his view. This suited Lohman because he found the activity on the plazas much more interesting than the imposing view of buildings one could get on higher floors. Since he was the Managing Partner there was also a large conference room adjacent to his office.

3 WEDNESDAY, JUNE 8th, 2011 - FIRM PROBLEMS

Early on a Wednesday morning in mid-June this plant was up and running. The factory was churning out billable hours and the sales force was selling the hours to clients in supposed need of them for tidy amounts per hour. Additional flat fees were added for excellence in performance. At base fees of $300 to $950 per hour you would think excellence was already being paid for. But this is not for ordinary people to inquire into. As with Mr. Goldman and Mr. Sachs, those who are truly deserving must be paid or the whole world will disappear. The real key to the matter is that large businesses were the clients. These businesses are run and controlled by hired management. Not the stockholders. Not the owners. Hired management wants to hire and associate with the best and, after all, it is not their money that is being paid. And the more you pay people you hire, the more important you are and the more you must be paid. Yes, Fenton, Pettigrew was moving along just fine.

Lohman was in his office going over billing reports for his clients when his secretary told him one of the associates wanted to see him. Ordinarily you can tell who is a lawyer and who is not a lawyer by whether you can get a hold of him, on the phone or otherwise. If someone will never return your phone calls or meet with you, then you know he is a bona fide lawyer. Lohman, however, got things done and if you wanted him you got him. The associate was John Sweeney and Lohman cringed. There were so many people around the firm. He didn't know them all very well, but he knew Sweeney. Sweeney had the manners of a toad on crack. He was, like, an exaggerated example of the modern hey dude, wasssup generation. He almost always had a backpack slung over one shoulder that looked like it contained about ten cinder blocks. If he didn't have a smart phone plastered up against his ear, he had his nose in the device and was fiddling with it. So far as Lohman knew Sweeney had sex with the thing. Lohman was not thrilled with Sweeney's use of the device. Sweeney was not the only one of his type in the firm and Lohman was trying to learn how to deal with them. Sweeney was different from most of them in one way. He got things done right and on time. Lohman found him actually easier to deal with than most of the rest. Since Lohman had Sweeney working with him a lot he was also using him to get acclimated to the new generation.

Sweeney also had one great advantage in the firm. He was beginning to bring in substantial business from internet and entertainment types. He was on the fast track to partnership. Fenton, Pettigrew knew excellence when they saw it.

So Sweeney comes in and Lohman is like, "Hey!" and Sweeney goes "Hey!"

This was as far as Lohman could go. He did not know the newspeak. He said, "Hey what?" Sweeney explained that an equity partner who he was doing some work for had objected to some of his pro bono work and had sent him to Lohman to resolve the matter. "Pro bono" came from Latin words meaning "for the good of". There was another word in the original phrase meaning "the republic", but lawyers only used the "for the good of" part. Who cares for who's good. What pro bono meant in modern day large law firms was work done for free. Lawyers from the firms, usually younger ones, got involved in noble and deserving matters for free. The younger lawyers never really got a chance to do anything outside a narrow area and their experience was very limited. Eventually, after many years of practice, they could claim to be the world's leading authority on the left side of the period in jury instructions under Section 12.16 of the Business Corporation Act. Letting them do pro bono work was a way of giving them experience they otherwise would not get. Also, these younger lawyers often wanted to get involved in these matters to advance what they saw as noble causes.

The partner who had sent Sweeney was Ellis Kirkland, a highly placed older equity partner whose practice was concentrated in the intellectual property area or IP for short. It used to be called patent, trademark and copyright. Then the name evolved to intellectual property. Apparently the patents got smart. Kirkland's clients had a lot of work in these areas. They also had a great variety of general legal work which Kirkland acted as lead lawyer on. Many of the clients were located in the north and northwest suburbs of Chicago and the Milwaukee and south east Wisconsin area so Kirkland used the Highland Park office a lot. Within the firm this was called the Lake County office. Kirkland was one of the St. Charles snob faction. Kirkland did not think Sweeney should be getting involved in a particular pro bono case and he was the one who had sent him to Lohman. Kirkland had called Lohman about it in advance.

Lohman said, "I know. Ellis says he wants you out of a pro bono matter you're handling." Lohman asked Sweeney about the case. Sweeney said, "Shit man, he never likes anything I do. All he cares about is money and the fuckin' dude can't even count much. He just wants me to bill more time on his files. I'm billing all the hours I can. I gotta sleep. Besides he creeps me out. You know what he told me the other day when he told me to ignore a court order to produce some papers? I asked him, don't the rules require us to produce? He said, 'Rules are for losers. Let the losers abide by them.' He's nothing but a weasely hyena."

Lohman couldn't agree more, but he said, "It's wise to keep our comments about those we associate with positive." There. He was on record as not approving.

Sweeney told Lohman the client was at a post card collectors' show where one of the dealers gave a kid free postcards and told the kid that would help start him a collection. The client then asked for free cards too and the dealer did not give him any. The collector had filed an age discrimination claim with the EEOC and now he wanted to go to court with it. Kirkland did not like pro bono work and did not like any age discrimination claim and did not like plaintiffs generally, except when a client of his was one. He could not even think of dealing with idiocy like this so he sent Sweeney to Lohman.

Lohman was a little surprised too. Sweeney ordinarily had some sense. Lohman asked, "Why are you representing someone who has money to collect post cards for free?"

Sweeney said, "He doesn't have anything, Dude. He's an old guy who came with his son who was taking care of him for the day. His son's the collector, man. Son's got 150,000 cards he says. Know how much they are worth? $75,000 or even $150,000 if sold to dealers and maybe $750,000 when sold by the dealers. At least that's what the son says."

"Why do you want to waste your time on this?" Lohman asked.

Sweeney admitted that it was a crock, but he said there technically may be a violation and he wanted to learn something about the area and about trying a case in court which he had never done and would never do on his own for years, or probably ever in a large firm. He told Lohman that he took the case in the first place because a rock show producer he knows asked him to. Sweeney was trying to get the producer's business.

The Dead Man Says

"What's going on in the case?" asked Lohman.

"We filed with the EEOC about a month ago. We named the dealer as well as the post card club hosting the show as respondents. The respondents made an offer to settle, but the claimant wants big bucks."

"It figures," said Lohman. "Does he have any actual damages?"

"Not really," said Sweeney. "These post card people are weird. I went out there to take a look at one of their shows. They hold it in an American Legion hall that has a big room. They have tables all over with boxes of cards set up on them and the dealers sit behind the tables. The potential customers go around and look at the cards. They're kinda strange people."

"You could probably say that about collectors of most things," said Lohman. "Do you collect anything?"

"What do you mean by that?" asked Sweeney.

"Just asking," said Lohman.

Then Lohman said, "That reminds me of a discrimination case I had a while ago. It involved the office at Great Lakes Iron and Steel. There was a lady there who was pregnant - in the later stages and quite big in the belly. Her manager kept calling her Ms. Fullabella. Naturally an EEOC claim was filed. The odd thing was that her name actually was Ms. Fullabella. But she wasn't complaining. A co-worker was complaining. Another lady who complained of sexual harassment because she had to hear this all day long."

"So what happened?" asked Sweeney.

The Dead Man Says

"Settled for $5000 I think," said Lohman.

"Wow Dude!" said Sweeney. "Why? I woulda dumped on her."

Lohman considered this. Did Sweeney mean he would have shit on her? Did he mean he would have defended the client with all the firm's considerable resources, thus making things difficult for the lady and her lawyer? Not to get into. He replied, "It's in the best interest of the client to settle most things. Also the hearing examiner was a pregnant lady who seemed rather sympathetic to the claimant."

Lohman concluded the meeting by saying Sweeney could do it and he would take care of Kirkland. Lohman then said, "I'll speak to Ellis about it. In the future, try to remember that he's from the last century so try to speak to him in English. You might get along with him better that way."

"You mean Olde English," said Sweeney. Throughout the entire conversation Sweeney had been fiddling on his phone and looking at things on the screen. On his way out he said, "You go Pops!" This was sort of an improvement. Usually Sweeney called Lohman Bumpy.

Lohman wondered what this would lead to. He had sent Sweeney over to court once on a minor matter and Sweeney had told the judge, "If this is a court, you are a kangaroo." The judge cited Sweeney for contempt and was going to go after the firm. Lohman had to send the firm's fixer to deal with the judge, which the fixer did by reminding the judge of how much the firm and its clients contributed to his campaign fund.

Lohman remembered talking to Sweeney later about how to behave in court. He remembered telling Sweeney that he had almost gotten the whole firm disbarred. He remembered what Sweeney had said. "Yo Dude! When you're disbarred you're barred from practicing. How come when you're barred you're called disbarred?" Sweeney did however let Lohman know that he understood what Lohman was trying to tell him. Anyway, Lohman generally wished he could get away with what Sweeney did.

The fixer was Bungus LaRue. He was held out to clients as being a maven in the government affairs area. That is how law firms referred to their lobbyists. LaRue was such a maven, but he backed it up with a little spiff and covert machinations. Bungus was no friend of Kirkland. Kirkland was trying to get him kicked out of the firm because of his background. Bungus was a former congressman of low origin who had gone to a night law school. He had been disbarred once, but the firm managed to get the ruling reversed. He was politically connected and often operated through third party lawyers. The client or whoever needed the appropriate "government affairs" would be referred to the third party lawyer who would collect an exorbitant fee. A lot of the fee was used to make a pay-off to the appropriate people. This way Fenton, Pettigrew had clean hands and could claim they knew nothing about the bribe. Bungus also worked extensively with campaign contributions. In Illinois, at least, politicians were of the opinion that it was legal to take campaign contributions for personal expenses so long as they were declared as income. Hence bribery was legal, at least if the recipient held elective office.

Kirkland knew that LaRue had fixed some of Kirkland's cases, but Kirkland did not want to be associated with such a low life anymore. Kirkland felt that his stature and skill were primarily responsible for the results in those cases. Bungus had told Lohman earlier that Kirkland was trying to blackmail him. Basically Kirkland was trying to get Bungus to resign from the firm and was threatening to turn him in if he didn't. Bungus didn't give Lohman any of the details, but he did assert that he did nothing wrong. Campaign contributions are moral and legal as are referrals to other lawyers.

4 THE CHAIRMAN AND THE POOFSTER

Just then Lohman was called to St. Charles' office. He went up to see him. St. Charles had come to Lohman's office once, but found the venture so distasteful that he would not repeat it. He had entered, took a look around, and had sniffed and said, "It looks like someone works in here. Can't you do something about that?"

Lohman entered St. Charles' office suite and nodded to St. Charles' secretary who said, "Mr. St. Charles is expecting you Mr. Lohman."

He then went to the door to St. Charles' office. He reached for the door handle and the door opened in front of him. The most delightful and beautiful young Asian woman came through it saying over her shoulder, "Right away Mr. St. Charles."

Lohman could hear St. Charles saying, "Excellent, excellent, my dear. I'll see you soon."

Lohman didn't know who the woman was, but he assumed it was one of the new summer hires. The firm hired law students each summer in hopes of getting a leg up on hiring them later. St. Charles liked to have the young and pretty female ones assigned to him.

St. Charles office was large. The largest. You could tell from it that he was important. It was furnished in traditional and expensive style and the art works were all of the most expensive sort. Interspersed with the art were framed degrees and certificates and licenses. Fully half the wall space though was covered with pictures of famous people, usually with some sort of language addressed to St. Charles. There were no files or papers anywhere. St. Charles did not touch paper or files. Subordinates did that for him and did it out of his sight. Zenon Cohenstein was there. Cohenstein was standing up behind St. Charles' desk and looking out the window when Lohman came in. St. Charles was seated at his desk.

"Good morning Graybourne," said Lohman as he sat next to St. Charles' desk. Upon being seated he looked at Cohenstein and said, "Good morning Zenon."

Cohenstein said, "'Morning Bumper. Did you get a look at Miss Suckagoya?"

"Who?" asked St. Charles. "I thought her name was Emily. Chan, I think."

"Well," said Cohenstein, "You're a Goy."

St. Charles just straightened up and stood there speechless. Finally he said, "That's not funny, especially considering what we asked Bumper here for today."

Watching over all this impassively was St. Charles' cat which was often found on a pedestal to the side of and behind St. Charles' desk chair. Yes, St. Charles had a cat in the office. At least he didn't have any mice.

Cohenstein looked at Lohman and said, "Anyway Bumper, good morning."

St. Charles said with a sniff, "It could be, but we have a problem. It has come to my attention that there are rumors circulating around the firm that one of the male file clerks is making advances of a sexual nature

24

to other males in the firm." His lip pulled up at the left and his eyes narrowed when he said this. "What do you think about that Lohman?"

Lohman asked, "Who is he hitting on, who is complaining?"

"What is 'hitting on'?" asked St. Charles.

"What you are describing," said Lohman.

"Well I didn't say anything about physical violence," said St. Charles.

"It's newspeak," said Lohman.

"Well don't speak new here." St. Charles looked out the window.

"Who?" reminded Lohman. "I haven't had any complaints. Firm policy says they are supposed to complain to my office."

St. Charles said, "The matter is largely confidential, but I hear the offender is one Jason Kunz who I understand is one of our file clerks. That's all I can tell you. I cannot betray a confidence." With St. Charles, everything was confidential. If you were him you probably would not tell people what you were up to either. In any event, so far as St. Charles was concerned, he ran things. He did not answer questions or inform people of anything. He told people what to do. Period.

St. Charles said, "I want this conduct stopped. I am appalled that such a thing could occur at this firm. My firm. What will people think if this gets out? People are going to think we are a bunch of fairies. This isn't like the normal sort of sexual intrigue in the work place. When that sort of thing gets out it can be good PR. It adds to the allure of the work place. At least it is good PR when it comes to hiring young people if it involves boys and girls. But I do not want any queer stuff going on at Fenton, Pettigrew." Whenever he mentioned the firm name he would straighten up and try to look even more dignified that usual, which usual level of dignity he thought very high indeed.

Cohenstein told Lohman, "Get on it Bumper. I could care less about this kind of thing, but I don't want to spend time on it. And I don't want any bad PR. And while you're at it get out a press release about Graybourne's little girls."

St. Charles shot him a dagger stare.

"Just joking," said Cohenstein.

Lohman thought for a moment about all the sexual harassment complaints he got. He had begun to think that everyone in the firm was a sex maniac. He did not seem to be getting through to them about what the danger was.

Lohman said, "There might be a sexual harassment problem if the firm doesn't do anything about it. I'll look into it."

St. Charles reminded Lohman and Cohenstein that the problem went far deeper than that. He went on about filth and depravity. He stated that in the past the firm did not have any of these types around. Cohenstein snorted and said, "Not that you knew of."

Lohman asked St. Charles again, "Who did you say told you this? It's kind of hard to track down what is going on without knowing who to ask about it." He suspected Kunz had turned down some old queen in the firm who then complained about Kunz. He said, "You know it is fairly common to get these kinds of complaints from old guys who are hitting on younger women in the firm. They claim the women are hitting on men in the firm and make them out to be the sexual aggressors. Sometimes they claim the women are hitting on them. The complaints are like a preemptive strike. Complain about the women before they complain about you, as it were. After all, we have a bunch of lawyers here. One legal principle is that the best defense is a good offense. And my experience is that a lot of these cases illustrate the principle that it is often the wrongdoer who first cries foul."

"Meaning what?" asked St. Charles. "What do chickens have to do with it?"

Lohman spelled out, "F-o-u-l."

St. Charles responded, "Oh. But I don't think any baseball is involved."

Lohman knew enough to avoid playing word games with St. Charles. St. Charles wasn't playing. Or even on the field.

Lohman was beginning to wonder if Kunz selected St. Charles for the foul deed. "Never mind," he replied. "It's just easier if we know who is the complaining party. Then I can ask him what happened."

St. Charles straightened and said, "I never betray a confidence. Besides, I told you what is going on." Then he said, "Enough of that. Do you know where Ellis is? Zenon and I were supposed to meet him this morning to discuss a somewhat sensitive matter."

"No," said Lohman. "What sensitive matter? Another sexual harassment claim?"

"One is enough," said St. Charles. "No, this involves Swifton. Someone at a subsidiary has supposedly been caught trying to hack into a competitor's computer system to get customer pricing information. We wanted to get his expertise in the IP area. He was supposed to be here half an hour ago. His secretary doesn't know where he is."

Lohman was well aware that any expertise from Kirkland would come in the form of some junior lawyer who would attend the meeting. Kirkland may have had extensive experience in the area and superior skill and judgment, but he usually carried it in someone else's head. In any event, with all those top partners in the conference there would be a bill fest, and nobody wanted to delay that.

5 KIRKLAND WAS KONKED ON TUESDAY, JUNE 7th 2011.

Lohman went back to his office and resumed working on the billing records. He hadn't even got settled when his secretary came in and told him that Kirkland had been found dead in the Lake County office. He had apparently been dead in his office all morning with the door closed. The doors were usually kept closed there and Kirkland had not been expected there this morning. The only reason he had been found was that a secretary, Jean Bean, had gone to his office to get a file. The office manager was called in and took one look at the scene and called the cops. The cops told her to do nothing till they got there. After calling them she called Lohman's office.

Lohman's secretary was Tina Goblat. Tete was her nickname. She was 6 feet tall and weighed almost 220 pounds. Her wrists were like a man's ankles. She made Golda Meir, the former Prime Minister of Israel, look like a sissy. She talked like a punch drunk boxer and called everyone "Hon". She often showed up on Monday morning with cuts and bruises and even black eyes. If she didn't like you she starred straight in your eyes and didn't say a thing. She was the perfect secretary for Lohman because everyone did everything she said, or at least they said they would. She was a great aid in running the firm. She was married to a little shrimp and everyone thought he must be beating her, although they wondered how.

Lohman was curious too, but he had the will power not to ask. Some things he did not want to know. He remembered his days in the legal aid office at his law school when he met his first divorce client. She was a big woman who wanted a divorce on the grounds of physical cruelty   He had asked her what happened and she said her husband had hit her. Then Lohman asked, "What did you do then?"

The lady answered, "I threw him out the window."

Tete said, "Call Beth. Kirkland's dead." Beth was Beth Morse, the Lake County office manager.

"What!" exclaimed Lohman. "What happened? Heart attack?"

"Probably not," said Tete. "Call Beth."

Lohman called Beth and said, "Beth, its Bumper."

"Oh, hello," she said.

"What happened?" asked Lohman.

She said, "Mr. Kirkland's dead. Jean went to the office he was using to get a file this morning. The door was closed. As you know we usually keep the office doors closed overnight. She went in when there was no answer after knocking and she found him dead, sprawled on the floor. She came screaming out of there and I went in and took a look. He was spread out on the floor with a lot of blood around him. There was a bust and dagger from the waiting room by his body. I suppose he had been there all morning while we were just a few feet away from him. I called the police."

"Are they there now?" asked Lohman

"No," she said. They came and went over the office and inspected the rest of the place. They wanted to take some of the papers on his desk, but I wouldn't let them. I told them the papers could contain client information and were protected by the attorney-client privilege. They sealed the room after a truck came and took away the body. There were a lot of police there off and on and they took pictures of everything and they interviewed everyone."

"Did they tell you anything?" asked Lohman.

"No," she said. "Just that the office was sealed and off limits. They asked who runs the firm and I referred them to you. They will probably contact you soon."

"Is there anything else you can tell me," asked Lohman.

"No. That's about it," she said. "Oh, his car is still here."

Lohman went out to Tete's desk and said, "Did she tell you the details?"

"Not much," said Tete. "She just said he had been found with a bust and dagger and the cops came and the place is sealed. Pain in the butt. We have enough to do. You know there are some people who are going to be glad he's gone."

"Speak no ill of the dead," said Lohman facetiously.

"So I can't say anything?" she replied.

Tete and Lohman then began working on redoing his schedule for the afternoon.

6 THE COPS SAY HOW KIRKLAND GOT KONKED

While Tete and Lohman were redoing his schedule the phone rang. Tete answered and told Lohman a Detective O'Malley of the Highland Park police was calling. He took the call and O'Malley asked him if he was the firm manager. Lohman said he was and O'Malley said he wanted to set up a meeting right away, but he wouldn't say about what. Lohman made an appointment with O'Malley for the afternoon.

Wednesday afternoon Detective O'Malley came in with a Sargent Fricknoodleh from the Lake County Sheriff's office. They exchanged greetings and pleasantries and then O'Malley said, "We're here about your partner Ellis Kirkland. I suppose you know about what happened?"

Lohman said, "I know he was found dead in our Lake County office this morning. I don't know much else."

O'Malley said, "It was probably a homicide and it probably happened last night. It looks like he had been hit over the head and stabbed. The murder weapons appear to be a marble bust and a dagger. What the office manager calls a ceremonial dagger. Maybe he had tea with someone shortly before it happened. There were two used tea cups on his desk with some other tea fixings. The medical examiner is still working on the body so we don't know the details yet. I hear you're the boss here so we want to find out what is going on in this firm from you."

Lohman said, "The boss I'm not. I report to the firm's Management Committee. I've got my own bosses. I am called the Managing Partner, which means I'm sort of the head manager in carrying out what the Committee decides. I don't have much to tell you about what happened, because I wasn't there and I haven't heard much about it. Just what our office manager there told me."

O'Malley said, "The office manager says the bust came from the waiting room. She says she doesn't know anything about it. There's still another one in the waiting room. Do you know anything about it? They look like Indians."

Lohman said, "I don't know much about them. They're part of the firm's art collection. Apparently one is CaCaPoo who was chief of the Kickapoos who inhabited this region when the Europeans came. Or was it Kickapoo who was chief of the CaCaPoos? I think it was CaCaPoo who was chief. Anyway the other bust is his squaw CaCaGooma."

"His wife?" asked O'Malley.

"I don't think they had marriage," said Lohman. "I'm not up on Indian things. All I've ever heard is squaw. Does it matter?"

"No," said O'Malley. "Are you serious? CaCaGooma? CaCaPoo?"

"Well," Lohman said, "that's what the head of the firm told me. Graybourne St. Charles. Ask him." Then he asked, "Which one hit him?"

"Must have been the squaw," said O'Malley. "The one with the necklace."

"That's the guy, I think," said Lohman.

"So," said Fricknoodleh, "once again we are seeing that we Indians are here first and you ones should get the Green Cards." He started laughing.

They started asking Lohman general questions about the firm.

33

Lohman told them who to see about what. O'Malley asked, "Who is usually there? I understand a lot of people use it part time."

Lohman said, "Yes. Only a few of our partners have their regular offices there. The rest of the offices are used by whoever needs the office at the moment. People who have litigation in Lake County or want to meet with someone who would find that office more convenient use it. Some of our semi-retired partners use it part time because they live up there. Mr. Kirkland used it a lot because he needed to see a lot of people north and northwest. Of the people who did not have a regular office there, he used it the most."

Lohman went on, "Monahan O'Reilley is a semi-retired partner who uses it daily. He has his own office there. The active partners who have their own offices there and practice up there are Gloria Nagelberg and Gerry Ruckus. They do almost exclusively litigation in Lake County. Two associates also have their own offices there and they work with Ms. Nagelberg and Mr. Ruckus. Lee Stein and Chen Liou -- those are the ones. Apart from that we have a regular crew of secretaries up there, Ms. Morse, the office manager, a receptionist, one clerk and one paralegal. Do you have the information on them?"

Fricknoodleh inserted, "We are having it."

"How can we find out who is there when?" asked O'Malley.

"Not easy," answered Lohman. "All you can do is ask people and look at the time and billing records. Those records don't usually say where the work was done, but you can sometimes tell. The office is automatically locked by our computer system at 5 p.m.. Anyone who wants to get in after that either has to ring the bell and be admitted or use their individual code on a key pad next to the door. This same system is used at all our offices and the computer keeps a record of who entered and when. As you know, some of these security systems get quite involved, but everyone has them these days, although I don't know why. There is no such thing as security, witness what happened here. However, when enough of the law abiding people are inconvenienced enough by what they call security, they feel safe."

Lohman caught himself and stopped before he went into a harangue on the subject. He did resent, however, that as 1739* he could get into the Lake County office at night and the firm's toilets, but as Bumper Lohman, the Managing Partner, he could not.

O'Malley asked, "Does the computer tell us if the door is opened? How about the windows? Does it tell us if the windows are opened?"

Lohman paused and thought. "I don't think the windows open. It's one of those new buildings." He was raised in an era when buildings had windows that opened. "I don't know about the doors."

The firm occupied all of a two story building. The space consisted of offices around a central 2 story reception and stair area. There were 15 lawyer's offices, 4 conference rooms and a small library. There were individual secretarial areas outside 5 of the offices that were occupied by lawyers who had their own offices there. There was also a central secretarial area and an office for the office manager.

Lohman explained, "The firm's computer tracks all calls and keeps a record of the phone numbers where the calls came from and the numbers where they went as well as the times of the calls. The computer can even record the calls, although that is done only with the knowledge and consent of all parties to the call."

Sargent Fricknoodleh then asked, "And is Mr. Kirkland having any enemies in the firm? Are there any bad things going on with him here? Is anyone having any resentments about him?"

Lohman looked innocent and said, "No.   Nothing out of the ordinary. In a firm this size you always have someone getting on someone else's nerves, but that is normal." What he thought to himself was, "God! No one liked him. Was there anyone who really disliked him more than all the others?"

Sargent Fricknoodleh said, "So be reviewing this issue and let us know of what you come up with."

The officers then told Lohman they had heard law firms keep the billing records he had referred to that show things that people are doing and when. Lohman explained that all the lawyers and paralegals kept records of their time and what they were doing during that time. He explained how these people entered the information on the firm's computer system and that the information was then used for billing the clients. He explained that each person's system for recording time varied. Some used paper and entered the information on the computer later. Some entered the time directly into the computer. He also explained that some people recorded the time as they spent it. Others did so later, perhaps at the end of the day, so the exact times may not be entirely accurate. He told them the firm could not release the records to them because they contained confidential information about client affairs and to release them would violate the firm's duty of confidentiality to its clients.

"Yeah?" said O'Malley in a not satisfied tone. "Same thing we were told about the papers in Kirkland's office. We want to see them."

"Well, if you got a court order you could," said Lohman. It's not that we want to keep them from you, but the attorney-client privilege is not ours to waive. It belongs to the client."

"We will be seeing," said Fricknoodleh.

Lohman called the firm's IT manager, Henner Pigman, and asked him to come to Lohman's office. When Pigman arrived Lohman introduced the officers to him and told Henner to cooperate with them. Lohman also asked if the firm's computer kept track of door openings or window openings at the Lake County office. The answer was no. Henner was pleased as punch to show his systems to the officers. Henner had been trained to keep client confidences, but Lohman reminded him again. The officers left with Pigman to go to his office and find out more about the computer system.

Lohman then called a junior partner named Joe DiBello who Lohman usually found capable and cooperative. "Joe," he said, "I want you to do me a favor. You can put down firm time for it." Since what the lawyers got paid depended a lot on their billings for work done for clients, no one wanted to spend time on internal firm matters. Firm time was a concept that allowed them to get credit for the hours spent on internal matters as if they had been billed to a client.

Lohman continued, "I don't know if you've heard, but Ellis Kirkland was killed last night."

Lohman waited for a reaction, but DiBello gave forth with a long silence. He could have expressed some regret. Or he could have expressed glee. Perhaps silence was the best policy under the circumstances. So Lohman said, "I don't have much time. The police are here and they are asking questions. We talked and then I sent them over to Henner so Henner could explain the computer set up to them. I want you to go there right away and see that we don't release any client confidences. Just go and play it by ear. You can ask them your questions when you get there. Can you do it?"

"Ok. Will do," said DiBello.

7 THE MANAGEMENT COMMITTEE MEETS

Tete had been working on setting up a meeting of the firm's Management Committee and told Lohman on the intercom that it was ready in the conference room next to his office. Lohman went in. Most of the Committee was there except a few who were tied up or out of town and some were on a conference call set up which Tete was testing. Tete had placed copies of the two main Chicago papers at each seat. Tete had also arranged to have reruns of the morning's TV newscasts shown on monitors set up in the room.

St. Charles and Cohenstein were not there. They did not wait for others to show up at firm meetings. When everyone else was ready they were informed. Cohenstein usually showed up right away. St. Charles would not move until he was told Cohenstein was there. Furthermore, he made it plain to everyone that he was in no hurry to show.

Cohenstein kept trying to bring up the subject of the waiting. He kept making the point that it was time no one could bill (or shouldn't) and it was the time of their partners with the highest billing rates and that the waiting time was costing them a fortune. However, no one really wanted to get into a fight over it. Besides, St. Charles was worth it, at least in his mind.

When St. Charles finally showed up the meeting started with a general discussion of what had happened. Some of the partners had heard about Kirkland and they had been discussing it with the others while they were waiting for his eminence. No one knew anything about the details and Lohman filled them in to the extent he knew anything. He told them the detectives had said Ellis was murdered and he explained

39

how the body was found and the other details he knew. Then Lohman had Tete run the videos of the newscasts.

The papers and the newscasts both reported the death as a murder and prominently mentioned the firm and that Kirkland was one of its most prominent partners. It was made very clear that he was killed in the firm's office under mysterious circumstances.

There was a lot of surprised conversation about the death being murder, but the talk soon turned to what was important. Who was going to get Kirkland's billings. The talk was not about who was going to do the work for Kirkland's clients, but which partner would get credit for the billings. The partners generally got paid in proportion to how much in billings they were credited with bringing into the firm. Who would do the work was a much simpler matter. Other lawyers were already doing it.

Who would feed on the Kirkland billings would not be resolved so quickly. The conversation soon turned to the next most important thing. What would people think? Put another way, the attention of the meeting turned to public relations. Here was a major modern law firm of the highest repute with a murder in its midst. On its own premises. One if its own people. Snobs did not think much of people who got themselves murdered. The Committee decided rather quickly to get in touch with its public relations firm and see what they could do.

Nothing else was accomplished and Lohman assumed the responsibilities of contacting the public relations firm. He also informed the Committee that he was going to contact all Kirkland's clients or have someone else contact them to arrange for continuation of service and to inform them of the firm's view of what had happened.

Like a newspaper, Fenton, Pettigrew kept draft obituaries for all its partners and other important employees on hand. As a matter of fact they were usually prepared by their subjects. The firm Business Manager, McDade, had been at the Management Committee meeting and Lohman had told him to get Kirkland's obituary ready and email it to the public relations firm Fenton, Pettigrew used. He also told McDade to get in touch with Kirkland's widow right away to coordinate things.

The obituary related how Kirkland was the preeminent intellectual property lawyer in the Midwest and related the bar associations he had headed and of which he was a director. It listed various companies and charities of which he was a director and related various other things about his professional and civic activities. It gave the usual information about his family and stated that he was "beloved". It claimed that he developed many leading edge patent and trademark strategies. It exaggerated a little.

Then Lohman called his contact at the public relations firm and informed her of the death. Lohman told her frankly that the police suspected murder, but that this should not be disclosed. "Just say he was found dead in our Lake County office this morning and concentrate on the fact that he was a pillar of the community. Concentrate on all the charitable and civic activities and organizations he was involved in and his awards. McDade emailed you his obit and Tete will email you a copy of his official resume we keep on file. She'll get back to you later as soon as she knows the details about the wake and funeral." Then Lohman thought, "What the Hell," and he said, "Let everyone know how much he will be missed by his friends and colleagues."

Lohman had already scheduled a meeting of the lawyers working on the Kirkland matters. After talking to McDade and the PR lady he went to a larger conference room in the conference center where they were waiting for him. Kirkland had several fairly senior partners working on his matters and those partners in turn supervised many more junior lawyers. At the meeting Lohman tried to identify all matters that Kirkland had pending. He brought Kirkland's billing records to help and Kirkland's secretary was there. Lohman told those present that he would handle some of Kirkland's upcoming appointments. Then he basically told the lawyers reporting direct to Kirkland on his matters to take over responsibility for dealing with the clients for the time being, except for the clients Lohman was going to meet in the next several days. He told them to contact the clients and tell them what had happened and, if they did not know, to explain to them. The emphasis was to be that their matters where being handled effectively. Lohman told them not to discuss how Kirkland died and to claim that they did not know any of the details if asked. He told them to try to deflect any conversation to the fact that the client's work was being attended to. If necessary, he told them, have the clients call him for details. He told them that some burglar or nut case probably was involved, but no one really knew yet. What he didn't tell them was that he had no idea of what had happened, but the public relations firm had suggested that suspicion be placed on forces outside the firm before people started suspecting forces inside the firm. Lohman would have loved to ask the group then what they knew about Kirkland's death, but he was late for a dinner appointment with a client. So he told them that if anyone had any knowledge about what had happened to contact him individually.

8 WEDNESDAY EVENING AT THE PULLMAN CLUB

Lohman was going to join St. Charles and George Pelton for dinner. Pelton was a client's chief financial officer. They were going to the Pullman Club along with an officer from the client's investment bank. The Pullman Club was Chicago's most prestigious. Its members were generally the top officers of the region's largest companies. The membership included few of the professionals or lesser business persons who were found in other clubs. However, a few of the very top law and accounting professionals were admitted. Sort of like pets. St. Charles was one of these and he was quite proud of it.

St. Charles liked to walk over to the Club after work with guests for dinner. It was a nice evening and the group left the firm. For city boys it was a short walk of 6 blocks. Pelton and his investment banker were not city boys. They seldom walked further than their driveways. As a result they were not in too good a mood. The client and the firm were in the middle of discussing a financing with the investment banker and everyone was trying to impress everyone else. Lohman didn't do any work for the client, but Lohman knew Pelton socially and St. Charles always took someone from the firm with him when he took clients to dinner. Then St. Charles would have someone present who the client could see was acting deferentially. This would demonstrate St. Charles's importance. Clients who did the same type of thing whenever they could really ate this up. One hears that you should never try to bullshit a bull-shitter, but in truth it is the bull-shitters who are the biggest buyers of bullshit.

The financing involved an acquisition. "Acquisition" is what the cognoscenti say instead of "the purchase of a business." To say "We are going to buy a business," is as common as mud. Besides, if you kept talking in a plain and simple way people could understand you. If they understood you, they would know you were a phony or at least that what you were doing was no big deal. Hence the "acquisition". Pelton's company was named Junegar Systems, in accordance with the modern tradition that you should never be able to tell what a company does from its name. One of Junegar's subsidiaries, Bax Brands, sold a popular soft drink. They made only the flavoring syrup which they sold to independent bottlers who held franchises and product licenses from Bax. Bax owned some of the bottlers itself. In this case Bax was buying one of its bottlers.

This would not be remarkable, except that Bax had just sold the bottler 2 years ago. And had bought it 7 years ago, after selling it originally 12 years ago. What gives? Earnings management. Any gain or loss on these transactions would be combined with the earnings from Bax's regular business operations. Bax's licensing of the brand gave it the ability to dictate when the bottler would be bought or sold. It had a lot of bottlers it could do this with. This gave Bax the ability to avoid bad years. If its normal business operations were going to show less profit than the prior year, it would just sell a bottler at a profit and show increased profits over all. Bax's earnings were consolidated with Junegar's so Junegar was controlling its earnings in this way. Junegar was a publicly held corporation and companies that reported a smoothly increasing earnings trend generally had higher stock prices than those that reported fluctuating earnings of the same overall amount. Since the big wigs were given company stock for a lot of their pay, they cared very much about the stock price.

The investment banker was going to arrange for a lender to supply the funds to Bax. Heaven forbid Bax should use its own money.

The Dead Man Says

On the way over to the Club Pelton was complaining about everything. The traffic, the weather, politics, the bums on the street. There were bums on the street near the Club. Pelton started in on that and how it demeaned the Club. He went on about how he was a member of a much better Club in New York where this was not allowed. Lohman explained that nothing could really be done about it. He explained that there were bums all over town, not just near the Club. He said, "Bums are like pigeons. They go where they're fed. What can we do? In Chicago, perhaps we are a bit too charitable." Pelton was not mollified, but he did change the subject of his complaints to how the Club building looked. But not until after he had pointed to one of the bums and said, "That one looks like Ellis."

They went in and went up to the dining room and began their dinner. Pelton continued with his general discourse on the defects of mankind and the world. St. Charles and the investment banker agreed with everything he said. Then Pelton brought up the subject of Kirkland. By now the news was out and Pelton had heard it. Kirkland had done work for Pelton's company from time to time and in the course of that work he had come into contact with Pelton. Pelton didn't like him and was angry about the fact that Kirkland was charging his company too much. Lohman knew that hired management hardly ever complained about high fees so long as the lawyer did not squeal on them and what they were up to and the extent to which they were soaking the company. Besides, the ultimate fallback of management after paying tons of money and getting a bad result was to point out that they had hired the best (most expensive) lawyers available. What more could they do? The quality of something is defined by what you pay for it. If you pay a million dollars for a cow pie it is a rare piece of Dresden china. This principle explains Rolls Royce.

The Dead Man Says

St. Charles told Pelton, "Our fees are quite competitive. You know that. You handle the finances. You see what other firms charge."

"I'm talking about Kirkland," said Pelton.

St. Charles said, "Ellis charged no more than other lawyers of lesser skill and repute. He was one of the true bargains in his area."

Pelton did not seem to want to pursue this any further and the conversation turned to what they should have for desert after the waiter came over and asked them.

Lohman wondered what Pelton really had had against Kirkland. He had heard Pelton make general disparaging comments about Kirkland before, but he had always assumed that he just didn't like Kirkland. Pelton never seemed to like anyone much and seemed to like people less as they descended on the social scale. He spoke very well of billionaires. Even if he had never met them. Lohman assumed Pelton did not like Kirkland because he had to work with him as an equal and he considered himself very far above Kirkland. It is irritating for a superior person to have to work with someone who considers themself to be the superior one. But Lohman wondered. He had never heard Pelton make specific complaints about Kirkland before.

After dinner Lohman took his leave of everyone. Pelton was going to the suburbs so he took a cab to one of the train stations. The investment banker was going to New York so he took a cab for one of the airports. St. Charles had had his walk before dinner so he was taking a cab to his apartment. He had a house in Lake Forest, but he maintained an apartment on the North Side of Chicago in the most fashionable Gold Coast area on the lake front which he often used during the week. He called it his pied-a-terre. Lohman once was at a party where some undeserving creature asked St. Charles what "pied-a-terre" meant and St. Charles had said, "It is French."

"Meaning what?" The creature asked.

"Well, if you don't know, I am not going to tell you," said St. Charles, meaning that he did not know himself. He did know that people of substance often referred to their in town apartments that way and that is all he needed to know.

Lohman lived in a house at the north end of the Gold Coast area on a street called Dearborn. Actually Swifton Plaza was bordered on one side by Dearborn. His house was about 2 miles straight north of the office. He often walked home up Dearborn or Michigan Avenue, the street through the fashionable shopping area. Michigan Avenue ran north into Lake Shore Drive which separated the Gold Coast from the lake. In the Gold Coast Dearborn was 3 blocks west of Lake Shore Drive. Lohman knew a lot of people from all walks of life and he often met some of them on his walks home. It was one of his favorite activities. The Pullman Club was on Michigan so tonight Lohman was walking up Michigan.

9 STROLLING UP MICHIGAN AVENUE AFTER DINNER

Lohman took his leave and began walking north. The sun was just setting and the temperature had come down a lot. A line of buildings was on his left and he was walking on the sidewalk in front of them. Across the Avenue to his right was Grant Park. He looked north and saw the white terra cotta wedding cake Wrigley Building all lit up at the apparent end of the Avenue a half mile away. He began thinking of the recent events regarding Kirkland and found himself hoping that whatever happened it wasn't going to be too much of a headache. He was soon passing by the Art Institute over on the other side of the street with a lion guarding each side of the wide staircase to the entrance. He reviewed the banners outside advertising the shows that were currently in progress. One touted an artist he was fond of and he remembered that the College Club where he was a member was having a dinner and view of the show as one of its activities which he had seen in the Club announcements. The College Club ranked just behind the Pullman Club in prestige downtown.

As he passed on beyond the Art Institute he came to the College Club itself. He thought of going in to see who was at the bar, but he reminded himself that it was late and it was a school night, as he called it. Just ahead and across the Avenue was a section of Grant Park that had been rebuilt and tarted up and renamed Millennium Park. It was very popular with the tourists and tonight it was full of them. First there was an area with two towers in a barren area that slanted towards drains. The towers showed pictures of some of the tourists and emitted a steady stream of water over themselves and the pictures. Lots of people liked to loiter around the towers, many with their shoes off on account of the water. Next going north along the Avenue came what looked like a shiny chrome plated jelly bean about thirty feet high and sixty feet long. The underside came up so people could pass under it. Many people liked to sit and mill around here.

Further on near the end of the park at Randolph Street was the band shell. It was designed by a famous architect and looked like crap. Lohman thought that anyone who can design stuff like that and manage to be acclaimed for it deserved to be famous, but for his ability to be acclaimed for crap, not his design ability. The band shell had rows of seats and behind them a vast open lawn. The lawn area was usually quite busy with people doing a variety of things, whether or not there was a performance.

On Lohman's side of the street at Randolph was the old Chicago Public Library, now being used as an exhibit and meeting building.

The Art Institute and old Library had been built in the late 1800s and were in the traditional Beaux Arts style of the time. Lohman liked them. Everyone liked them. But it was the crap across the street to Lohman's right that drew the flies.

Ahead of Lohman on his side of the street, north across the street from the old Chicago Public Library, Lohman remembered another library, a privately endowed library for scientific and technological materials that had once stood there. It too had been in traditional style. It had been replaced by a modern high rise office building.

Millennium Park had ended and the Avenue now had buildings on both sides. This was perhaps the least popular part of the Avenue. It led up an incline to a bridge over the Chicago River. Originally there had been no bridge there. The old bridge went over the river slightly to the west of where the current Michigan Avenue Bridge was. What is now Michigan Avenue here was once on the west side of the largest rail yard in the world. It belonged to the Illinois Central Railroad which came into town along the lake front in the area that was now Grant Park and Millennium Park. The yard was just south of the river to the east of Michigan Avenue. There was no longer a railroad yard there and the area had been filled in with the usual assortment of new high rises found in any large city. It was called Illinois Center after the railroad that had owned it. The tracks still came up to the north end of Millennium Park to serve a commuter line, but they were now underground and there was no more yard.

Chicago's is a city of bridges. The Chicago River goes right through downtown and at one time in the 1880s the River hosted the busiest port in the world. It isn't a wide river and you wouldn't think of it as any kind of port now. But it was then and it remained busy for years. All this activity took place in the midst of downtown and many bridges were built to handle all the traffic crossing the River. Part of old Chicago activity was waiting for bridges to open and close. Some of this activity was still going on when Lohman was a child and he remembered waiting for the bridges. Nowadays this didn't happen. About all the bridges opened for were yachts going to and from their lake berths in the spring and fall. They were stored along the river in the winter. Almost all heavy freight traffic now went to a port based around another river at the south end of the city. The traffic left in the Chicago River was mostly tourist and commuter boats and the occasional barge and these could all fit under the unopened bridges

As the Avenue rose to the bridge it became apparent that it did not end at the Wrigley Building. Instead it jogged to the right. The bridge crossed the river in a northeasterly direction. The Wrigley building was at the northwest corner of the bridge and that is why it looked like it ended the Avenue from the south.

As Lohman walked across the bridge he entered the glare of the flood lights on the river bank and the bridge itself which lit up the Wrigley Building. He looked down at the water. It looked black. "Why not?" he thought. "It is night." Then he recalled what it looked like in the day time. Black. It was largely muddy sewage.

Years ago the River, like any other river would, flowed into the lake. Chicago got its water supply from the lake and it dumped its waste in the river. Not good. So the flow of the Chicago River was reversed. Now Chicago sent its poo to Peoria and St. Louis. The poo was treated a little and much of it was kept out of the River, but it still made the River look like liquid mud. Since the amount of water that came from the Lake was limited the poo got into the main stem of the River, even near to the locks at the Lake.

Near the end of the bridge Lohman ran into an old schoolmate of his from college, Brad Zane. Zane was an editor at the Chicago Tribune and he was just leaving work. The Tribune was in a gothic style building across the street from the Wrigley Building. They greeted each other.

"So Bumper," said Zane, "What's going on at your place. Kirkland murdered. A big shot. Big story."

Lohman cringed inside. Zane put things in print. In public. "You probably know as much about it as I do. The police say he was killed with a marble bust and a ceremonial dagger."

"Yeah, well our people can't find out much either. Who did it?" asked Zane. "Seems like you have a lot of candidates. Did anyone like him?"

51

The Dead Man Says

"No one knows who did it that I know of," said Lohman. He knew what people thought of Kirkland would get out. He added, "There's no evidence it was anyone in the firm. Maybe a burglar."

Fortunately Zane had to hurry to get his train and he departed after wishing Lohman good night.

Lohman continued on up the Avenue. Here it turned straight north again and started descending from the bridge height. It went as far as the Water Tower before turning northeast again. This meant the Water Tower was in the center of the Avenue as you looked north. Like the Wrigley Building, it was lit up too. It wasn't as tall and it wasn't white, but it was still quite visible about a half mile north. It was made out of limestone and was a yellowish cream color. It had been built in the 1860s and contained, as the name implied, a tower of water which supplied the pressure for the north side water system. The pumping station was across the street to the east and both buildings were still there. They had nothing to do with water anymore though.

Michigan Avenue from the river on north was one of the primary high end shopping centers of the world. It was also a stroll for hordes of people, both Chicagoans and tourists. It was usually very crowded. The old shopping center in Chicago had been on State Street south of the River. State was two blocks west of Michigan. At one time it had eight huge department stores on it and a host of other stores, some themselves as large as department stores. The neighboring streets also had many stores. But the new retail system worked differently and it was located north of the River on Michigan.

Lohman sighed. He liked the sightseeing on this part of the Avenue, but the walking was tough. He told himself, "You're in Metown now." Everyone had the right of way. The Divine Right of way. Many of them were talking on phones and oblivious to anyone else. Groups of people walked abreast, often blocking the whole sidewalk. Many people were just standing around, sometimes moving from side to side, in the process blocking the sidewalk. Some were shoppers. Despite the late hour, many were women with children in strollers. And women with a baby think they can go anywhere at any time. It was hard to make steady progress through this crowd, especially since all these hordes of people blocking the way expected everyone else to get out of their way.

Street traffic was also interesting. Cars were regularly going through red lights and many of the drivers were talking on the phone. Bicycles were all over the place and naturally the riders paid no heed to the traffic signals. Lohman remembered how the police used to do something about such conditions because they got pay offs from the people they stopped. Maybe, he thought, that wasn't such a bad system. Now they weren't even there. And if they were they wouldn't see anything. If they saw something they would have to do something. Lohman thought that if you took the typical modern cop's mother and put her in front of the cop's car and held a gun to her head, the cop would look the other way so he wouldn't see anything that required him to do anything or - God Forbid! - get out of his car with no donut shop around.

Lohman reminded himself that he was going up Michigan for the people watching, not because it was the fastest way to get home. He walked on up the Avenue, looking at the interesting people, sometimes looking at the window displays, sometimes looking down the side streets. Soon he came to the Women's Athletic Association, one of the most prestigious women's clubs. His wife was a member and they had attended many events there. The food was good.

The Dead Man Says

He came to the Water Tower and walked around it. One block north and across the street was the Water Tower shopping center, Chicago's first vertical mall. It was packed with people going in and coming out. North of that and still on the east side of the street was the John Hancock tower, Chicago's first 100 story building. Lohman looked up at its top. There was a restaurant there and he wondered if any of his friends were there. He recalled the last time he was there. Kirkland had asked him up there for lunch on an emergency basis because Kirkland wanted some more associates assigned to him that day for a project he was behind on. Kirkland was in that neighborhood and saw little reason why he should travel back to the office to see Lohman. Kirkland made Lohman pay for it. The firm reimbursed him, but he was the one who had to deal with the menial aspects of credit card usage, not Kirkland.

The Hancock tower occupied all of its block except for the northeast corner where Lohman could see the one story Refectory Club, the other prestigious women's club. He remembered how upset many of the lawyers in his firm were in the past when the private clubs realized that they could no longer restrict their membership to one sex. The members of the Pullman Club and the College Club especially were up in arms. Now it was no big deal. There were many women members of the formerly male clubs. The women's clubs accepted male members too. Not many men joined. So the Refectory Club and the Women's Athletic Association were still mostly female, mostly social climbers, mostly rich house wives with time on their hands. Working women who wanted to schmooze with other working sorts joined the formerly male clubs.

Lohman had been at events in the Refectory Club many times and his wife was a member. He remembered how he had her arrange a lunch with another member whose husband he was trying to get as a client. The prospect kept saying he had to consult his wife about everything so

Lohman went straight to the source. He and the wife got along well and Lohman got the client.

On Lohman's side of the street across from Hancock was the 7th Presbyterian Church. It was a society church. Many of its members passed countless other Presbyterian churches to get there. They wanted to go to the church with the right people. Lohman and his wife were members, but did not go much. Lohman had attended a Presbyterian church ever since he was a child. He sent his children to Sunday school at 7th. Lohman, after all these years, did not know what Presbyterianism was, except that he gathered from what he had heard around the church that the central belief was that Roman Catholicism and Roman Catholics were no good.

Now we all know that there is only one God. Likewise there is only one true religion. That is the Presbyterian religion. On the other hand there is the Father, the Son and the Holy Ghost. Maybe one is three. And there is the Catholic Church which seems to be OK. But it is not Roman. It is merely the church universal. Goodness is complicated.

Lohman thought to himself that something was wrong when all religions said they were the only valid ones and that all others and their subscribers were bad people. But he reminded himself that the Devil oft times lurks in the house of the Lord. He also found it interesting that the most prominent churches in Chicago of a variety of religions were in the area. In fact the main Roman Catholic cathedral and their business offices were just short distances away. Lohman passed by the church and crossed Delaware Street to its north where a very tall building had been built in recent years. This building contained a vertical mall, a hotel, and on top, very expensive condominiums. Just then he saw Lady Fitch-Bennington coming out of the building. She had an apartment there. She was a memorable creature to Lohman because she had the misfortune of having a dyslectic butler who often referred to her as Lady Bitch-Fennington. In informal moments he often referred to her as Lady Bitch. She had the grace not to notice, so those around her pretended not to notice either. Her first name was Elizabeth, but her friends called her Pansy.

She was a client of Fenton, Pettigrew and her lawyer, naturally, was St. Charles. They were like peas in a pod. She was a bigger snob than he was. She maintained that her visits to Buckingham Palace were limited to one per year because her presence made the Queen appear common. St. Charles loved it.

Lohman reflected on this oft expressed claim of hers. What does common look like? What does the opposite look like? What is the opposite of common? Probably noble. Did Pansy look noble? She did look like she had expensive jewelry and clothing on. It was in good taste. She was well manicured and her hair was done well. But other than that she still looked like shit.

Her main residence was in London, but she had extensive American agricultural interests. These were managed for her by the trust department at the Swifton Bank and she came to Chicago often enough that she had bought a condominium. Her husband usually stayed in London or at their English country estate.

She liked to give parties and her condo was huge. Lohman was well acquainted with her from her parties and other parties that they both attended. He had also been consulted about a few of her legal matters and had some contact with her as a client. While she was a big snob and poseur, she was good natured and Lohman got along well with her.

Lohman waived at her and she waived back. She started moving toward him and motioned for him to come over to her. Lohman turned west on Delaware and walked up to her.

"Oh good Heavens!" she said. "How delightful to see you Bumper."

"It's my pleasure," said Lohman. "A wonderful night isn't it."

"Yes," she said. "I was just going out to dinner with friends. I am going to meet them at Les Garcons." Les Garcons was the most expensive restaurant in Chicago. Pansy ate there the same way other people ate at McDonalds. Just then a man came out of the building and glanced around, saw Pansy and Lohman, and walked over to them. While the cat's away the mice will play and Pansy, her husband not being present, always seemed to have a string of gentlemen to keep her company.

"Johnny," she said, "Meet Bumper Lohman, one of my solicitors. Bumper, meet Johnny Miller, my friend."

Johnny was a lot younger that Pansy, as were most of her companions. "Pleased to meet you," said Lohman.

"Hello," said Johnny.

Pansy said, "What's all this about Ellis? It's all over the news that he was killed in one of your offices. Is that true?"

"Apparently so," said Lohman. "It's a great loss."

"Oh I am so sure it is, "said Pansy. "Mourning and sorrow - times of woe. You have my condolences."

The Dead Man Says

Lohman was not particularly in mourning, but the story he was trying to get over to all comers was that Kirkland was a respected and valuable human being and his passing was a great loss. He was trying to cover up the story that he was a jerk whose passing was applauded.

"Isn't it odd," Pansy remarked, "but Graybourne and I were discussing a matter just the other day where we decided we wanted Ellis' help. Somebody used 3,000 bushels of the wrong wheat seed out in our South Dakota fields last year. It was sold to us as Agrimerica seed and it turned out to be someone else's inferior seed that they had put the Agrimerica name on. Now there is all sorts of controversy about it. Agrimerica says we were complicit in it. We, of course, suffered untold losses because of the inferior wheat that was produced. Everyone wants to sue everyone else. We wanted to talk to Ellis because of the...I think Graybourne called it the trademark problem. So Graybourne said he was going to drop in and see Ellis on Tuesday night because he was going to stay in Lake Forest that night. Did Graybourne see him? Think of seeing someone who is about to be murdered."

Lohman did not know what to make of this. Was St. Charles there? He hadn't mentioned it. And if he was and he had something to do with it, then maybe he wouldn't mention it. Lohman made a note to ask St.Charles about it.

"You haven't talked to him since then?" asked Lohman.

"No. I haven't had a chance. I've been so busy with other matters. Right Johnny?"

Johnny grinned and said, "Somewhat." Lohman could imagine some of what.

The Dead Man Says

"Well," said Lohman, "This is the first I've heard of it and I haven't talked to him about it either. We've talked since then, but he didn't say anything about it."

"Well we have to go so night, night," she said and then she put her right hand on Lohman's left shoulder and pecked him on the cheek.

Johnny then grabbed his hand and shook it and said, "Nice to meet you," and the two went off to get a cab from the cab rank in front of the building.

Lohman then went back to Michigan and turned to his left and went on north up the Avenue. He passed by an art deco skyscraper on the other side of the street that was originally named after a soap company. It had had a powerful revolving beacon at the top that could be seen far in the distance and was originally used as a navigation aid for planes. It was one of the landmarks of the town while it lasted. Which it did not. As taller buildings were built nearby the beacon became a nuisance to their occupants at night and it was permanently turned off.

Lohman came to a cross street named Walton. Northeast across the intersection was the Gander Hotel, the traditional best hotel of the Gold Coast. Lohman fondly remembered many of the events he had attended there. The hotel contained what were once some of his favorite restaurants. The next street was Oak Street and that is where Michigan Avenue ended. The street that had been Michigan now turned into Lake Shore Drive as it continued north. On the west, nearest the buildings, was what was called the Inner Drive. It had two lanes in each direction. Parallel to the Inner Drive and to its east was what was called the Outer Drive. This was one of the nation's first limited access urban roads and it ran up and down most of Chicago's lake front.

The Dead Man Says

The neighborhood was now residential. Mostly tall apartment buildings. Lohman continued north along the Drive. He met a few dog walkers he knew and passed the time of day (or night) with them and finally he turned left and walked 3 blocks west to Dearborn and turned north again and arrived home.

He let himself in and said "Glor, I'm home."

She already had heard him coming in and was coming into the hallway to hug him. Louie had heard him too and was already there greeting him. Gloria and Bumper hugged and kissed and Bumper went upstairs to change to his pajamas. Then he came down and they met in the kitchen for some milk and cookies.

"What did you do today?" she asked. She always did. Bumper did not think any of what he did was of any interest to her, but he always told her. He realized talking was the point, not what was talked about. Tonight, however, she was definitely interested in the subject. "I've been watching the news. Sounds like you were busy."

"You mean Ellis?" he asked.

"No. I heard there was a sale on gardening accessories at Sears so I suppose you spent all day there." Sometimes she was kidding. Sometimes Lohman could tell. This time he could.

"Well, a little. It takes time to find out about something like this, but it's the police who are working on it."

"What happened?" she asked.

"Everyone thinks I know," he said. "I probably don't know any more than you heard. This morning Tete told me he had been found dead

60

and I called Beth, she's the office manager, and Beth tells me he was found dead in his office with a marble bust and a ceremonial dagger from the waiting room so she called the police. They came to the Lake County office and then they came to see me and asked all sorts of questions about the firm and I sent them off to see Henner about the computer system. The police think it was murder. I don't know much more."

"Do they know who did it?" she asked. "The news didn't say. They didn't even say specifically it was murder, but it sure sounded like it."

"They aren't saying." Lohman sighed. "They wanted to know who had it in for him. Who his enemies were. What could I tell them? Every one? I have to think of the firm's image."

Gloria said, "Good luck."

"What did you do today?" asked Lohman.

"I did a lot of house work." Gloria did her own house work, even though they could have afforded maids. She was proud of it. "Noontime I went to the Refectory Club for lunch with Trina." That was Trina LaRue, wife of Bungus. She and Gloria were friends and liked to go shopping and have lunch and gossip every now and then.

"Anything interesting come up?" asked Lohman.

"No. Just the usual stuff. We trashed everybody. She was dying to get out. She said she had been home for two days. Didn't get out once. No visitors. Just her, the maids and at night Bungus for dinner. No one exciting. You know how she likes to be with people."

10 THE CODE WAS FEATHERBOTTOM'S

Thursday morning Lohman got in early and rang St. Charles. St. Charles was in too. "Hello," said St. Charles.

Lohman said, "Good morning Graybourne. How are you?"

"Quite satisfactory," stated St. Charles. He didn't care how Lohman was and didn't ask.

Lohman went on, "Guess who I saw last night?"

"Pelton. You were with us," said St. Charles.

"No, Graybourne. On the way home. I ran into Pansy." Lohman was patient.

"Pansy? How is she? Dear woman," said St. Charles.

"Fine," said Lohman. "She was with another one of her companions if you know what I mean. Anyway she told me about the South Dakota wheat seed problem and said you were going to see Ellis Tuesday night. What gives? Did you see him?"

"Of course not! Who do you think I am! I wasn't there." St. Charles was quite assertive. "You know I don't like working after five." Lohman thought he didn't mind billing after five. "I just told Pansy that - you know. The usual. We want our clients to think that we are getting right on their matters - nothing could be more important, etc."

"So where were you?" asked Lohman.

The Dead Man Says

"That's confidential," said St. Charles.

"I hope he doesn't tell the cops that if they ask him about it," thought Lohman. He said to St. Charles, "Well I was just curious. I'll talk to you later." he hung up.

Lohman reoriented himself and started wading through client matters, looking at documents and conferring with associates and talking to people on the phone. He had to clear enough of his work to free time for him to meet with a client Kirkland had been scheduled to see that afternoon. As he was doing this he got a call from Pigman, the firm's IT manager. Pigman was excited.

Pigman said, "We know who did it. You won't believe it. It was that kid Featherbottom."

"How do you know that?" asked Lohman.

Pigman said, "His code was used to get in. He went in about 9:30. As you know, keys are not used to get into the Lake County office. Everyone in the firm who would ordinarily have a key has a separate code instead. This code consists of numbers and symbols which are found on a telephone key pad. For instance Sean's code was 3059*. The firm's computer system keeps a record of all codes used and stores the record for 6 months. It's for security."

"Yes I know," said Lohman with a sigh. He had found it useless to reason with computer types. "Security" was their justification for everything. It justified having so many constantly changing codes and passwords that he couldn't remember them. It seems like each of us must be identified by some code that no one else knows. So how does it identify us? Well, someone knows it - the keeper of the secrets. So someone does know it. And what someone knows another can find out. So the game is on. Lohman sighed again. Rather than argue about it he just said, "You know, all software is made by the Taliban."

"What?" said Pigman.

"Forget it," said Lohman. Then he asked, "What about anyone else? Were any other codes used?"

"No. None were used that night after the doors were locked," said Pigman. "The computer system automatically locks the doors of all our offices at 5:00 p.m.. People have to use their codes or ring the doorbells after that to get in. And we change the codes every six months. No one used a code except Featherbottom. And I checked to see if anyone looked at it, accessed it, in our computer. No one did."

Lohman said, "That wouldn't tell us if anyone was still there after 5 who was there before the doors were locked. And it wouldn't tell us if someone was let in after ringing the bell. And even if no one else was there, did Sean stay there and kill Kirkland?"

"But no one else came in. He came in about 9:30," said Pigman. "And who else would be there that late?"

"Oh come on!" said Lohman. Both Pigman and Lohman knew that lawyers often work all night.

"But why would he come in at 9:30?" asked Pigman.

"He could have gone out to dinner," said Lohman. "Was he there earlier?"

"I don't know," said Pigman.

The Dead Man Says

"Well check his time records and check everyone else's' to see who was there," said Lohman. "Can you do that? And look to see what kind of records Ellis kept on the system. I think he used it for notes sometimes. And get his time entries. Get everything he did and get it to my office please."

Pigman reminded Lohman that he had access to everything on the system himself. Then he reminded Lohman that the firms' software could perform various types of searches, such as all hours billed on a certain date or all hours billed on a certain date at certain times. Then they could see who was billing hours at that time and could get their records and see if the records indicated where they were at the time. If not, they could be asked. While lawyers often worked late, most of them would be off the bill at 9:30 p.m. so the task should not be too complex. It might not be done quickly though. Pigman said, "It will probably take a while. You know a lot of our people are not current with their time keeping."

"Yeah, I know," said Lohman. "Let me know what you find out when you can. Did you tell this to the police?"

"Not yet," said Pigman, but they know I can get this type of information and I told them I would look for it. I'm just telling you first."

"OK, tell them," said Lohman. "But, for Christ's sake don't tell them Featherbottom did it. We don't know that and anyway he doesn't seem like the type. At any rate it is bad PR to have a murder in the firm so just give them the facts and remind them that we don't know who else was there or when he left."

Lohman then went to his computer and looked at Featherbottom's time records. As the firm manager he had access to everyone's records. Featherbottom had already entered his time and it showed that he billed time on Tuesday. The firm required the lawyers to show when they started and finished a task as well as the total time spent so there was a record of when Featherbottom put in his hours. The records showed he stopped billing at 7:45 p.m. The records also showed that he had been in a conference with Kirkland soon before that. That placed him in the Lake County office till 7:45 at least, if the times were accurate.

11 CUSTOMER SERVICE?

Lohman didn't have any more time to spend on this because he had to prepare to meet the client.   The client was Victor Stone and he was coming in with his IT guy, Dung Nao. Stone owned Stone Systems, Inc., which developed and sold software for just about anything it could get a customer to bite on. Stone had come up with a customer service program, as he called it, and he wanted to get a patent for it. He had been set to meet with Kirkland, Sweeney and Jack Sprack, a partner working in the IP area. Lohman had met Stone before and was going to fill in for Kirkland.

For a large law firm this meager a turnout was pathetic. Usually they assembled as many lawyers as they could to impress a client. Very often a client would complain about not having enough lawyers there. They would refer to other meetings where lawyers were present and compare the number of lawyers there to the number in their meeting. This was especially true when more than one side had lawyers present. No lawyer wanted to hear, "How come they have ten lawyers and I only have nine?"

Stone, however, owned all of his company. It was the hired management that wanted the numbers. Sole owners merely saw each lawyer as an additional item on the bill which they saw as being paid for right out of their own pockets. So why three lawyers? Stone and others like him still had egos and they would not want to think they were low level clients who were assigned the low level lawyers who took their own notes. All clients also bought the idea that specialists had to be called in for their matters.

The Dead Man Says

The meeting was going to be in Lohman's conference room. The first to arrive was Sweeney. Tete sent him in to Lohman's office. "Yo dude!" said Sweeney, "How're they hangin' Bumpy?"

Lohman by now could avoid rolling his eyes or grunting when he heard this stuff. "Hey!" he said. Not long before this whenever Lohman said "Hey!" to anyone in the firm they were in trouble. Whatever Lohman said, Sweeney probably didn't hear, since he had his iPod playing.

Sweeney took his backpack off and put his smart phone down and sat down and took out the iPod earplugs. Yes, phone and iPod both. He hadn't got the combined model yet. Lohman asked Sweeney if he knew what the conference was about. Sweeney's phone rang and he held up his hand to Lohman and took the call. "Yo!" Then a pause. Then, "Oh Wow!" Then he closed the phone and said to Lohman, "Sorry Man. Had to take it."

Lohman wondered if he could write some sort of pamphlet for the younger lawyers in the office telling them in gentle tones how to behave, but he did not have any confidence that it would work. "Well," he thought, "at least the clients and everybody else are starting to do it too." This gave rise to a thought he did think would work and that was to keep the younger lawyers away from the older clients, unless the elders were accompanied by young ones too. He also thought the firm should spend more time on getting the younger lawyers more exposure to the younger people the firm dealt with, clients or not. Vice versa? No. You can't get most old fogeys to accept "Hey dude!" He made a note of these thoughts to develop later.

Sprack then showed up and the three of them went over the matter. Sprack and Sweeney knew what the client wanted and had given it some preliminary thought. They basically told Lohman that the client's purported invention had patentability problems, but that they needed to learn more about it. Tete rang Lohman and told him Stone and Nao were in the conference room.

Lohman, Sprack and Sweeney went in. Stone was sitting at the head of the table with Nao on his right. Stone was one of those people who always sat at the head of the table. His table or anyone else's table. As he would say, "I'm the dog with the big balls here."

Lohman would have said, "Sit anywhere where there is room enough for your balls," but he felt he did not need to since that is what Stone was doing anyway. Lohman didn't give a damn. He was more interested in the substance of the meeting.

Sprack had big balls too so he sat at the other end of the table. Unfortunately the table seated 22 so he was rather out of it. He moved closer and sat on the side of the table. A defeat.

After pleasantries were exchanged Stone asked, "What happened to Ellis? Is all that stuff on the news right?"

"I'm afraid so," said Lohman. "It's a great shock to us all."

"Do they know who did it?" asked Stone.

"Are they saying someone did it now?" asked Lohman.

"Well, dead on the floor with blood and a marble bust and a dagger? What do you think?" said Stone.

"We have no idea," said Lohman. "You know as much as we do. We are just trying to help the family at what is a very difficult time."

The Dead Man Says

Lohman felt like a big phony, because he was being a big phony. But one of his jobs was policing the firm image. What should he have said? "It could have been anyone in the firm?"

Stone said, "Yeah, I know. You know I was up there Tuesday night. I had been having dinner with a customer at a restaurant in Highland Park and on the way back I drove past your office. Maybe 10:00 or so. I saw his car there in the lot. You can hardly miss a bright chrome yellow Mercedes S class. It was standing there all alone except for one of those black Fords the cops and government agencies use. Crown Victoria I think is the model name. What a contrast. I thought of going in to say hello, but it was too late."

Lohman and Sprack looked at each other. Sweeney was absorbed with his smart phone.

"Did you notice anything else? Was your wife with you? Could she have seen anything?" asked Lohman.

"No. Nothing.   I was alone. Boys night out, you know," said Stone. "You don't have much time to see things when you are driving by somewhere."

Lohman was deflated. No one knows anything. "How," he thought, "can someone be killed in a law office and no one know anything about it."

"Well let's get on with it," Stone said. "I want to get my patent."

Stone's company had created lots of customer service software. He started explaining his new idea. "Some people think customer service is an oxymoron. It isn't once you understand it. Customers and service are involved. Most people think the system exists to give service to the customers. But get this - the central idea. The service is not to the customers. It is to the corporations who hire us. Remember that once a service or product has been sold, dealing with the customer is nothing but a cost. The less you deal with him the better."

Stone went on. "We use a variety of devices to do this. We combine the devices into one system and separate them all into discrete steps and create wait times between them. Eventually the customer gives up. We have the waits between steps timed. A caller cannot go on to the next step or level or device until they have spent a specified amount of time at the prior step. Our software does this."

Lohman began to reflect upon one of his favorite quips which was the one about the Taliban creating all software. Maybe not. Maybe it was Al Qaeda.

Stone continued, "We will charge our customers based on how difficult they want us to make it for the caller. The starting line is the usual voice recognition software. Our voice recognition software says that it can't understand what you are trying to say. It has a volume meter so if you get angry and yell at it, it tells you it can't understand you and you will have to lower the volume. This infuriates people who are already angry and a lot hang up right there. Over a certain volume level it never lets you go on to the next step. It just keeps saying it can't understand you. Of course if you cough or sneeze or if there is background noise it reverts to the can't understand you mode. After a set time and after the volume level comes down it lets you go on to the next step which is the recorded message with a variety of choices to be selected by pushing numbers on the phone. In our more sophisticated systems you are told to press combinations of numbers, letters and symbols and before you can do it you are told time has expired and to try again."

The Dead Man Says

Stone went on. "Our software is set up to provide as many steps as the customer wants. We have at least 10 levels of phone menus. If each phone menu has 6 choices you can see at the third level we have 196 choices. It is highly likely the caller will make a mistake and have to start over again. At the next level, if the caller can get to it, the caller talks to a human. These people are computer operators. All they can do is match up the caller with options they are given on a computer screen. These are usually the same options we gave the caller in the phone menus. They are usually not employees of the customer's company and know nothing about the company or its products. They are usually handling calls for a lot of different companies. They get yelled at a lot and it is a minimum wage job. The job attracts a lot of kids with low skills. To get even with the callers they often put callers on permanent hold or put them back in the voice recognition system or use a variety of other techniques. This is encouraged by their employers who hold meetings with them where the various techniques are described in detail under the guise of telling the kids not to use them."

"Callers often ask to speak to a supervisor at some stage. If they do they are switched to another level of operator. The system actually works with up to ten levels of operators if the customer wants to pay for it. The same operators handle all the levels, but the caller is told he or she is going on to the next level. Our software tracks who the caller has talked to already so the caller doesn't get the same one again. The software also tells whoever is speaking to the caller what level the caller is supposed to be at. All the operators at a call center handle all the customer companies' calls. They just have different software and computer screens for each customer company. At some level selected by the company the caller can get an operator who can actually do something if it isn't too difficult. These are a separate group of operators and have slightly better skills. If the problem is at all out of the ordinary the caller is told to use email."

Stone seemed to brighten up and get excited here. "For email we have fantastic software. There are lots of screens with lots of stuff on them, but it is very hard to find the 'contact us' part. Of course there are no phone numbers or addresses. If the user does get an email through the system it goes to a computer which sends an automated response. It is like voice recognition, except it is letter recognition. Usually, a stock response is sent saying the sender's email is being evaluated. These responses are automated. Eventually the customer is referred to the same operators at the call center that the caller started out with."

Now Stone seemed to be brimming with pride. "So how does the customer get service? He doesn't. Somewhere along the line he gives up. It is a beautiful system. It cuts customer service costs to the bone. If a company wants we can tie up a caller all day, or even indefinitely, and make it so he never gets anywhere."

The lawyers looked at each other. Sweeney asked, "So Dude, why bother with the operators? Why not hook up the caller straight to the computer and leave him there?"

Stone didn't see this as anything but an honest question and said, "That is one of our options. But most customers want the operators included so the caller thinks the system is really an effort to give service."

"So Dude," said Sweeney, "Why doesn't somebody just invent voice recognition software for customers to use to deal with your software?"

Stone looked at Sweeney with surprise. Then he turned to Nao and asked, "Why didn't we think of that?"

Lohman interrupted. "That's pretty impressive Victor. But to patent something you have to have something that's not obvious. If I were going to try to discourage callers wouldn't this system be obvious?" Lohman was mindful of the fact that the ancient Greeks or whoever, did not invent math. God did. The Greeks just opened the book. But he didn't tell Stone this.

Stone said, "Of course it is. That's why I want to keep anyone else from doing it. Pretty soon my potential customers are going to realize that they can get away with this because everyone else has lousy customer service too and I want to be the one to get the business. Can't you get a patent for software or business methods?"

Lohman tried to look knowledgeable and said, "Yes, sometimes you can. Let us look at this and check out the applicable rules and get back to you. First we will do a patent search to see if anything else like this has been tried. We may have some suggestions for what can be done." Lohman didn't know what could be done. He didn't think there was any true invention, but he knew he was not up on patent law. He was aware that Kirkland would have told Stone that he had an earth shaking invention. Kirkland would have proceeded with a gold plated and top priced patent application. Somewhere along the way, if no patent could be secured, Kirkland would deal with it. One usual technique was to tell the client that the Patent Office was wrong, but that the client had kept others out of the field for the time being with his application.

Some lawyers like Kirkland who maintained that they were the most skilled and eminent in their field had skills that a client would rather an opposing client was availing himself of. However, they truly did have world class skills in explaining away their lack of results.

Stone and the lawyers finished up with small talk about the weather and their families and Stone and Nao left.

Sprack and Sweeney went into Lohman's office where they discussed what they were going to do. Sprack was the new kind of snob. Old style snobs like St. Charles pretended to superior lineage and manners. The new style snob pretended to be of the highest skill level and therefore superior to everyone else. The modern law firm, including Fenton, Pettigrew, had many of these. They were just as contemptuous of everyone else as the old style snobs. Sprack wanted to stick it to Stone on the bill. He said, "God! Stone is just like all of Kirkland's clients. Just as big an asshole as Ellis was. Boy, birds of a feather flock together." Ordinarily lawyers at Fenton, Pettigrew did not criticize each other, especially their superiors, but Kirkland was dead and Sprack knew that Sweeney and Lohman both knew he did not like Kirkland. Sweeney did not know why Sprack disliked Kirkland, although he had the same opinion of Kirkland. Lohman did know why. Several years ago Sprack had been out for an extended period because of a serious illness. During that time Kirkland assumed responsibility for Sprack's biggest client. Kirkland managed to get the Management Committee to assign the client to him, meaning he got credit for producing the billings, even though Sprack continued to do work for the client when he came back. Kirkland had the clout in the firm to make it stick.

12 PATEL PROMISES PATENTS – PERHAPS

Lohman then had to go on to another Kirkland client. This was Hodie Patel who ran a company that held itself out to the general public as a firm that would get patents for their inventions. The firm charged high fees and filed patent applications even when there was no chance of getting a patent. They did not expect to get more business from the customer so what did they care if the customer beefed. Besides, they could explain that the Patent Office said no so what did the customer expect. In the rare instance when a customer had a viable and valuable patent, the customer wound up owning very little of it. Patel referred patent, trademark and copyright matters to Kirkland occasionally. Patel was being charged with consumer fraud by the Illinois Attorney General.

Lohman went to the firm's reception area to meet Patel and took him to Lohman's office. Lohman preferred to meet people in his office rather than conference rooms, but he ordinarily would have seen Patel in a conference room where Lohman could leave if necessary. However, Lohman had to talk to Patel about the sensitive matter of his unpaid bill and wanted to have access to the records in his office. The unpaid bill is why Lohman was taking the responsibility of dealing with Patel.

Patel seated himself and asked where Kirkland was. Patel said he wanted to discuss some errors in the bill with Kirkland. Patel said Kirkland had called him at 9:00 p.m. on Tuesday to make the appointment so he was expecting to see him. He was going out to pick up his wife and he got the call on his cell phone. Evidently he had not heard the news about Kirkland.

Lohman asked, "Haven't you heard the news? Ellis was found

The Dead Man Says

dead Tuesday night in our Lake County office. Apparently someone got in there and killed him." Lohman found it difficult to believe Patel hadn't heard about it since it had been constantly on TV and radio for a while.

Patel appeared surprised. "How did it happen?" he asked.

Lohman said, "I don't know. The police are still investigating. You say he called you at 9?"

"Yes," said Patel.

"How can you be sure of the time?" asked Lohman.

Patel responded, "Because when he called me I was trying to get out of the house to pick up my wife and I was late. I got the call on my cell phone and I was looking at the time when the call came in."

"You're sure it was him?" asked Lohman.

"It certainly sounded like him," said Patel.

Lohman noted that the appointment had been entered in the firm's computer system, which is where he got the information that Patel was coming in.

Lohman got into the subject of the meeting. "I've been reviewing the file Hodie. I see you're way behind on paying your bill. What arrangements can we make to get it paid?"

Patel did not address that point. He started complaining about Kirkland. "Kirkland lied to me about what he could do for me. You know that. He lied about what it was going to cost too. That guy was just an asshole who didn't know what he was doing. I am telling you what he did to me."

The Dead Man Says

"What?" asked Lohman.

"He delivered documents he shouldn't have to the Attorney General," said Patel. "You think I am giving you documents so you can show them to everyone? Kirkland is saying he got something he called a document request and he had to deliver them." Discovery requests are made by parties in litigation before a court to get documents or other information from the opposite party who is supposed to deliver the documents or information if they could be at all helpful in finding out what the facts are, unless they are subject to some kind of privilege.

Patel went on. "Now the Attorney General is saying that he has files showing my firm is making no patent searches or is using patent searches that are bad. Kirkland says he is not knowing at the time what the files would show. Is he not supposed to ask me?"

Patel paused and then continued. "And do you think I can find him when I am wanting him? Calls and messages. That is what I am doing. I am paying for a phantom?"

Lohman said, "That's just it. You are not paying."

Patel had a variety of other complaints about Kirkland. Lohman was tempted to tell Patel that the way lawyers prove they are lawyers is by not returning their calls, so what else is new? However, it is never a good idea for a lawyer to make light of lawyers in general. He was also mindful of the fact that the non-paying clients are often the most demanding, so he decided to get on with Patel's case.

Lohman reviewed the status of Patel's case with him. Lohman suggested that the Attorney General had some powerful ammunition, including the documents Patel was complaining about Kirkland delivering in discovery. Lohman went through Patel's claimed defenses. He pointed out that in many cases his firm had not done patent searches before recommending filing patent applications, even though the customer was charged for them. He pointed out that the Attorney General had obtained independent patent searches on some of the matters where Patel's firm did get searches and the searches obtained by the Attorney General showed existing patents that would bar Patel's customer from getting a patent.

"You know," said Lohman, "The Attorney General has something. You could get stung here."

"I am thanking Mr. Ellis Kirkland for that," said Patel.

"He's not the one that didn't do adequate searches," said Lohman. "Anyway, you might want to consider settlement. You can never tell what a court is going to do. If we could tell what a court is going to do there would be no trials. Even if you think you have a flat out winner. Remember, they say justice is blind. Sometimes it is. And deaf too. And even in cases where you win, you can lose because of the costs. And if you are going to lose, you can lose big. Settlement precludes the loss you can't handle." Lohman knew it was best to settle almost any significant litigation. Many clients thought litigation was like the trials on TV. The right person always wins. It takes no more than half an hour or an hour including commercials. And there is no discussion of a fee or costs. And they never heard of a TV case being settled.

Patel did not want to explore settlement. He wanted to fight it to the hilt. He said, "This is crucial to what I do! Don't you understand that? I am fighting this and winning. Cost is no object! We are going to win this thing! If it wasn't for that prick Ellis I wouldn't be in this mess." Patel was born in India and he spoke with a combined Indian/upper-class English accent, but he pronounced "Prick" in American.

Lohman had heard this kind of thing before. Of course cost was no object. Patel wasn't paying. What did he care about the cost? As to fighting the matter to the hilt, well Patel was really saying he wanted to fight it to the extent of Fenton, Pettigrew's ability (or willingness) to pay for it. Rather than point these things out to Patel, Lohman said, "We will. We will do that. But first you have to make some significant progress on your bill."

The two parted civilly, but Lohman knew this was just the first in what would probably be a series of contacts leading to a parting of the ways and the firm's motion to withdraw from the case. In the meantime he planned to coax some money out of the guy. It is easier to get the money under threat of withdrawing or not doing further work than it is to collect after you have withdrawn. Lohman began dictating a memo to all the lawyers billing on Patel's matters that they should do no further work without contacting him.

Lohman then began reviewing the client files for his Friday meetings.

13 ARGONE AND SO IS YOUR MONEY

Friday morning Lohman met with Wiegur Polanski. Polanski ran a TV marketing company that ran ads for consumer products that were claimed to do miraculous things. Knives that never needed sharpening. Choppers that could make mincemeat out of a rock in three easy swipes. Hearing improvement devices for the elderly that would help them hear the rescuers ringing their door bell after they had fallen and could not get up and had summoned the rescuers on their emergency pagers which Polanski had sold them. Polanski sold millions of bottles of an allegedly completely safe herbal supplement guaranteed to alleviate the symptoms of arthritis in four weeks of use or "your money back". The supplement was called "Argone" as in arthritis gone. The ads claimed that "studies have shown" it worked. It consisted of pills containing sodium bicarbonate, fennel seed, sugar and some flour. It didn't do anything. Some of the customers asked for their money back. Polanski's firm then trotted out an agreement it said the customers had subscribed to when they got the product.

Customers could order the product by phone or on the internet. If they ordered on the internet there was a screen containing the agreement which they had to click "agreed" on before going to the next screen. If they ordered by phone they were told (allegedly) that the terms of sale were on the product wrapper. The product wrapper did contain these terms and it said that, "By removing this wrapper and using the product you agree to these terms."

The terms of the supposed agreement were that in consideration of being furnished with the product and by using it the user released all claims against Polanski's firm. The agreement also called for arbitration of any claims. The so called agreement did not explain how, if you do not have any claims, you can proceed to assert them in arbitration or otherwise. The arbitration was to be under the commercial arbitration rules of the North American Arbitration Association. This outfit last decided for a consumer claimant 17 years ago. The Association was formed by a group of consumer sales outfits like Polanski's and held itself out as independent and impartial. Almost all of its business came from companies that used arbitration clauses in their consumer contracts. If the Association's arbitrators decided against those companies it would have very little more business. The commercial arbitration rules called for the complainant to put up a $7,000 deposit to cover costs.

Some plaintiffs' lawyers had found out about the Argone and Polanski's firm was the defendant in several class actions. The actions were alleging that consumer fraud statutes of various states had been violated. There were also allegations of actual fraud committed with malice, something harder to prove, but having the potential for higher damages. They had just recently been filed and Polanski's firm had just been served with process so the courts had not yet ruled that the actions could proceed as class actions rather than a lot of individual actions. No plaintiffs' lawyer wanted the individual actions because the possible damages would come nowhere near covering the costs and, even if there was a statute allowing the recovery of costs, the work was too hard. Most courts previously took the view that arbitration did not apply to class action claims, but just after the claims were filed the Supreme Court ruled that it does. Lohman knew that if you could get to the plaintiffs' lawyers before the classes were certified you could often settle for way less than immediately after the class was certified, although this was more true if there were a lot of other defendants who had been selling the same things. The plaintiffs' lawyers then used the settlement money to pay for their work against the other defendants. There were no other defendants here, but Lohman was operating on the principle that you can sometimes settle a case up front for way less than it takes later. And, while it could be expected that the plaintiffs' lawyers would now claim there was no enforceable contract to arbitrate under the law of contracts, the new Supreme Court ruling would give him much more leverage.

Even where the client maintains that he is absolutely not liable, it is still advisable to settle. Besides not knowing up front what the ultimate result will be, the question really is how much the suit will cost the client, even if the client wins. The question is not who is right and who is wrong. The question is how much it is going to cost. Polanski was not really telling Lohman that he didn't do it anyway. They agreed that Lohman should try to settle it quick and talked over possible amounts that the plaintiffs' lawyers might agree to.

The ultimate fall back was that Polanski used a separate corporation for each product. They didn't have much in the way of assets since they had other companies make the product for them and had those suppliers ship direct to the customers. The people taking the orders worked for other companies too. Companies that supplied customer service employees. The TV ads were also done by outside companies. The companies that the customers bought from essentially had nothing. So if the plaintiffs won, they could collect their judgments from nothing.

Many lawyers would have been supremely proud of setting up this situation for Polanski. Lohman had not set it up and probably would not have had Polanski come to him in the first instance. Polanski was using this system already when Lohman became his lawyer. But Lohman was a lawyer and Polanski was his client. So Lohman went ahead like a good little officer of the court. At least he would have some other lawyers do the work. That was the advantage of being a big shot in a firm. You could get someone else to do the real work, even if you had the ability to do it yourself.

After Polanski left Lohman rang another partner in the firm named Cory Hastings. Hastings had done work for Polanski before. "Cory," said Lohman, "We've got another Polanski suit. It's Argone this time. Stands for arthritis gone. Seems someone disputes the claim. It's a class action with fraud and consumer fraud counts."

Hastings said, "I just saw an ad for that last night. I wondered when we would get the case."

"Try to remember that the plaintiffs' case is without merit," said Lohman sarcastically.   A standard claim for a defendant's lawyer to mouth, as are, "baseless claim" and 'absurd".   Lohman added these adjectives too.

"Yeah," said Hastings.

"Tete will get you the file," said Lohman. "Take a look at it and get back to me. Tell me what you think." Lohman paused and then said, "About how we can help him. I think I know what you think about his products."

"His advertising is good," volunteered Hastings.

14 AT THE GOOSE

Lohman then went to lunch with someone he knew from serving on a hospital board of directors. Lohman was trying to get business out of him. His company was getting sued all over the place and it was constantly buying and selling other companies. The guy liked fancy restaurants and Lohman was taking him to the Puce Goose that got about $200 per person at lunch, exclusive of booze. Lohman did not have any real interest in hospitals, much less the New American Hospital where they served, but he was engaging in what he called "sales". This is a dirty word amongst lawyers. It is only in the last 20 years or so that they admitted to "marketing" activities. But Lohman was doing what lawyers have always done. You get business out of people you know. The richer the people you know, the better the business you get. You work your way into leading roles in institutions and organizations as one way of meeting such people. The more important the group, the more important the people you meet. In other words, to get good business, hang around with rich people. Lohman did not generally like these people and he did not kid himself. He was doing it for business, just like a salesman of industrial machinery takes his potential and current customers to lunch, whether he likes them or not.

The guy's name was Ken Tuckman. He headed up a large public company which he owned a large part of. The company was Trans Global Logistics. This was not a consortium of wizards solving problems. It was basically a nationwide trucking company. They started out talking about their families and what they had been doing with their wives - social activities, not what you are thinking of. Along the way Tuckman said, "What's all this about your partner? Kirkland. Killed in Highland Park.

85

Right in your own office. How did that happen?"

Lohman said, "We don't know yet." Lohman wanted to say, and a proper caca spewing lawyer would have said, "I know there is talk, but we don't know he was killed. It could have been from natural causes." He wasn't up to it. He asked himself, "So he hit himself over the head and then stabbed himself?" He just said, "We don't know the circumstances yet."

Tuckman went on. "It's pretty dramatic. The news said he was hit over the head with something and then stabbed with a ceremonial dagger. Or maybe the other way around. And you guys don't know who did it? It was in your own office. How come you don't know anything? Or are you just keeping quiet until you nail the guy? What kind of people do you have around your place?"

"No, we don't know," said Lohman. "We really don't know who did it. The police are following up on some leads, but nothing yet"

"Well," chuckled Tuckman, "you should find out quick. Who wants a law firm with murderers hanging around?"

"We're working on it," said Lohman. He made a note to talk to the PR firm about what could be done about people's perceptions. Shift their thinking to someone outside the firm? But what if it was someone inside the firm?

"What kind of work did he do?" asked Tuckman.

Lohman responded. "He had a lot of tech clients. His main area of expertise was patent, trademark and copyright law. We call it IP law nowadays. So most of his clients were companies doing a lot of inventing or in areas where brands are a major factor. A lot of planning, a lot of litigation, that type of thing."

"Yeah. I've heard of those guys," said Tuckman. "That reminds me of the Sales Manager at one of our suppliers who was murdered. We bought trucks from the supplier, but they had a lot of car dealerships too. Just last year. Hoverington Ford was their big dealership around here. You've heard of them. Ads all over the radio and TV. He was found dead in his office one morning. They charged a salesman. They said he had lot of gambling debts and he was mad at the Sales Manager because he nixed 5 straight deals. They couldn't prove it though so the guy got off. Several months later he supposedly committed suicide. Some people thought it was a Syndicate hit instead of a suicide. Because of the gambling debts. He was in to the juice people. The guy had been beaten up bad just before he died."

The Syndicate, also called the Outfit, is the Chicago version of the Mafia.

Tuckman said, "The guy was hit over the head with a large wrench from the shop and then stabbed with one of those huge screw drivers. Jesus, I hope he was out of it. Anyway, it sounds like what happened at your place. If I were you I would be looking out for suicides now. Know what I mean?" He chuckled.

"I hope not," said Lohman. "When did this happen? I don't recall hearing about it. You'd think it'd be big news."

"I'd think it would be big news too, but who wants that kind of news about their company? Hoverington is one of the biggest advertisers around here. They got it toned down."

Lohman made a note of this as a way to handle his own firm's PR problems.

Tuckman changed the subject. "While we are talking about lawyers, what do you think about the hospital's proposal for that new proctology center it wants to build? Did you look at the financial projections?"

"Yes," said Lohman.

"So what do you think? Will it pay? It seems too expensive to me. The whole thing is based on an increase in Medicare reimbursements and I don't think that'll happen - long term at least."

"I think you're right," said Lohman, "but try voicing that view. Everyone thinks Medicare money is unlimited."

"Yeah," said Tuckman. "Well, if we can get the reimbursement there sure are enough assholes around."

They soon concluded their lunch and were off on their separate ways.

15 A DEBT OF HONOR

After lunch Lohman met with one of his associates to go over the status of several matters. Then he had a meeting with Qwen Lohfahrt. Lohfahrt had originally been scheduled to see Kirkland. Lohfahrt knew another client of Kirkland's named Gordon Weinstein. Weinstein had referred him to Kirkland. Lohfahrt had been parking his income in a Panamanian corporation and the IRS had found out about it somehow. He was being charged with tax fraud. Lohfahrt said he knew that Weinstein used offshore entities and other devices a lot and that is why he had approached Weinstein about the matter.

Many people of his type had heard about Panamanian corporations that have only bearer stock. The stock is issued to a bearer. The certificate for the stock says "Bearer." No name is given. No record of who owns it is kept. The person who has the stock certificate owns the corporation. An agent in Panama exists to serve as an officer and director and keep the corporate records, but the records do not show who the shareholder is. Thus, even if the authorities can trace the income to the corporation, they cannot find out who is the true recipient. Unless, that is, the recipient makes a little mistake like having a corporate account the money can be traced to which shows all the money paid out of the account going to him. In other words, disguising to whom the money flows - or money laundering - is involved too. Lohfahrt had made a mistake in this regard. His Panamanian corporation had an account in Nigeria that the IRS had managed to find and get records from. The records showed that he got the money. In his own name. No. No. No. It should have gone to another mysterious untraceable entity.

An additional thing is required to avoid tax with this device and a lot of other "off shore" tax evasion schemes. The recipient of the income files a tax return which does not declare the income. This is tax fraud. Lohfahrt was being charged with criminal tax fraud. Ordinarily Fenton, Pettigrew did not do criminal work. However, it did do something called white collar criminal work. This usually involved charges of crime in business or investing activities. Or tax evasion charges. They key was that the crooks involved could pay a lot. Rich crooks are OK.

Lohfahrt was like a lot of people who evaded taxes. He had a high income and he avoided a lot of taxes with his schemes. However, the amount of taxes he avoided did not cover his costs in doing so. All the foreign entities and accounts and cash transfer services he used cost a bundle in setting up and maintenance charges. But he and people like him would do anything if it involved not paying taxes. He was a class A sucker prospect for a "tax shelter" which is an enticing name given to a bad investment sold by a variety of people in the finance, accounting and law industries to their rich clients and customers.

Lohman was going over Lohfahrt's financial matters and he was reviewing Lohfahrt's financial statement. One item was a receivable identified as "loan to private party". Lohman said, "What's this loan to private party? $500,000. What is that?"

Lohfahrt said, "Let me see," and took the financial statement from Lohman. "Oh that! Yeah! That's Kirkland. He told me he needed cash for a short period until he sold some securities and I helped him out."

"What?" exclaimed Lohman. "When was this?"

"Last month," said Lohfahrt. "What do I have to do to collect it? I thought it was only going to be a day or two. My accountant put it on there and it doesn't look like the best asset in the world."

The Dead Man Says

So Lohfahrt gives his lawyer $500,000 just because the lawyer asked him for it? Sure. Just because you have money does not mean you know what to do with it. Did he do a credit check? Did he get security? Did he even document the loan? The loaded are no more careful than the poor when dealing with someone who they believe in, in whom they have confidence. The people they have confidence in are often called con men. And a client is supposed to have confidence in his or her lawyer - right?

Lawyers are not supposed to have business dealing with their clients under the Rules of Professional Conduct and this worried Lohman. Lohman had heard Kirkland complaining about bad investments and losses and he wondered if Kirkland had been in financial trouble. Kirkland had been getting about $1,750,000 a year out of the firm in recent years, but Lohman knew that did not preclude him from having financial problems.

Lohman tried to act like there was no problem and told Lohfahrt that he would look into it. They parted and once again Lohman called in another lawyer to assign the matter to him. Lohman entered the money owed to Lohfahrt in his to do list. Hopefully he could get Lohfahrt repaid before the matter became public knowledge. He determined to ask the Management Committee to pay Lohfahrt and take an assignment of the note and then try to collect it from Kirkland's remaining assets.

16 GOODBYE ELLIS

Lohman then headed down to the lobby where his wife picked him up in their car. They were going to Kirkland's wake. The wake had been going on since Thursday morning and was being held at one of the few remaining funeral homes on the North Shore. The firm's standard policy was to have as many of its partners attend wakes of prominent people as possible. The firm viewed wakes as just another way of meeting people and stirring up contacts that could eventually lead to business. Firm partners had been in constant attendance at the wake. Their sorrow was untold. (Since if it be told, they were mostly glad the bastard was gone.)

The funeral home, Carroll's, was the home favored by the socially elite of the North Shore. The Kirkland wake occupied the whole place. Lohman and Gloria parked in the adjacent lot and went in. They knew many of the people there, since many were F, P & C people or clients. They went to the alcove where the attendance register was kept and signed in. Then they headed for the line of people waiting to give their condolences to Helen Kirkland, the widow, and members of her family. Once that was done they were free to circulate and did, like good little partners and their wives. Like many wakes, apart from the location and receiving line, you couldn't distinguish it from a refined party. Eventually they left and headed for home, stopping for dinner on the way.

Saturday morning Lohman and his wife went to Kirkland's funeral. The funeral ceremony was held in Christ the Redeemer church, the most socially correct Episcopal Church on the North Shore. The church was packed. While the Kirkland's were members of the church, they had not been in regular attendance. Thus it was perhaps understandable that the minister seemed not to know much about Kirkland. Lohman recognized much of what the minister said about Ellis as coming from the firm's pre-prepared obituary.

From the church there was the trip to the cemetery. Because of traffic problems funeral processions were no longer in vogue and it was up to each person to get themselves to the cemetery. The cemetery was in Chicago. It was Grace The Land Cemetery where all sorts of prominent people had been buried over the years. Kirkland fancied that he would like to associate with the most prominent and superior citizens of Chicago in perpetuity so he had bought a plot there long before. The funeral was mercifully brief as such things went.

17 AT THE GANDER

Then Lohman went in to the office and attended conferences all day with other lawyers to review the status of his client matters. Later he was due for a rare night off. Most of the time was devoted to a conference with a group of younger lawyers Lohman had working on a bankruptcy matter. A large company had filed in bankruptcy court for reorganization. Chapter 11 it is called. This is a court supervised process where all those who hold claims against a company that can no longer pay its bills assert their claims against the company and try to get a bigger share of the pie. This involves trying to see everyone else gets less. Large company bankruptcies have turned into one of the most lucrative fields of practice for large law firms. Lohman's client was a secured lender to the bankrupt company. This means it had a lien on the bankrupt's assets to secure its loan. In this case it had a mortgage on some of the bankrupt's plants. Other creditors were claiming the mortgages were no good. This is not unusual since everything in these large bankruptcies is contested. And the more the lawyers make off them, the more they advise contesting everything.

Finally the conference ended and Lohman was free. He walked up Michigan Avenue to the Gander Hotel at its north end. Michigan was packed with shoppers and the weekend tourists. It was jammed with strolling and lingering hordes. Lohman enjoyed watching what was going on just as the people he was watching did, but it took a long time to get to the hotel.

As he was passing good old 7th Presbyterian he saw a crowd of people outside. They were gathered around the time of services sign outside the church. Lohman went into the crowd and inched forward to where he could see what they were looking at. Someone had placed a cardboard overlay sign on the glass fronted case with the times of services in it. The cardboard was taped on. The overlay was white and had the type of lettering on it that you might see on a flier for a horror movie. It was simulated red blood lettering, complete with places where the blood had run or spattered. It proclaimed:

THE GREAT GLOBULICIOUS **EVIL SHOW**

HOSTED By The Naughty DEVIL

DIRECT FROM **HELL**

The ONE And ONLY CHICAGO APPEARANCE

RAPTURE Without GOD?

DELIGHT Without ONE SINGLE ANGEL PRESENT?

MESSAGES FROM BEYOND WITHOUT ONE SINGLE PRAYER?

YOUR FONDEST WISHES GRANTED!!!

NOT EVEN ON MARS DO THEY HAVE THIS!

YOU WILL BE ASTONISHED IF STILL AWAKE!!

COME! SEE! HEAR! BARGAIN!

GET WHATEVER YOU WANT - ALL WISHES GRANTED!

The Dead Man Says

ABSOFUCKINLUTELY FREE!!!

Sunday, June 11, 2011 11 a.m.

Soul Productions

Lohman just read this and tried to comprehend it, which he couldn't. He thought it must have just been put up recently because surely the church would not leave it there once they became aware of it. In any event, being a member of the church he thought he would find out about it later. One thing he noticed though was that the only thing the crowd was discussing was the word "globulicious". They were divided on whether it was a word or not. And those who thought it was an accepted word were divided about what it meant. Many were asking what it meant. The rest were telling them. Apparently it meant a wide variety of things. No one thought the sign out of place. Apparently it was just another Saturday night amusement on Michigan Avenue. Lohman walked on.

He met his wife Gloria at the Gander in the Cohasset Room, one of the oldest Chicago restaurants with a very private and cozy atmosphere. He called her Glor. She was sitting in a booth when he arrived. He slipped in next to her and kissed her. "Glor," he said.

"Bumper," she said.

She had told him she was going shopping with Bungus LaRue's wife Trina earlier. Trina was one of her best friends. "Did you and Trina have fun?" asked Bumper. "How much did it cost us?"

Gloria was not a big spender, but Trina was. Gloria mostly helped

Trina spend. "Not much," she said. "I just got a few shorts and summer blouses." Bumper knew this could cost thousands on Michigan. "At Latham's. $350," she volunteered. "Mostly we were trying things on and gossiping. She was all stressed out about all the things Bungus says she should keep her mouth shut about. For instance, last Tuesday she says she and Bungus were having dinner alone, except for someone from the firm who delivered something. At least that is what Bungus told her to say. But she says they were having dinner with someone named Gordon Winkleman who works for the State. I asked her what they were talking about, but she said it was only man stuff like the Cubs and stuff. She says they went off into the library to talk just between the two of them. She says she can never keep straight what she is supposed to say and what she is supposed to keep private."

"Yes, I can imagine," said Bumper. "I never really press Bungus on what is going on. I probably don't want to know." Just then he remembered something. "Oh. Didn't you tell me that you had lunch with her recently at the Refectory Club and she told you no one was with them that night?"

"Yes, that's just the thing she was talking about. She mentioned this about the Winkleman fellow. She says it's hard for her to know what she's supposed to say. So she said she used to take notes, but Bungus found her note book and told her not to do that anymore. What is he up to? Are you supposed to have someone like that for a partner?"

Lohman sighed. "Well, whatever Bungus is up to, we are probably more at risk from some of our most supposedly respectable of partners than we are from him. Anyway, if there were no Devil, there would be no need for lawyers. Or, I know I say it all the time, but bad guys are found in lawyer's offices and on both sides of the desk. Whenever I ask Bungus what he is up to he says I don't want to know. Everyone else I ask says the same thing. Lets' face it. He's a fixer, an influence peddler, a bribe arranger, but at least not the briber himself. I don't know the details, but I'm sure the less people know about it the better. And you know I don't choose all the partners, or even most of them."

They then got off on other subjects and went to a movie after they had finished eating. Then they went home and engaged in unseemly conduct.

18 SUNDAY GOLF

Sunday was for golf. Business golf. Lohman did not like golf. He had better things to do. But there was business to drum up and golf, like wakes and funerals, was a way to mingle with the prospects and current clients. The golf club of choice that day was Olgosia in Lake Forest, another high toned North Shore suburb. It was the country club with the highest social standing in the Chicago area. But the course wasn't too hard. The Club was called Old Goatsia by some. Lohman spent most of Sunday at the Club playing golf with St. Charles and the general counsel of a large organization they were trying to get business out of. The general counsel was Herman Schlot. The organization was a large worldwide religious society which generally kept to itself and did not seek publicity. It was loaded and its investment activities are what generated the legal activity. The name of the organization was ECOTAG. St. Charles was the one who had stirred up the prospect so Lohman did not know much about the outfit. At first Lohman had thought it was some kind of combined religious and environmental movement, but luckily St. Charles had given him the full name before he made a booboo by asking Schlot what it stood for. Evangelical Congregation Of The Angel Gabriel.

Schlot brought one of his chief aides along. Fang Lo apparently was his name, although no one cared to make sure. Lohman was good at this sort of golf thing because he always arranged his play so that he or his pair lost by just a little. Hence his presence.

Schlot was a newbie. He did not come from a distinguished (or even rich) background and St. Charles was trying to impress him and his aide, Fang Lo. While they were waiting to tee off Schlot kept talking about the golf clubs where he played and how they were much tougher and better than Olgosia. He said, "And my own club, Fairfield Hills where they hold the Open. It's the toughest course in Illinois. And it's next to the Creighton Polo Club. One of the few polo clubs in the country. Our Angelic Leader plays there."

"Oh yes, "said St. Charles. "I've met him. A superb fellow! The very best!"

Actually St. Charles was getting very upset. He did not take kindly to an inferior who failed to recognize the superiority of his club. So Lohman tried to carry on in a friendly manner. He started talking up Fairfield Hills where he said he liked to play.

St. Charles had talked to Lohman at the funeral when they were matching notes about the upcoming golf outing. St. Charles had explained that Schlot was "new" and that he was going to be over his head socially so Lohman should make allowances. St. Charles explained that Schlot and his crowd did not know the proper social etiquette in many matters. For instance, St. Charles told Lohman that the Leader of Schlot's organization was running a string of polo horses at Creighton, even though he was new money which he had made himself. As St. Charles put it, "He has the nerve to enter polo with new money!"

"What about Lo?" asked Lohman. He could not help it.

St. Charles rose up and said, "I understand he is some kind of aide. Like a caddy that is allowed to talk. Try not to get too involved with him."

It came their turn to tee off and they all got up and went towards the tee. Schlot was the guest and he would go first. His golf bag was made out of white patent leather with black margins. ECOTAG was spelled out on it in sequins. He went to his bag and pulled out something with a shaft. Not a golf club. A shaft with one end pointed and a gold cross at the other end. He gave it to Lo Fang who thrust it into the ground at the side of the tee. Then Schlot and Fang Lo fell to their knees in front of the cross. St. Charles motioned to Lohman to get down and the two of them managed to do so like a couple of arthritic walruses.

Then, right in front of all the people waiting for their own turn to tee off, Schlot said, "Let us pray." He proceeded to ask for God's favor for the representatives of the holy Evangelical Congregation Of The Angel Gabriel and vowed eternal obedience to God's commands. He did not ask God to let the best man win. He then said his amens and got up and teed off.

Then St. Charles. Then it was Fang Lo's turn. He went to his golf bag and got - what - his phone. He called his wife and carried on a conversation with her about when he would be home. Then he teed off. Then Lohman.

With God on their side and Lohman going last, Schlot and Fang Lo won by several strokes.

After Lohman ended the matter with his final put the party proceeded to the clubhouse for drinks. They got seated at a table with drinks and St. Charles toasted Schlot's victory. They started talking.

"What's all this about one of your partners getting murdered?" asked Schlot.

St Charles said, "Extremely unfortunate. Ellis was the salt of the earth. It is a great loss. To us and the bar and his family and friends. And they are numerous."

Schlot thought about this for a moment and then said, "You know, most people who are murdered are complicit in it. They have brought it on. God sees that they get justice. What was he up to? What was your firm up to?"

"Good Heavens!" said St. Charles. "I can't imagine what you mean. He was not up to anything. The firm is pure. The purest. It was someone - well we don't know who. But no one in the firm is up to anything wrong. Why, we have prayer sessions."

Lohman almost choked. He started coughing. "Allergies," he said.

Schlot said, "Well God will be pleased about that. But you shouldn't have had daggers around a law office. Sooner or later someone around a place like that will use them."

St. Charles said, "You are so right. We are conducting a search of the entire premises for devices like that and other instruments of the Devil. I myself have given the order. You can't be too careful with so many people around. Some will always go wrong. You understand don't you Herman."

"Yes I do," he said. "That's why I ask what is wrong at your place."

St. Charles was hoisted on his own petard. He looked at Schlot with widened eyes and a slack mouth.

Fang Lo said, "Right. Hallelujah!"

"This reminds me of what happened with one of our suppliers," said Schlot. "We purchased bibles from them. Our own edition with the parts about the Angel Gabriel restored. The ones the so-called Christians took out under the influence of the Devil. The manager of the printing plant was closing up one night when he was murdered. A witness said he saw one of those Fords pull up. One like the detectives use. The witness says he saw two people get out and go into the plant and come out a little while later. The next day the manager was found. He had been brutally beaten and then stabbed. The police told us that they thought someone from what they called the Syndicate did it, but they never solved the crime. Needless to say we got a new supplier. We don't have anything to do with crime."

"Oh, we don't either," said St. Charles.

Finally Lohman got to go home. When he got home he reflected on how holy he felt after his day long association with the agents of God. Holy like having a hole in the head.

19 KIRKLAND'S SECOND

Monday morning Lohman had a conference with Egon Fitzhubery. He was a second level partner and Kirkland's chief aide. Kirkland didn't like too many of his juniors, but he liked Fitzhubery because Egon could document the fact that he had noble ancestry once long ago in Europe. Fitzhubery had the best relationship with many of Kirkland's clients and he would be taking them over. He was a brown nose and a social climber. One lawyer in the firm had said of him that he was stuck up. That is - his head was stuck so far up his ass that it came out on top. Another firm lawyer had described him as, "Smile up. Shit down." Fitzhubery was continually in a state of outrage about someone and was always trying to get people in the firm fired. He was not anyone's favorite. Kirkland had liked him though. This was another example of birds of a feather sticking together. Especially when covered with gooey slime.

Fitzhubery was especially the hawk when it came to the poor clerks and secretaries without clout. Just out of curiosity Lohman asked him if he had heard about Jason Kunz hitting on some other male.

For once Egon was not on his high horse. He just said, "That is of little import. Everyone knows he is a degenerate homosexual. I do not know why you let him stay here. He will just do it again and again. That is what homosexuals do." Fitzhubery was one of those people who always used full proper words. It is amazing the filth that can spew out of your mouth without the use of one naughty word. Fitzhubery then went on about other affairs in the firm, including those indulged in by Kirkland. He claimed everyone knew Kirkland was porking his secretaries which is why there was so high a turnover among them. Of course Fitzhubery did not say "porking". But Lohman heard it that way. Lohman was a real low life, at least to people like his honor Fitzhubery.

Then Fitzhubery said, "You might have taken note of the fact that one of the associates assigned to me, Sean Featherbottom, is homosexual too. Everyone knows that."

"He is?" said Lohman. "How can you tell?"

"Oh please," said Egon. "Do not pretend you do not know. He lisps when he gets excited and he flaps his wrists like he is going to take off. But you notice that I put up with him. I am well known throughout the firm to be of open mind and liberal demeanor."

Lohman was mindful of the fact that Sean was one of their best associates and that Sean did a lot of Fitzhubery's difficult work. Now that he thought about it, Sean did flap about a bit when he got excited. Anyway, he could see that Fitzhubery wasn't trying to get anyone fired at the moment. He just said, "I don't think the issue is sexual preference. It's hitting on someone."

Fitzhubery said, "Whatever you call it," in a pained, but obviously tolerant manner. Lohman thought that maybe newspeak is not so different from the properspeak of our superiors. Sweeney, Lohman thought, would just have said, "Whatever". Score one for the young. Much more succinct.

"He does some work for you, doesn't he?" asked Fitzhubery. Lohman nodded his head. Egon continued, "Yes. Good. But you know I don't think he liked Ellis very much. He was there Tuesday night, you know. To help Ellis. He very well could have killed Ellis."

"How do you know what he was doing?" asked Lohman.

"He told me," said Fitzhubery.

"Well," said Lohman, "If you really think we have a killer running around here we should do something about it."

Fitzhubery did not respond so Lohman said, "Let's get to the clients."

Lohman and Fitzhubery then started reviewing the Kirkland clients and what was going on with their files. They got to Gordon Weinstein. Weinstein was just plain rich. He had come up with some important inventions in the computer, communications and chip areas. Weinstein was not Kirkland's type. Weinstein was an intellectual old wizard Jew of plain talk and good will. Kirkland had inherited his business from an older lawyer in the firm who was part of the Cohenstein faction. Primarily because Kirkland was supposedly an IP master.

Kirkland was waiting on Weinstein to approve something. Weinstein was an old client of the firm and he wanted to review his patents and companies to see that they all fit in with his estate plan. An estate plan is legalese for your plan for your assets when you die. Who gets them and how? How can you avoid taxes? How should things be arranged to achieve the desired results? Kirkland was working with lawyers from the estate planning, tax, corporate and international departments on this. Kirkland was waiting to hear from Weinstein to see if Weinstein wanted Kirkland to prepare an outline of the work to be done and the fees and costs involved. Since Weinstein had extensive interests this would be quite involved. And lucrative.

Egon said, "He approved it. Gordon approved it. Gordon told me he approved the work on the outline."

The Dead Man Says

They got to talking about Kirkland and his death and in the course of the discussion Lohman asked Egon, "Where were you when he was killed?"

Egon said, "Oh, Heavens. How should I know? When was he killed?"

Lohman said, "Well, we all know it was Tuesday night."

"When on Tuesday night?" asked Egon.

"The police haven't said yet," said Lohman.

Egon said, "While I may not know when Ellis was killed, I do know where I was Tuesday night. My wife and I were at the opera with a Clay Fenger and his wife. You know. We get a substantial amount of business from them. We were at the opera till about 10:30 and then we went home from there. The driver took us and the Fengers and dropped us off first. Where were you?"

Lohman said, "I was at home with my wife too."

"So there," said Egon.

"So there what?" thought Lohman, but he did not want to pursue it. But opera in June? "So what is with opera in June? I thought it was a winter sport." No acceptable person would ever have referred to opera that way. "I mean, I always thought they only performed in the winter, or fall or spring. Never in the summer."

Egon sighed. He paused. He needed to compose himself. One does not get upset by a peasant. One disposes of him. Even if he is the estate manager. "Usually you are correct. This year however, the Lyric is experimenting with a longer schedule. The main reason being that they are trying to see what they can do at the box office with no incremental expense for the house except utilities. They have the theater there all year at great expense so why not use it. And they have equipped the theater with that new silent air conditioning system."

"That's new?" asked Lohman.

"Yes," said Egon. "Go to Orchestra Hall on a warm day in the early spring when they are still there and listen. Just before the conductor gives the down beat they turn it off. You aren't aware of how much noise it makes until then. Actually you can notice this in the winter so it must be the fans. Anyway, you can't have an un-airconditioned house in the summer."

Lohman changed the subject to Kirkland's clients and the status of their matters. After they had gone over all Kirkland's clients Fitzhubery left. Lohman thought to himself, "A stable hand has to shovel shit all day. I have to talk to people like Egon all day. Not much difference, except the shit doesn't talk back. At least I get paid a lot more".

20 MORE FIRM BUSINESS

Lohman then met with Monica Platt. Tete announced her and Lohman went out to Tete's desk to greet Monica. He said, "Monica! How lovely you look. Is that a new dress?" Tete rolled her eyes. They went into Lohman's office.

Monica Platt was a partner and she was seeing Lohman about a client she wanted to take on. The lawyers in the firm could not take on new clients without getting firm approval. The firm did not want to take on a matter that conflicted with a current client's interests and it wanted to screen the clients for suitability in other ways. In this case the prospect wanted to haggle over the retainer, which is a term for a deposit lawyers take from a client for a new matter. It serves as security for payment of fees that may be quite large. Monica and Lohman discussed that matter and Lohman reminded Monica that if a client will not pay a retainer up front when he wants the service, he will not pay later when the job is done. With this reminder she resolved to just insist on the amount she had quoted and let the prospect take it or leave it.

Monica and Bumper were the subject of much gossip in the firm, even though both were married to others. Monica was one of Bumper's wife's best friends. Monica and Bumper sometimes worked on the same matter together, but Monica was always running in to his office on business and other matters too.

On the way out Monica turned in front of Tete's desk and went into general conversation. "So what else is going on Bumper?"

"Not much out of the ordinary," he said, "except a dead partner or so. Don't forget we're having lunch next week."

Tete's eyes practically rolled up into her forehead.

Lohman got back to work on his own clients' matters. Then to dinner with a client and then home.

Kirkland's secretary was Elizabeth Gordon. The next day, Tuesday, Lohman went to see her. He questioned her about what records Kirkland kept and how. He told her to assemble all the time records and notes on everything Kirkland was working on and the file for Gordon Weinstein. Lohman also told her to get him Kirkland's appointment records.

As soon as Lohman got back to his office he met with a former client of Kirkland's named Biff McCain about the status of the purchase of a company Kirkland had been working on for McCain's company. Biff came from an old line social register family that owned a large chunk of a conglomerate that started out with his great-great grandfather's store in a small town. Biff was the CEO of the conglomerate. Biff was an idiot. His real name was Biffster if you can believe that. Biff remarked that the news about Kirkland was terrible and that he had been so looking forward to seeing Kirkland at the monthly meeting of the wine tasting committee at the club they both belonged to. The meeting was held on Tuesday night. Kirkland had not called to cancel. Members who could not make the meetings rarely called to cancel. The club was the College Club, the most prestigious of the downtown clubs after the Pullman Club.

After the meeting with McCain Lohman went to Kirkland's office and talked to Elizabeth Gordon to see if she had the records. She did. She had assembled them on Kirkland's desk so they went into Kirkland's office and she showed Lohman the records. Lohman asked her, "Did you know anything about what he was doing Tuesday night? Did he say anything?"

The Dead Man Says

She said, "He didn't tell me much. I know he was due at the wine tasting committee at his club, but he didn't tell me he had a change of plans. I know he was waiting to hear from Mr. Weinstein on something. He was here until about 3 or 3:30 in the afternoon and then he told me he was going to the Lake County office. I didn't hear from him after that."

A lot of lawyers were not very good at keeping records of what they did and how much time it took. They tended not to keep a record of their activities while they were doing them. They wrote the information up later. For many this resulted in recording less time than they actually spent because they couldn't remember what they did. For others though, this resulted in magnifying the time spent and the tasks done. What was written up was fiction of magnified importance. Kirkland used this system, although he did keep a note pad on which he wrote things throughout the day. Lohman was ultimately in charge of the firm's billing activities and McDade, the Business Manager, had pointed out to Lohman that Kirkland was often billing about 20 hours a day. McDade had pointed to similar billings from other lawyers in the firm. This was a delicate matter, since the firm made money from hours. Lohman wanted to add a feature to the firm's computer system that would flag consistently high daily hour totals in the billing records, but the Management Committee opposed it.

At any rate, Lohman wanted to go through Kirkland's records to see if they would indicate if he was missing anything that had to be done for Kirkland's clients. He frankly was also curious about what Kirkland was up to and wanted to see if the records would shed any light on the death.

He told Ms. Gordon, "Ms. Gordon, have the papers sent to my office, please." She then called one of the clerks and had the papers delivered. In his office Lohman started reviewing them and the billing and time records that had been entered in the firm's computer so far. The rest of the day Lohman caught up on his phone calls and reviewed memos from associates about various client matters they were working on.

21 THE STALKER

Wednesday morning Lohman found one of the young associates waiting for him when he came in. She was Tambola Cook who was one of those high class rank people large law firms like to hire. She had been second in her class at Yale and was a whiz at turning out legal memoranda and spending a lot of billable time doing it. The legal memoranda were statements of the law applying to a specific fact situation. The associate would do what is called legal research, which consists of looking through all the applicable law to see what applies to the fact situation. Once upon a time this would involve looking through books and indexes listing law on various subjects and then finding the particular legal material and reading it. The legal materials were reports of decisions by courts, statutes, administrative agency rules and a lot of other miscellaneous statements of the law. Then, in a writing called a memorandum, how all these sources of law applied to the facts would be discussed and a conclusion reached.

Most lawyers now use computers to do the looking up of the law. Almost all the younger lawyers do because that is how they have been trained. What was in books has been transferred to computers and what was done with books and indexes is now done by computers. Some lawyers love this because they do not have to search through indexes to find things. Besides being laborious, this requires knowledge of English and an ability to use it to think of alternate words and combinations thereof. With a computer you can just enter the words you are looking for law on and tell the computer to go fish. The Software God then supposedly gives you all the applicable law on those words.

The Dead Man Says

Many young lawyers like doing legal research because they do not have to deal with anyone else. There are many of these sorts among the high ranking top law school youngsters. And they love playing with the computer. Tambola was one of these. She was not a people person. She was a nerdess. And she dressed and acted the part. She was about 5'4" tall and weighed about 180 pounds. Her clothes looked like she got them at the resale store and she often wore running shoes in the office. After law school many of the top graduates often serve as clerks to judges for a short period. Someone who is second in her class at Yale would ordinarily get a clerkship with a judge on one of the federal appeals courts at least. Tambola did not interview well, however, so she had served with a judge in a federal trial court.

You want to know what is the law applicable to your client's situation? Ask Tambola - in a written memo. She will tell you all you need to know - so long as it does not involve analyzing what people will do. She will tell you this in writing. On time. Guaranteed. Just do not speak to her about it.

Tambola was wrapped up in herself. She walked the halls of Fenton, Pettigrew in a trance, often fiddling with her smart phone. She always walked on her left of any hallway or other way she was on and hugged the wall. She did this outside too, even if she was with a group of people. Anyone who was walking towards her and was keeping to their right would just have to get out of her way. Sweeney had come up with a nickname for her which stuck. It was Miss Leftwitch, because of her keeping to the left and because her favorite hat was a little black conical thing she stuck on her head. Anyone who complained about having to dodge her in the halls was told that they had better keep out of her way because she had the left of way. Loony bin or law office? Same thing.

114

The Dead Man Says

As Lohman came up to his office he saw Tambola waiting for him. He almost said, "Good morning Lefty," but he caught himself. He said, "Good morning Miss Cook."

Tambola said, "Can I see you for a second?" Whenever a lawyer mentions a span of time, beware.

Lohman opened his office door and held it open for Tambola and invited her in. She wanted to take some time off which ordinarily could be arranged. She had done a lot of her work for Kirkland and Egon, but she also did a lot for Lohman so she was asking him about it for that reason. And because he ran the joint day to day. He, however, had a mess in IP just at the moment because of the sudden absence of Kirkland and he wanted to keep her available for the time being. He told her this and asked what she wanted the time for. She said, "I just need to refresh myself. There is a course in meditation I want to take with the Meditation Institute in Karachi. It will be good for me and the firm too. I will come back in a much more productive frame of mind."

"Karachi!" said Lohman. "Who runs this? The Taliban?"

"No. No.," said Tambola, "It's interdenominational."

"What do you want to go to Karachi for?" asked Lohman. "How can you meditate in the middle of a war? And you're probably going to get on someone's national enemies list. Can you get a visa? Are there any travel restrictions?"

Tambola said, "That's the thing. The presence of the war is used as a training tool. If you can meditate in that environment, you can meditate anywhere, maybe even in a law firm. There are times when meditation would be just the thing for lawyers you know."

115

"Well, think about it," said Lohman. "Think about what our government might want to do to people who travel to enemyland. In the meantime I need you in IP. You can go there later after you have investigated the risks."

"But I have been under extreme stress and I need the time to recover," said Tambola. "Mr. Stine has been driving me insane. He keeps telling me to drop everything and work on an emergency matter. Then when I get into the matter he does it again for some other matter."

Stine was Felder Stine, an aggressive junior partner who Ms. Cook had been temporarily assigned to lately. Stine was continually bringing in new business. Sometimes several new clients a day. He wanted associates to get right to work on the new matters so he could make a favorable impression on the clients. His world was limited to the latest prospect. He had no use for or memory of the client he brought in yesterday. Consequently he was constantly telling associates he put to work on something the previous day to drop it and pursue the new client's matter. While he brought in more new matters than anyone else, he also lost more clients than anyone else. Yesterday's clients who had been ignored also were hard to collect from. All in all, not a satisfactory situation.

Lohman had talked to Stine about this several times. If the firm could get him to continue paying attention to the clients he had brought in he would be a huge producer. Stine did not get the point. Finally Lohman had told him, "Look. If you ever want to get laid you have to fuck the one you've got before chasing the next one!" Apparently Stine was still not getting the point so Lohman made a note to talk to him about it again.

The Dead Man Says

To Tambola he said, "I'll talk to him. But we need you here right now."

Pouting seemed the best response to Tambola. Then she said, "You're just like Mr. Kirkland. He wouldn't let me go either."

Lohman said, "You asked him?"

"Yes," she said. "He wouldn't let me go either. He wasn't very nice. He said he would just as well fire me. He said no work, no pay. He abused me." Then she added, "Look what happened to him." She apparently didn't think this comment out of place. "Now that he's gone, I thought it would be OK." Then she said, "Sean thinks it's a good idea"

Sean was Sean Featherbottom. Sean was one of the best associates in the firm and did a lot of Egon's work. God knows Egon didn't do much besides the talking parts. Tambola was always talking about Sean and was very often seen with him in the firm. Sometimes she just followed him around. It was a topic of some gossip.

Lohman had heard it too and he couldn't help asking, "Are you stalking Sean?"

"No. Of course not," she said. "We just work together on a lot of matters and I just run into him a lot. I see him everywhere. For instance, last Tuesday I got home late and when I was coming home I stopped in the 7/11 near my place and I saw Sean and Jason Kunz going into a bar across the street. It was dark, but I'm sure it was them. I would recognize Sean anywhere."

"Oh," said Lohman jokingly, "so he is stalking you."

"No," she said, "it's just that I see him everywhere."

117

"So did you talk to him? What was he doing in your neighborhood? He doesn't live around there does he?" asked Lohman.

"No," she said. "They were going into a bar. A place called Drinker's. Come to think of it, I wonder why. It was kind of late for that kind of thing."

"So what time was this," asked Lohman.

"About 10:30," she said.

"Where is Drinker's?" he asked.

"It's by me," she said.

"Where is that?" he asked.

"On Halsted near Roscoe," she said

Lohman then told Tambola to contact Egon and tell him she would be helping him out and that he would reconsider her request for time off after IP was straightened out and she had checked on her ability to go to Pakistan.

"Mr. Fitzhubery?" she asked. "He took me to see a client last week. My first time to see a client outside the office."

"Really," remarked Lohman. He thought to himself that Egon must have been desperate. A lot of lawyers in the firm hardly ever saw a client alone. They added other junior lawyers to the meeting to impress the client and, most importantly, add to the bill. Another reason for this was that many large firm lawyers could not do anything by themselves. Many couldn't even go the john by themselves. But when they selected the troops to see a client with, they usually selected more people friendly associates. "Who was it?" he asked.

"I don't know," she said. "It was out on Elston Avenue. You know that street that runs out northwest? Pretty far out. It was something Pipe Works."

"Ah yes," said Lohman. "Illinois Pipe Works. What was going on? Are you doing work for them?"

"I don't know," said Tambola. "Mr. Fitzhubery just called me late Monday and told me he would pick me up the next morning and we would go there, and he told me to pay attention and take notes. I don't know what it was about."

"So who were you talking to about what?" asked Lohman.

"It was a Phil. I didn't get his last name. He and Mr. Fitzhubery acted like old friends. They were talking about several different law suits, but mostly about their wives and families and cars and baseball. Guy stuff. They didn't pay any attention to me."

"And what about the suits?" asked Lohman"

"Some supplier was suing for payment and apparently the defense was defective goods and Mr. Fitzhubery was telling Phil about summary judgment, He was explaining to Phil we were going to make a motion to get the case thrown out, as he put it. Then they were talking how Phil was suing some customer for non-payment and the customer was making the same defense in a motion for summary judgment. Mr. Fitzhubery said we were going to win both cases. I don't think Mr. Fitzhubery was being entirely consistent in what he was telling Phil."

"So he picked you up at home in the morning and drove you

there?" asked Lohman.

"Sure. I don't have a car. I could have taken a cab, but he said he would be in town anyway because he had to get his parents' car because his was in the shop. Boy was he put out about it."

"What?" asked Lohman.

"The car. He was telling me all about his BMW. A Seven he called it. Some series or whatever. That's a fancy car, isn't it? So he was complaining all the way out there."

"Yes," said Lohman, "About what?"

"The Mercury," said Tambola. "His parents' car was a Mercury. I remember what he called it." Here she started to talk with a nasal mock high class accent. "He called it a Grand Marquis." She repeated it and drew out the words. "While he was so upset he had to drive it I could hardly keep from laughing. Grand Marquis fits him perfectly. Why should he complain? It was all nice and a shiny deep blue. Nice car. "

"Well," said Lohman, "Egon is very particular about his things. While you may have liked the car it is merely a fairly low priced car that is not even made any more. Egon would not want anyone to see him using one. You know how he is about matters of status and social rank."

"So that's why!" said Tambola. "He said he was tired of driving and had me drive there. He told Phil it was my car. You could see it in the lot from Phil's office. Phil and Mr. Fitzhubery were talking about cars and Phil told Mr. Fitzhubery he had a new car and he pointed it out to us. They he asked Mr. Fitzhubery where his car was and that's when he told Phil it was my car. So this is a lot of stress. You see I have to go to meditation school."

"Soon," said Lohman. "But not just now. We need you here. What happened after you left Illinois Pipe Works?"

"Well," said Tambola, "Mr. Fitzhubery had me drive away and then, like after we got away, he had me pull into a Burger King and we changed places. I had to go up to a client in North Chicago and deliver them some forms and check to see how their HR department was using the forms they had and to show them how to use the new forms. I don't usually go to the clients' places. So he drove me up there and dropped me off at about 4 and said he was going to go home. I was there for a while and then everybody else started leaving and they started getting very antsy and finally they told me they had to go home. I guess they don't work like we do. Anyway, about 8 I left and took the train back down town. Then I took the el back home. So I dropped into the 7/11 and saw Sean. So then I went home and went to bed."

Lohman asked, "Did Sean see you? Did you speak? Jason?"

Tambola said, "No. I don't think they saw me. I was in the store and they were across the street. They weren't looking in my direction."

Once again Lohman told Tambola he would check into getting her time off. They concluded their meeting with a standoff and Tambola's secret delight in the prospect of doing more work in the same department as Sean.

Lohman spent the rest of the day on his own client matters.

22 KIRKLANDS' WORK IN PROCESS

Thursday morning Lohman was able to go through Kirkland's records and notes. He also was able to review Kirkland's time and other records on the computer more thoroughly. He was looking for client or firm matters that needed attention, but he was curious as to what had happened as well. He found Kirkland's notes about Patel and Stone which had been made in preparation for the meetings with them that Lohman had conducted. He also found Kirkland's notes about Lohfahrt's financial situation, which were quite interesting, especially since Lohfahrt seemed to have given Kirkland a different story about the sources of some of his income than he had given Lohman. There was a note that Lohfahrt had threatened him and was coming in and that Kirkland told him not to and to call next week.

An interesting set of notes listed wines and Kirkland's opinions of them. Evidently for the wine tasting committee of his club.

Of further interest in Kirkland's computer files was a lot of porn. Kirkland seemed to like women in tight black leather bras and pants, high heels and studded belts. Most had whips of some kind.

There was also a to do list for the Wednesday that Kirkland was never to see. There were things listed to do for Weinstein. Evidently Kirkland had gotten the go ahead from Weinstein. Upon further going through the papers Lohman found notes of a meeting or phone call, he couldn't tell which, with Weinstein. The notes included, "Weinstein approves - go ahead." the notes, like most of Kirkland's notes, were on a separate sheet of paper and were dated and bore a time. The date was the Tuesday before last and the time was 9:10 p.m..

The Dead Man Says

By now Lohman was aware of what Kirkland was talking to Weinstein about. Kirkland had proposed a large and intricate asset protection and tax plan with off shore entities and accounts. Weinstein and Kirkland had been discussing it and Weinstein had to approve going ahead with it. He also had to review the estimated cost and come up with a deposit. There were extensive notes in the files describing ideas for what was proposed to be done. Now Lohman had to see that all the ideas were refined into a workable plan that could be outlined and explained to Weinstein. He noted that he should contact Weinstein to see he had not changed his mind. He determined that he would be able to take this matter over, since it involved the types of projects he often did for clients and since he liked Weinstein and thought he could do a good job for him. And get credit for Weinstein's business. No lawyer who has to produce prodigious amounts of money each year to survive amongst his cannibalistic partners is immune from these types of thoughts. If you've got the money honey, I've got the time.

Later that day Lohman had called another conference of associates and partners working on Kirkland's matters to see what they knew about what was going on and what needed doing. They did not tell Lohman anything much he did not know already about the work, but he did pick up some other tidbits. Kirkland had a lot of things going on and there were 18 associates and 5 partners in the room. Some were there already when Lohman came in and just as he entered he heard one say that whoever offed Kirkland should get a medal. This he pretended not to hear.

Another of the associates, Gilbert Crane, in the course of the discussions said Kirkland had told him to see Bungus LaRue about some building code matters for a Kirkland client. The client had a large warehouse and shipping center in Chicago and it was not in very good repair. The client didn't want to spend much on it because they were looking for a new location in the suburbs. They wanted to redevelop the property, perhaps with offices.

Crane said, "LaRue told me to see a lawyer named Oscar Toschi about this. I called Toschi and made an appointment with him. I went there and met with him. I was going to tell him all about the problem and all about how the building code applied to it and what I thought we could do. LaRue didn't tell me exactly what Toschi was going to do so I thought he was sort of an expert who would help us out. He didn't want to discuss the details at all. All he wanted to do was talk about his fee which would be $250,000. I couldn't believe it. This guy operates out of an old building west of the river and he doesn't even have a secretary. The office is a dump. I didn't even want to sit down because I was afraid of what I would catch. It was that kind of place. One of those creepy solo guys. $250,000 for what? I couldn't imagine paying this guy anything. He had a law degree on the wall and I never heard of the place."

"Toschi gave me a sealed envelope and told me to give it to Mr. LaRue. I delivered it to LaRue's house the night Kirkland was killed. LaRue's wife answered the door and I gave the envelope to her. She didn't invite me in so I didn't see Mr. LaRue or anyone else there. But there was a Ford with State government plates on it parked in the street so I figured LaRue must be meeting with some government type, since he's a lobbyist."

"So what is the status of the matter?" asked Lohman.

"I told LaRue about it later," said Crane. "LaRue just wanted to know what the fee would be. He didn't say anything else. Then he just switched to another subject."

The Dead Man Says

Lohman hadn't heard about the building code matter. Not surprising he thought, since Kirkland might not have wanted to put anything about it on paper. He knew the developer of the building involved was a Kirkland client and the real estate department was handling the normal construction matters on it. He knew there was a building code question, but he didn't know anything about the involvement of LaRue or the outside lawyer. The property involved was going to be developed with a large office building to be put up where the main stem of the Chicago River, coming from the east, split into north and south branches. It was going up on the west bank over railroad tracks that came out of one of the train stations. The warehouse and shipping center now on the property was on both sides of the tracks.

Lohman got ahold of LaRue and asked him to come to Lohman's office. LaRue showed up after a short interval. Lohman asked him about the building code matter. LaRue described the problem and said they were trying to work out a settlement with the City. He said the outside lawyer was an expert in these matters. Lohman knew enough not to go into this much further.

Lohman wanted to ask what was in the envelope the associate delivered to LaRue. He knew he shouldn't. But he wanted to. He asked, "Did you get the envelope from Crane?"

"Who?" asked LaRue.

"Crane. Gilbert Crane. He said he delivered an envelope to you after he met that guy," said Lohman.

"Is that his name," said LaRue. "Yeah, I got it. My wife gave it to me."

The Dead Man Says

Lohman resisted. He did not ask what was in the envelope, but the instinct pushed him. "Was it helpful?" he asked.

"We'll see," said LaRue.

Lohman's instinct screamed "What was in the envelope! What was in the envelope! Find out! Find out!" Like many lawyers he spent half his waking hours finding out what was happening in any given situation and he did not rest until he did.

But curiosity killed the cat. Especially the cat who thought he could kill the curiosity. So Lohman retreated. "So why was the State car there?"

"What State car?" asked LaRue.

"I'm told there was a Ford with State plates on it outside your place. Crane said so," said Lohman.

"I didn't see it," said LaRue. "Trina and I were having dinner and the bell rang and Trina went and got the envelope. I wasn't looking outside. I didn't see any car."

Lohman thought to himself that now was the time to quit. God knows what LaRue was doing. Lohman did know that a client of LaRue's was trying to get a contract to sell computers to the State. Then he remembered Gloria saying that Trina had mentioned a Winkleman being there. A Winkleman who worked for the State. "Later," he thought. He was not certain he wanted to know about it.

Lohman spent Friday traveling to see a client in St. Louis and getting back. On Saturday he took several clients to see a White Sox game. The firm had a sky box at the stadium for entertaining clients and some other firm lawyers were there too with other clients. Traditionally Chicago baseball has been quite exciting if you like tight races - for last place. The current teams were trying to win a few games so things were no longer so exciting.

23 THE POLICE - AGAIN

Monday morning Lohman met with the police officers again. O'Malley and Fricknoodleh told him they had been checking out people who had been dealing with Kirkland lately or who had been at the Lake County office that Tuesday. They had learned from Pigman, the firm's computer or tech support guy, that Sean's code had been used to get into the office that night after everyone except Kirkland had left. Sean himself insisted that he had already left for the night by the time Kirkland apparently died.

O'Malley said, "You sure lose a lot of things. The office manager says Kirkland was looking for a file and she got it for him that afternoon and gave it to him. She says she couldn't find it after that. Then some old guy up there says an expensive vase was missing from his office. He says he left about 5 and it was there then. He says he locks his office door when he leaves. He says when he came in the next day the door was still locked, but the vase was gone."

Lohman said, "Every day everyone misplaces something. Do you know what file was missing?"

Fricknoodleh looked at his notes. "World Systems vs. Global Internet Solutions. Your office manager is telling us this. She is saying it is only part of the whole file. 4 file folders she says. What is that involving?"

"Well," Lohman said, "it involves litigation. The case is in court so it is public knowledge so I can tell you some things about it, at least to the extent I know. World Systems is a fairly large company producing and selling a lot of software and what are called 'systems' these days. Most of their products perform some function for businesses, like accounting software. They also set up and manage internet sites for businesses that do not want to set up or run their own sites. That is their main line of business and they are suing Global Internet Solutions for infringing on some of their patents. It is a major piece of litigation. Most of the file is not on paper. It's in our computer. The four folders you were told about were probably just Kirkland's own personal file on the matter."

Lohman called Tete on the intercom and asked her to find out who had the file if she could.

"Right Hon," she growled.

He turned to Fricknoodleh and said, "We'll try to find it for you. Most of us work from documents that have been scanned into the firm's computers so we don't have too many files around, but many of the older lawyers still want to use the paper documents and files and sometimes we all have to look at the actual papers. When the paper file is used it is checked out to whoever has it so we should be able to find out something. Four file folders would only be a small part of the file on this case and it would probably be just a sub file. Maybe just Kirkland's personal file as I told you. Why the office manager can't track it down, I don't know."

"As for the vase," said Lohman, "You are probably talking about Monahan O'Reilley's vase. Monahan is one of our semi-retired partners. We call him 'Of Counsel'. He gets confused sometimes. In particular he loses the vase lots of times. It usually turns up later."

What Lohman didn't tell them was that O'Reilley usually drank his lunch and often what he called mid-afternoon tea with some of his drinking buddies, and very often did not remember much. It was an open secret that he often took the vase with him when he left the office and looked like he was trying to hide it. There was much gossip about it, but no one knew what he was doing. Lohman did, having walked in on O'Reilley one afternoon without warning. Good old Monahan was barfing in his vase. Monahan made up the excuse that he was not feeling well that day because of a "bug" and then said, "I guess I'll have to take it home and clean it up now."

"Again," thought Lohman. "You forgot to say 'again'".

"We will investigate," said Fricknoodleh. "What are you knowing about Featherbottom? We are told Mr. Kirkland did not like him and tried to get him fired."

"And Mr. LaRue," said O'Malley. "We hear Kirkland had it in for him too. What do you know about that?"

"And Mr. Weinstein and Mr. Patel," said Fricknoodleh. "How are they liking Mr.Kirkland?"

"Who did you hear all this from?" Lohman wanted to know who was leaking this to the cops. He said, "I don't have any knowledge of these matters, but I have heard there were some rumors about Featherbottom. So far as I know Kirkland got along well with the others."

"Who did you hear these rumors from?" asked O'Malley.

"I can't remember," Lohman parried.

Lohman was beginning to wonder. "Sean's one of our best associates. Kirkland did very intellectually demanding work which he really -" Lohman paused because he had about said "wasn't up to", but he recovered and went on, "excelled at and for which he needed associates with superior skills. Of course he was assisted on many matters by Mr. Fitzhubery, who also had similar skills, but they worked on so many matters of such size that they needed a lot of other lawyers working with them."

In truth Egon was no legal wizard either, but both he and Kirkland thought they were. If anything out of the ordinary came up they just parried any discussion of the topic by stating that they had people who handled such mundane matters for them. To Kirkland and Egon ignorance of the law was not an excuse. It was something to be proud of. Their ignorance was matched only by their arrogance. In retail you cannot sell something you do not have. In law you can.

Lohman also recalled what Kirkland and Fitzhubery thought about Sean. Sean was very working class according to them. Sean's father had been a steelworker and they often made cracks about Sean's background and his consequent inability to appreciate or understand some supposedly sophisticated or upper class thing. Sean dated a lawyer named Tammy Fine who worked at a small law firm in town and Kirkland and Fitzhubery did not approve of her either. She handled consumer class actions on the plaintiffs' side and that by itself was reprehensible. As a matter of fact her firm usually had a few cases pending against Fenton, Pettigrew clients. She was kind of a rough critter who could drop dirty words without notice - just like the men. One time Sean and she came to a party involving some clients, one of whom was being sued by Tammy's firm. Tammy and that client met and talked. Civilly, curtly and shortly. Kirkland and Fitzhubery never stopped talking about it.

However, just as defense lawyers would be out of a job without all the plaintiffs' lawyers they complain about, snobs would be out of business without lowlifes. Kirkland and Fitzhubery were the type of people who need a steady stream of people they could look down on in order to reassure themselves that they occupied the penthouse. So Sean and Tammy were necessary parts of their existence.

Lohman wasn't about to tell the detectives any more about Sean. They knew how he was treated by Kirkland and Lohman did not want to add any of the details. He was beginning to wonder about Sean, but he also had a duty to present a good face for the firm to the world.

Then O'Malley asked about Egon's wife. Lohman said he didn't know her too well, but she seemed to be nice. What Lohman really knew was the Egon's wife was a drunk. Everyone knew it. Egon constantly complained about it. If O'Malley hadn't heard that yet, Lohman wasn't going to tell him.

O'Malley asked, "Would she be the reason there are rumors about Mr. Fitzhubery?"

"What rumors?" asked Lohman. As if he didn't know. Actually, if left to his own devices he wouldn't know. He didn't much engage in office gossip, but Tete knew all and told him all.

O'Malley continued, "We've been told that Mr. Fitzhubery has had affairs with more than one woman in your firm and even Mrs. Kirkland."

The last was news to Lohman. "Maybe," he thought to himself, "that's why she did not call in about his absence." He made a note to talk to Tete about it. He said, "I am aware that there were some rumors, but I don't think any of them has been substantiated. Certainly we have never had any trouble in the firm because of them that I am aware of."

"You know," said O'Malley, "the younger people here know a lot

132

more than the older people. Talking to the people who have been here a while is like talking to a bunch of crooks."

Lohman's radar started sending warning signals. Lawyer jokes were one thing, but criminal charges are another thing. To his relief O'Malley finished with, "None of them saw anything or heard anything."

Lohman's fears subsided and he was comforted that the constant reminders to firm personnel not to talk or gossip about the firm, but to refer all inquiries about sensitive matters to him, were having some effect, at least on the older element. Of course they generally had more to hide themselves

Then O'Malley asked, "Mr. Fitzhubery was found sleeping in his office the day after the murder. The next morning one of the secretaries said she saw him sleeping there when she came in early and went by his open door. Do you know anything about that?"

"No," said Lohman, "but very often people in a firm like this work long hours or even all night and it is not uncommon to find someone asleep here in the morning. We try to get them to close their doors though. Have you found out anything more about what happened?"

O'Malley told him that the medical examiner had narrowed the time of death down to between 8 p.m. and midnight. O'Malley said, "We found a marble bust and a ceremonial dagger in his office. The ones that you had in the waiting room. Apparently he was hit over the head with the bust and then stabbed with the dagger. We couldn't find any prints on those items, but we found a lot of prints around Mr. Kirkland's office that belong to people in the firm and the cleaning crew. There were a lot of other prints we couldn't identify and a lot of partials. As you know he was using one of the smaller offices off the conference room area and those offices are not exclusive to any one person, but are used by whoever is using the Lake County office at the time. That would account for so many prints."

"So do you know who did it?" asked Lohman.

"We are not knowing now," said Fricknoodleh.

O'Malley took over again. "We are piecing things together. We talked to a lot of people up there who use this office downtown too. The night Mr. Kirkland was killed all the other partners and secretaries had left by 5:30. Except for Kirkland of course. All the associates except Featherbottom had left by 7:30 and they all alibied each other except Mr. Featherbottom. Apparently he was the last to leave. Except for one of the cleaning crew - she was there. I forget her.. ."

"She is Kazmerski. Wanda she is called," said Fricknoodleh.

"Yeah," said O'Malley. "We talked to her. She saw him leave. Couldn't say exactly when. She says when she left only Kirkland was there. She left about 9:15 she says. Says she stopped at a convenience store and then drove home. We found someone at the store who remembers her. Says she comes in there about the same time every night after work. So except for her Featherbottom was the last to leave. She says she had gone to Kirkland's office after Sean left to get the wastebasket and Kirkland was still alive. He told her to get the Hell out."

O'Malley went on. "Featherbottom. He couldn't name anyone who could vouch for his whereabouts later. Says he went home from there. We got something Mr. Pigman calls redacted time sheets. He says no client specific material is in them. Featherbottom's time sheets show he had been talking to Mr. Kirkland earlier and then was reviewing documents. His time records end at 7:45. As you know, even if he left, his code was used to get in later. He says he didn't come back."

Lohman remembered what Tambola Cook had said, "There's someone who said she saw him later that night. Tambola Cook. Did you talk to her? She says she saw him in town that night near where she lives."

Fricknoodleh said, "He is saying he went home and he was staying there."

"Well, talk to her," said Lohman. "Maybe I'm mistaken, but I thought she said she saw him. And I think she said he was with Jason Kunz who is one of our file clerks."

O'Malley and Fricknoodleh both made notes of this. Then O'Malley asked, "Do you know where Mr. LaRue was that night?"

Lohman wondered why they were asking about LaRue all of a sudden. Maybe they had heard that Kirkland had tried to get him kicked out of the firm. Did they know what LaRue was up to? Was LaRue actually there? At home with his wife? In the Lake County office? Trina LaRue had told Gloria that LaRue was at home. He said he was at home. But what about Winkleman? If necessary Winkleman could provide an alibi. Maybe. Would he admit to being there? What were they doing? "So far as I know," said Lohman, "he was at home having dinner with his wife."

O'Malley asked, "How do you know that?"

"He told me," said Lohman.

O'Malley said, "His wife told us that only she and LaRue were there."

135

The Dead Man Says

Lohman said, "Well, so that's where he was."

"So no one is seeing Mr. LaRue there except his wife?" asked Fricknoodleh.

"Not that I know of," said Lohman. Then he told them about Crane going there. "Crane said there was a State car parked outside. LaRue told me he didn't know anything about it."

"We are being investigating," said Fricknoodleh.

"We'd like some corroboration as to where LaRue was," said O'Malley.

"Are you knowing of anyone who can corroborate?" asked Fricknoodleh.

"The only one I can think of who knows anything is Crane," said Lohman. "Ask him."

Fricknoodleh said, "Be asking him about the tea cups."

"Oh yeah," said O'Malley. "There were two used tea cups on Mr. Kirkland's desk. No prints were found on them. Do you know anything about that?"

"Not really," said Lohman. "Ellis did like to have tea once in a while. He made quite a thing out of it." What Lohman really knew is that Kirkland conceived of tea as a social ritual for the upper classes. He would not ordinarily drink tea with just anyone. He would not do so with most of the people in the firm or most of his clients. He would though, talk about his tea rituals to impress various people. One of the few firm people Lohman had ever heard Kirkland speak of having had tea with was Egon

Fitzhubery. St. Charles was another. And he was supposed to see Ellis that night. Since Egon had not been there, who did Kirkland have the tea with? Had the Queen of England slipped into town unnoticed? Had Kirkland been confronted with such a conundrum he would have spared nothing to find out who the exalted guest was. Lohman could care less. Except for the idea that it could have been the murderer. Who was it? "So what else did you find out?" he asked.

Fricknoodleh said, "We have been talking to your tech support."

"Henner Pigman?" asked Lohman.

"Correct," said Fricknoodleh. "That is the one. Besides the codes for getting in the office he is explaining your phone system to us. You are having a very sophisticated system. We are tracking all the calls that are going there that night and only two calls are coming in or out of the office after 7:34 p.m. At 7:34 a call is coming to the office where Mr. Featherbottom is working. It is being forwarded from his office here in downtown. It is coming from outside the firm. We are tracking it down and it is coming from one of the few pay phones being left in Chicago. The phone is being just outside a 7-11 store on Halsted Street. At a cross street named Roscoe. We are having no information on who is placing the call or what is being said. Mr. Featherbottom is saying it is being a wrong number."

"After that call," Fricknoodleh continued, "there are two more calls. Both are coming to or from Mr. Kirkland's office. One is coming from Mr. Kirkland to a number registered to Mr. Patel and one is coming from a number registered to Mr. Weinstein. Patel's is going out around 9:00 and Weinstein's is coming in around 9:15."

"So," said O'Malley, "we have Kirkland up there. Maybe

137

The Dead Man Says

Featherbotton came back and killed him. We have to talk to this Patel and Weinstein still. Featherbottom says he was not there. The tech guy says the codes are personal and no one but the person to whom the code is issued is supposed to know the code. You say this, what's her name?" He looked at his notes. "She says she saw Featherbottom in town later. It looks like we have a few more details to tie up. Anyway, whatever we find out, it looks like Featherbottom was the only one who could have been there. Of course that does not preclude someone having gotten in by ringing the bell and being let it."

Lohman said, "I think the computer is supposed to keep track of all door openings. Let's call Pigman." Lohman did so and Pigman was in. Pigman informed Lohman that the computer did not keep track of all door openings. Lohman told the officers.

O'Malley continued. "We haven't been able to find any witnesses yet to what happened there. As you know, the office is on a service road next to a major road and not within sight of any homes or businesses that are open at that hour. Your firm is the only occupant of that building. And you have your own parking lot. The cleaning people had all left by 9:15 when the last one says she left. So we don't have anyone up there who saw anything, at least to tell us."

Lohman liked Sean. What was going on, Lohman did not know. Maybe Sean did kill Kirkland. Not a bad thing, he thought. So he said, "You know, Ellis would never have had tea with Sean. Ellis was very particular about who he had tea with." Now Lohman went for another little lie. Instead of telling them what Kirkland thought about Sean and what a snob Kirkland was, he merely said, "Ellis never had tea with the associates."

The Dead Man Says

After the detectives left Lohman caught up on some client matters and then attended a lunch conference with the firm's marketing director and some of his assistants in one of the conference rooms.

24 SO WHO'S A POOF?

After lunch Lohman went back to his office and started to follow up on some things. He remembered that Tambola Cook had said she saw Sean and Jason at Drinkers on the fatal Tuesday night. He looked up Drinkers in the phone book. (Yes he still had one and used it). He noted its address. It was on North Halsted Street at Roscoe. Then he looked it up on the internet (yes he could do that too). He found more information on the internet. Apparently it was a gay bar and was located in a part of town called Boystown. At least Lohman concluded this from the statements and pictures he saw. "Boystown's cutest guys!" The pictures did not include any women - or much in the way of clothing either.

Lohman printed out the internet page he was looking at and got up and walked out to Tete's desk. He showed her the print out and asked her if she had ever heard of the place. She took a quick look and said, "What do you want with a place like that?"

"I just want to know if you ever heard of it. Tambola says she saw Sean going in there with Jason the night Ellis was killed," said Lohman.

Tete had set the page down on her desk. She picked it up and took a longer look. "Oh crapola!" she said. "One of those places. Look at this! I believe our beneficent Saint would call that a place of sordid adventure." She straightened up and put her nose in the air when she said this. "No. I never heard of it." She sometimes referred to St. Charles merely as the Saint. "Wasn't he supposed to be up in Lake County?"

"So I thought," said Lohman.

The Dead Man Says

Lohman got ahold of Jason Kunz and asked him to come to his office. Kunz came in a little while later after being announced by Tete. He seemed a little nervous, which was natural for a file clerk who has just been called to one of the big bosses' offices. Lohman said, "Take it easy. Nothing is wrong, no problems with your work or any of the people around here. That's not why I asked to see you."

Lohman then got to the point, "I am told you were with Sean Featherbottom the night Mr. Kirkland died. Is that so?"

"Who wants to know?" asked Jason. "Why do you want to know?"

Lohman tried a different tack. "Where were you that night?"

Jason said, "I was at Drinkers. Alone. I came home about 11:30. I didn't hook up with anyone."

Lohman was unclear about the exact meaning of "hook up", but he gathered it involved the presence of another person. Lohman asked, "Do you know where Sean was that night?"

"How should I know!" said Jason.

"Just wondered," said Lohman. "You have probably been asked where you were and a lot of other things by people trying to sort out this Kirkland mess. We're trying to find out where everyone was."

Then Lohman tried to calm him. "You don't have anything to worry about. I'm just following up about Kirkland. You should know that we are very pleased with your performance here and all this does not involve you. I want you to be at ease. We're very happy with you."

The Dead Man Says

Kunz looked to one side and then to the other and then said tentatively, "Thanks."

"What it is, is that Tambola Cook says she saw you and Sean going into Drinkers together. Did you see her?" asked Lohman.

"Oh her," said Jason. "I know her. Whenever I take files to her office she's always on about two things. She wants to complain about things here or she wants to talk about Sean. She knows we're friends. The last time I was there a few weeks ago she was telling me that Mr. Kirkland was interfering with her personal development she called it. She said she was going to fix him. Then she wanted to ask me about Sean. When did I see him last, what was he doing, and like that. It's hard to get out of her office without just leaving while she's talking, if you know what I mean."

Lohman asked, "What - how was she going to fix him?"

"I don't know," said Jason. "I didn't ask. I just wanted to get out of there."

Now Lohman decided to follow up on St. Charles's concerns. He asked Jason if he was making unwanted sexual comments or overtures to anyone in the firm. Lohman had been so busy that he hadn't gotten around to this yet. "You know that sexual harassment violates the civil rights laws, and at least under the Chicago Code, sexual preference is a protected category."

"It is?" Jason was taken aback. (Yes, young people can do what old phrases describe.)

"Yes," said Lohman. "If you take action with respect to someone on the basis of a protected category you violate the law. So if sex or sexual preference is a protected category and you treat someone differently because of it, you violate the law. For instance making sexual overtures to someone, say a woman, would be a violation. At least if the overtures are not consented to. This is because the action is based on sex. And if it is job related and the firm knows about it and does nothing about it the firm can be in violation of the law as well."

"I don't do none of that," said Jason.

"Which?" asked Lohman. "The women?"

"Men either," said Jason. "How come that's against the law? If there are pants or panties around here someone's trying to get in 'em."

"It just is," said Lohman. "Now, please just conduct yourself accordingly."

"I can't do anyone here?" asked Jason incredulously. "Everyone else does it."

Lohman sighed. "If they consent or ask for it, it's OK," he said.

"They're all asking for it," said Jason.

"I mean if they initiate it," said Lohman. "At any rate they can change their story afterwards, but I'm just trying to make sure you don't generate any more complaints."

"Someone complained about me?" said Jason.

"Yes," said Lohman.

"Who?"

"I was told by a third person and that third person told me it was confidential. I was not told who complained," said Lohman. "Do you have any idea who it was?"

Jason said he didn't.

"All right. Just be careful in the future," said Lohman. "Now if you have any questions or concerns, just give me a call."

Lohman told him he could go. Then he called Tete in and discussed the matter with her. He went over what Tambola Cook had told him and what Jason had just told him and what Egon had told him about Sean being gay. "Is something going on here I'm missing?" he asked. "Is someone trying to set Sean up? Is someone trying to set him up with an alibi? Can he be in two places at once? Is he gay?"

Tete said, "Why don't you ask Winter Goren? He's the official Firm Fruit. He seems to know everybody's sexual habits and all the gossip. Maybe Sean's a closet case. You know his so called girl friend is a lesbian, don't you."

"How do you know that?" asked Lohman.

Tete just said, "Oh please Hon," and turned on her heel and left.

Lohman called Goren. Goren was indeed the Firm Fruit. He was out, effeminate and flamboyant. He was fond of double breasted cream colored suits with lavender shirts and cream colored ties and hats with wide brims. He wore white rimmed sun glasses with glitter on them and cream colored patent leather shoes. Not that he was always a screamer. He wore black patent leather shoes at wakes. He had a lot of got-bucks clients so he was OK. The firm often trotted him out to show how open minded and non-discriminatory it was. St. Charles, though, refused to acknowledge that Goren was gay. St. Charles referred to Goren as being

The Dead Man Says

"creative" or "artistic".

Lohman asked Winter if he could come to his office. Goren was agreeable and Lohman arrived there shortly.

"Winter," said Lohman, "I have a favor to ask of you. I don't want to go into the details, but I want to know if someone is gay. It has nothing to do with his performance review or his progress in the firm."

"Why Honey," said Winter, "are you interested in him? I know how you so-called straight boys are." Goren held out his hand in front of his face with the fingers spread and examined his nails.

"Oh Christ!" said Lohman. "What guy around here haven't you tried? No. I'm not interested in him. I just can't tell you what it's about right now. It's Sean Featherbottom. Do you know anything about him?"

"Oh him!" exclaimed Winter. "What a cutie. I think you're on target there. Haven't you ever seen a closet case before? Anyway, I have it on good authority that he's been done by at least one of the guy's here."

"Who?" asked Lohman.

"You shouldn't ask and I shouldn't tell," said Winter.

They chatted a little more and Lohman went back to his office.

Lohman got ahold of Sean and had him come into his office. They made nice talk and then Lohman told Sean that his code had been used to get into the Lake County office the night when Kirkland was killed. After Sean said he had left.

Sean said, "I know. The police told me. I don't know how that can be. I didn't come back after I left.

Lohman said, "Yes, O'Malley and Fricknoodleh told me they found out your code was used and it sounds to me like you are a suspect. What did you do that night? You want to tell me before this gets out of hand?"

Sean said he had been in the office working on a brief in the World Systems v Global Internet Solutions case and he left between 8:30 and 9:00, although he wasn't certain about the exact time. He said he went home and stayed there the rest of the night.

"Can anyone confirm that?" asked Lohman. "Can anyone say when you left and what you did after that?"

"Not that I know of," said Sean. He was beginning to look uncomfortable.

"Were you at Drinkers that night with Jason Kunz?" asked Lohman.

"What is Drinkers?" asked Sean.

"Are you gay?" asked Lohman

"Isn't that an improper question?" asked Sean.

"When we had that associates' lunch over at the College Club last month, you remember, you were sitting next to me, and the waiter called you sweetie. What was that all about?" asked Lohman.

"I don't remember that," said Sean. "What did he look like?"

Lohman did not reply. Instead he went on to questions about

The Dead Man Says

Kirkland. "Did you have contact with Ellis that night? Did Ellis mention anyone else? Did you see anyone else with him? Did he say anything to you? Did he mention having tea with anyone?"

Sean said, "No. We didn't have any contact other than a conversation about the Weinstein file. He told me some things he wanted me to do, but he told me to hold off until he got confirmation from Weinstein. He said he hadn't got the go ahead from Weinstein. Why is everyone asking about Weinstein?"

Lohman asked, "Who wants to know about it?"

Sean said, "Well, the police. And several days before Mr. Fitzhubery and I went up there to see Mr. Kirkland in the evening. The door was locked as usual and I was opening it for Mr. Fitzhubery. You know how he always wants people to open doors for him and things. Mr. Fitzhubery was waiting behind me. He started asking about Weinstein. It startled me. I was putting in my code on the key pad and he was almost speaking in my ear. Mr. Fitzhubery had told me earlier that he wanted me to go up there with him. I had told him that I had a deadline to meet on another matter, but he insisted that I come up there with him. I don't know what I was there for. All the two of them did was discuss the Weinstein matter and who was going to do what and how much they thought they could bill. Mr. Kirkland even complimented Mr. Fitzhubery for bringing me. He said they should be sure to see that everything for Mr. Weinstein should have similar levels of adequate staffing, as he put it, in the future."

Lohman then asked Sean about Tambola Cook. Sean said, "She's a pain in the ass. She is always showing up in my office and wants to talk about useless things. A lot of the time she asks about files we are working on together, but what she says or asks about them isn't very work-related. When we aren't working on the same things she talks about the things we worked on before or about firm policies or firm gossip. It's just made up talk. She even makes up things like she needs an excuse to talk to me. She is always calling me too. Just about made up things and inane stuff. I think she likes me, if you know what I mean, but please. She's hardly my type."

"What type of things does she talk about? What does she make up?" asked Lohman.

"Oh, just anything," said Sean. "Here's a good one. A while ago she calls me in the evening and says she is at the Lake County office and can't get in because she forgot her code. She wanted my code. So I gave it to her. The next day I found out she wasn't even there. She makes things up. She even makes things up about me. Once she told someone I was on a date with her the night before. I was so embarrassed. She even said where. I asked her why she did that and she just said we should have been there together."

"When was this that you gave her your code?" asked Lohman.

Sean said, "Just after the codes were changed last time. I can't remember exactly when." The firm changed the codes periodically for security reasons. Naturally people who had enough trouble remembering their original codes had more trouble every time the codes were changed.

Lohman asked, "Did you ever give your code to anyone else?"

"No," said Sean.

25 MONDAY EVENING - A PARTY

Clayton Fenger had bucks. He was retired, but he still held a controlling interest in some of the firm's corporate clients. On top of that he had numerous investments that needed tending to. While he had others doing his business for him, he was still the owner and still the ultimate control person. Someone to know and be on the good side of. He was known to one and all as Clay and lately he and his wife had been getting a little eccentric. Like having big parties on week nights. They didn't seem to care what day it was. Some people were saying they didn't know. So Monday evening Lohman and others from the firm were invited to a large party at Clay's house.

It was very large house on a high bluff overlooking Lake Michigan in Kenilworth, one of the North Shore suburbs. The house had been designed by Chicago's most prominent society architect of the early part of the 20th century and it was in the Americanized Beaux Arts style. The furnishings resembled those found at Versailles or Buckingham Palace. The grounds were lavish and kept up by a crew of gardeners.

The Fengers subscribed to and applied the principle that nothing shows success like excess. Dinner was served on a large terrace overlooking the Lake and there was an orchestra for after dinner dancing in the old style. The Fengers liked this, but many of their guests, especially the younger ones, had no idea of how to do it. Periodically the band took a break and old disco tunes were played over the loudspeakers. The younger ones (in their late 40's and 50's) did like that. Whenever the women heard a song they liked they would come flocking to the dance floor en mass, hauling their men behind them. Lohman thought it odd that such old people who dressed so well should be doing kids' dances. He forgot how long ago the disco scene was and that these people were young then.

In one of the interludes Lohman and his wife got to talking with the Fengers. Lohman asked them how they liked the opera they went to with Egon several weeks ago. "What opera?" asked Clayton. His wife didn't seem to remember it either. However they proclaimed that they had season tickets for the opera and enjoyed it immensely. They said they often went with the Fitzhuberys.

Mrs. Fenger went on about various operas and singers and opera companies. Clayton kept asking what day they had gone and even called her Shirley. Her name was Joan, but he got it right most of the time. Joan was in better shape, but she was still a bit of a duzz bucket. She went into an adjoining room and got a calendar out of a desk and showed it to Clayton and the Lohmans. "There," she said. "It was Tuesday the week before last. Look here." She pointed to the book. "It's right here in your calendar Clayton."

He looked and said "Did you put that there?"

"No. Of course not," she said. "You know I don't make entries in your book." Then she showed the book to the Lohmans. Bumper looked and saw the entry for "Opera with the Fitzhuberys" on Tuesday.

"Now I remember," said Clayton. "When Egon was here last time we were discussing it and I remember he showed me that entry." The Fengers went on more about the opera, but it was a bit over the Lohmans' heads. Other guests rescued them soon enough and they took their leave and went home.

26 WEINSTEIN'S BUSINESS AND KIRKLAND'S FILE

Tuesday Lohman got ahold of Weinstein and asked him to come in. He did later that afternoon. They met in Lohman's office and Lohman reviewed Weinstein's project and who was working on it and the status of various things. Lohman told Weinstein, "By now you know all about Ellis and I'm sure the police and a lot of other people have talked to you about him. However, there are some questions I want to get straight so I thought I'd ask you rather than depend on hearsay. For instance, did you tell Ellis that you wanted to go ahead with your project? When?"

"The night he died," said Weinstein. "I called him about 9 or 9:30 and told him to go ahead with it."

"Who else did you tell," asked Lohman.

"No one, at least not then," said Weinstein. "I can remember telling Egon that I wanted to go ahead, but that was a day or two later. When I found out about Ellis, I called Egon because I knew he was working on some of my things. I don't think I mentioned it to anybody till then. Why? Is it important?"

"It isn't that important really," said Lohman. "I just wanted to check it out and to see that everyone has been doing their job since you gave the green light."

"I remember," said Weinstein. "I told Egon Thursday. I was going to the barber that day. I always go on Thursday. I remember telling him."

Lohman asked, "Did you tell anyone else before you told Egon? Did you discuss it with anyone?"

151

The Dead Man Says

"Hold on," said Weinstein. "I remember having lunch with Qwen Lohfahrt the day after. We were having lunch at the club and we were discussing what could be done with offshore entities."

"And you told him you had approved our going ahead with your arrangements?" asked Lohman.

"No. No," said Weinstein. "I didn't tell him I had decided to go ahead with you. I just told him about the subject."

"Did you discuss your phone conversation with Ellis the night before?"

"No," said Weinstein. "I'm sure we did not discuss that."

Lohman and Weinstein parted and Weinstein went to the conference center to meet with some of the lawyers working on his project who had some things to go over with him. Lohman spent the rest of the day on his own clients' matters.

The next morning Tete came into Lohman's office. She had news about the file that was missing from Kirkland's office. Normally whoever has a file has to check it out so the file center knew where it was. If people do not bring a file back, and instead give it to another person, they are supposed to inform the file center of that. The person who checked a file out was responsible for it. The firm wanted to know where all its files were at all times.

The file in question was checked out to Kirkland. No change had been entered in the system. However, Tete had put her nose in the firm's computer and found out that Egon was now the head partner on the World Systems case and she had gone to his office to ask him about the file. He told her he didn't know anything about the file, but it was sitting on his desk while he told her this. She took it. Nobody argued with Tete. She put it on Lohman's desk.

"What's in it." he asked.

Tete said, "It's a sub-file. It has a lot of Kirkland's notes and summaries of who is going to do what and all sorts of general information about the client and Kirkland's usual client stuff."

Kirkland's usual client stuff included all sorts of information about the client and contact people for the client. As much information as he could get. For instance, names of children and their ages. Who went to what school and when. Resumes. Credit reports. Notes about criminal convictions and law suits. Everything he could get his hands on. He used this information in dealing with the clients. The more you remember about a client the more a client likes it - at least as to some things. The other things were sometimes handy for controlling the clients and the contact people. Kirkland kept this information on his computer in a form only accessible to him. He also put a copy into the file for each client matter.

Why Egon would want this was obvious. He was trying to take over as much of Kirkland's businesses as possible. Kirkland had had the file. When did Egon get it?

Lohman called Egon. He was out and Lohman called his cell phone. As it turned out Egon was shopping. Lohman wondered who he was billing for it. "Egon," said Lohman, "remember the World Systems file Tete got from you? When did you get it?"

"A day or so after Ellis died," said Egon. "I wanted to get up to speed on the file so I took it out of the Lake County office when I was coming downtown. I stopped in there on the way. I think it was Thursday morning. We had discussed it before and he told me where it was. It was in his credenza."

"So how come you didn't tell files you had it?" asked Lohman.

"I forgot," said Egon. More nearly such a matter was beneath his attention.

Just out of curiosity Lohman called Beth Morse, the Lake County office manager. "Hi Beth. This is Bumper."

"Hello Mr. Lohman," she said. "How are you?"

"Fine," he said. "When did you notice that World Systems file was missing?"

Beth said, "I don't know. I just remember I couldn't

find it. Why?"

"When did you tell the officers about it?"

"That day when they were up here I think," she said.

"Is that when you told them it was missing?" he asked.

"Oh I don't know. Maybe. I don't think so. We talked about it later too."

Lohman sighed and said, "Well, if you can remember, let me know."

27 THE DAMN COPS AGAIN

Just then Tete rang Lohman and told him, "Cops again. They're down at reception."

Lohman had other things to do. "What the hell for?" he said.

"Got me," she said. "They're cops. Strange ones. Who knows what they want. Maybe donuts."

Lohman didn't want to offend them and cause trouble. "Send them up," he said.

Soon O'Malley and Fricknoodleh were in his office. They exchanged greetings. "So what's up?" asked Lohman.

"We are tying up ends," said Fricknoodleh.

O'Malley said, "We just need to straighten out a few things."

"So how can I help?" asked Lohman

"We talked to Crane again," said O'Malley. He told us about going to LaRue's home Tuesday night. He told us about the car, you know."

"You mean the Ford?" asked Lohman.

"Yes, we are meaning that," said Fricknoodleh. "It is being a Ford Crown Victoria. Black sedan. It is what we are being driving. Except our one is labeled Police Interceptor and is having stiffer springs."

O'Malley said, "You probably have seen them. Ford doesn't make them anymore and even when they did most were sold for police or government use. The police versions are called Police Interceptor. The name plate is on the back on the trunk lid. After we're done with them they usually become cabs. If you have noticed, most of the cabs are Ford Police Interceptors. Some are the Crown Vics. We're switching to other vehicles now, but there are still a lot of the Fords in use."

"So what about it?" asked Lohman.

O'Malley said, "Crane remembered some of the license plate. We got some of the numbers from him and then ran them and got a list of all the State cars with those numbers on the plates. Some weren't Ford Crown Vics so we narrowed it down just to the plates on Crown Vics. Then we contacted the departments the plates were assigned to and got a list of who the cars were assigned to. Most weren't assigned to anyone in particular. Here's the list. Do you know anyone on it?" He pulled a list out of a folder and gave it to Lohman.

The list consisted of two pages with two columns of names on each page. Most of the names had notations of what position or what department the person was in. Lohman looked at the list. He didn't know anyone on it off hand, but he had heard of a few of the people through their being in the news. He was about to hand the list back to O'Malley when he saw the name Gordon Winkleman on it. The position listed was State Purchasing Director. For God's sake! He had asked LaRue if anyone was at LaRue's house that night. La Rue had denied it, but his wife had told Gloria a Gordon Winkleman was there. And Lohman knew LaRue was trying to get a large state contract for one of his clients.

He had retracted his arm holding the document while he was thinking about all this.

The Dead Man Says

"Yes?" asked Fricknoodleh. "What are you seeing?"

"Oh nothing," said Lohman. Just someone I have heard of on the news. I thought they would give him a better car." He handed the list back to O'Malley.

"Tell us about Featherbottom," said O'Malley. "What kind of car does he drive?"

Lohman did not know. "I don't know," he said. "I don't even know for sure if he drives. All I ever heard him talking about is riding his bicycle. And taking the train."

"So," said O'Malley, "what did he have against Mr. Kirkland? What was the trouble there?"

"I don't know that there was any trouble. Ellis wasn't the easiest person to work for and he sort of looked down on Sean's social background, but Sean did not seem to react more adversely to that than any other associate who had to work for Ellis or a lot of the other partners around here. Frankly, being a young lawyer in a large law firm these days is not so pleasant. If they aren't asleep they are working and some of the people they work for are rather difficult."

"That is what all you guys say," said O'Malley. "But we are used to this in a murder investigation. Everyone covers up and says there aren't any problems here. It's ridiculous. You don't have anything to worry about. We aren't going to tell your secrets to the world."

"So what's all this about Sean? Tambola Cook saw him in town that night," said Lohman.

"She is saying anything Featherbottom wants," said Fricknoodleh.

The Dead Man Says

"You are knowing that. And who is saying she herself was there?"

"I see," said Lohman. "Well is that all you are trying to find out? Just about Featherbottom?"

"Oh no. We're following up on everyone," said O'Malley.

Lohman suspected they were focusing on Sean, but he didn't say anything. He and the officers then got into discussing what they had been doing earlier that day. Evidently they had been in the office talking to a lot of other people and no one had told Lohman. He tried to ask them nicely to let him know they were coming beforehand next time as they were saying goodbye, but he realized that this might lead to a confrontation and warrants being obtained and other unpleasant things. He began to feel annoyed at the time this was taking and the disruption it was causing. If they talked to 10 lawyers for half an hour each that was 5 hours. And how many people had they been talking to already for how many hours? Lots of money. The Management Committee wouldn't like this. But to Lohman personally what really mattered was that this was one more problem he had to deal with.

Lohman began to think about Sean. Did he kill Ellis? Why? Should he talk to Sean about it? If Sean was the killer, would that tip him off to get out of town as it were? And what about Tambola? Was she in on it? Or did she use the code? Just then Tete rang him again.

28 MAKE IT GO AWAY BUMPER

"It's hot button time Hon. The Saint called. It's big time. He was on the phone himself. He wants you up in his office right now. 'Damn office', he said. I think it's the fourth time in his life he said a naughty word. He had trouble pronouncing it. So Charlie wants to see you bad. Good Luck!"

Lohman had used naughty words more than four times in his life and he said one out loud. Then he grabbed a note pad and pen and headed for St. Charles' office.

When he got there St. Charles' secretary looked pale as a ghost. She looked scared. She mumbled that he was expected and motioned him in. She looked like she had just swallowed a cow. Lohman heard noise coming through the door from St. Charles' office. Lohman went up to the door, opened it and stepped into pandemonium. St. Charles was running across the office with his arms out-stretched shouting, "Get your hands off my Pussy!"

It was like a nursing home exercise session on crack. A lot of the members of the Management Committee were there and most were standing around. One was standing up on a chair. Lohman was not listening to the precise words, but most of them were emitting some kind of sounds. Some seemed to be trying to get out of the way of something.

St. Charles was running towards one of the partners who was holding Pussy, St. Charles' cat. The cat's fur was standing up on end and it was hissing. Another one of the partners was holding a Rottweiler on a leash that was trying to get at the cat and growling and barking. St. Charles reached the cat and snatched it out of the partner's hands and

159

shouted at the partner with the dog. "Get that beast out of here!"

Another partner who owned the dog came forward and took the leash and grabbed the dog by the collar and dragged it out. The rest of the partners started brushing themselves off and straightening out their clothing and preparing to sit down.

Lohman asked, "What's going on?"

"Ruhlman!" said St. Charles. "His beast! We have to outlaw it!" By now he was cuddling and kissing Pussy. "Oh poor Pussy. Dear, dear Pussy. Did big bad dog scare you? Was you-ums hurt? Oh, I'll make it up to you. We'll get fresh salmon tonight." He continued on with a lot of goo-goo sounds Lohman really couldn't interpret.

Ruhlman was the dog owner. Pincus Ruhlman. Who brings a dog to a law office? An equity partner generally does whatever he wants and sometimes Ruhlman wanted to bring his dog to the office. Whenever he did there was a problem because he could not stand to be without the dog. Wherever he went the dog went. This time though, he had apparently been busy and had told his secretary to take the dog out for a walk. While they were out the call came to get up to St. Charles' office on an emergency basis and he had gone there before his secretary came back with the dog. When the secretary came back and learned Ruhlman was in St. Charles' office she took the dog up there. Since St. Charles secretary was away from her desk, Ruhlman's secretary just opened the door and let the dog in. She was not thinking about St. Charles' cat. The dog headed straight for the cat and scarred the Viagra residue out of all the old coots.

At this point I wish to remind you that I am not allied or affiliated with or connected to these people in any way. Nor do I have contact with them if I can avoid it. I am merely informing you of these affairs as a good citizen of Chicago.

After a while everyone had calmed down and Pussy was restored to her perch on the little pedestal above and behind St. Charles' desk. Then they could get on with the business. "Look here Lohman," St. Charles started off, "what is going on here? The police have overrun our entire practice. This morning they were here all day asking all sorts of questions to all sorts of people. They are disrupting our practice. And the press keeps talking about this as an unsolved murder and mentioning all sorts of suggestive things about people here." St. Charles continued in the same vein for a while and then the rest of the partners there chimed in. They wanted Lohman to stop it. What? It! Lohman was told it was up to him and he better get to it. Why him? Because whenever they felt they were in trouble they told Lohman it was his job to get them out of it and quick. In this case Lohman was also tired of the time this was taking and he wanted to get rid of it too. If the problem was going to be resolved, his distinguished fellow equity partners weren't going to do it, so he accepted the fact that he had to get to work, find out who offed Ellis, and get the cops out of the office and the firm out of the news.

Cohenstein said, "Everyone thinks Featherbottom did it. The cops keep asking about him. But they don't arrest him. Do you know why Lohman?"

"No," said Lohman. He actually didn't know. But he was going to find out. He had had it. As the meeting was breaking up he made an appointment to see St. Charles the next morning. He might as well start at the top.

29 WHERE WERE YOU GUYS?

The next day Lohman kept his appointment with St. Charles. When he got into St. Charles' office Egon was there. They were talking about fox hunting and gossiping about some of their fellow fox hunters. Very often when Lohman had to see St. Charles Egon was there. To Egon, everything St. Charles said was right and terribly insightful. Egon couldn't compliment St. Charles enough. Egon could not solicit his opinions enough. Egon's nose was very brown.

When Lohman came in he greeted the two. They engaged in some small talk and then Egon left after telling St. Charles how helpful he had been.

"Graybourne," Lohman said, "you know I have to get to the bottom of this Kirkland thing. The cops seem like they are going to take all year. In the meantime it is interfering with all our schedules and some members of the firm are under a cloud of suspicion. Not good. And you know the Committee told me to resolve it. Now, I don't know anything about murder or being a detective, but I'm going to try. So I am going to start with you."

"If you must," said St. Charles with his usual tone of condescension. "I don't see how I can help you."

Lohman knew he had a sensitive issue on his hands and he did not know of any easy way to handle it. So he proceeded. "Now this is just something we have to do. We have to eliminate you as a suspect."

St. Charles immediately straightened up and jutted his chin in the air. "How dare you! You are here to clear this matter up, not to cast aspersions! What's got into you!"

"I know, I know Graybourne," said Lohman. "It could hardly be you. But as a lawyer you know we have to demonstrate that."

"I don't have to show anything to anyone," said St. Charles. "Everyone knows I could not conceivably be involved in this! Those officers who came here - they asked me where I was. I told them it was confidential. They understand these things. They understand the necessity for confidentiality in a law office setting. Besides, they told me that someone like me could never be subject to question or doubt."

"Really?" asked Lohman.

"Why certainly," said St. Charles.

"Well," said Lohman, "Pansy did say you told her you were going to see Kirkland up there on Tuesday night. So we have to show that you were not there. So where were you?"

St. Charles stiffened up, chin in the air, again. "I told you that is confidential. It is absurd to think I could be involved in this and even more absurd to think I should explain anything to anyone." A lot of lawyers like the word "absurd". It is absurd that they should use it so much.

Lohman said, "It's probably not a good idea to take that position with the police."

"Oh good Heavens," said St. Charles. "When you find out who did it my personal affairs will be irrelevant. Get to it."

Lohman sighed. "OK Graybourne. I'll see what I can do." He got up to leave and just as he was about to turn and walk towards the door a glint of light reflected from the sun shining on something on St. Charles' desk caught his eye. He looked more closely and saw a bejeweled letter opener. Lohman had seen it before. The handle was gold. Real gold. It had red rubies set in it along with several green emeralds. Yes, Lohman had seen it before. On Kirkland's desk. It was Kirkland's. He had been proud of it and had placed it prominently on his desk so visitors would notice it and inquire about it, whereupon he would describe it to them and gloat about it. When he went to the Lake County office he took it with him, along with several other conversation pieces.

"Where did you get that?" he asked as he motioned to the letter opener.

"What?" asked St. Charles with all innocence.

"Ellis' letter opener," said Lohman.

"Oh that," said St. Charles. "He won't be needing it anymore."

Just like St. Charles, Lohman thought. Whatever he likes is his. "When did you get it?" he asked.

"Oh I don't remember," said St. Charles with his best tone of insignificance. "Now, if you will excuse me, I have an important phone call to make."

Lohman didn't know what to make of this. He got up, said goodbye, and left.

Next Lohman had scheduled a visit with Zenon Cohenstein. He went across the floor and was admitted. Cohenstein was standing with a legal brief in his hand looking out the window. He liked to look out windows and he liked to been seen in pensive moods and settings. Lohman seated himself in a chair next to Cohenstein's desk. Cohenstein came over to the desk and sat down.

"Good morning Bumper," said Cohenstein.

"Zenon," said Lohman with a nod.

"So what is it?" asked Cohenstein.

"Well," said Lohman, "you know I have to get rid of this problem about Ellis. So we are going to have to find out who did this. Only that is going to put this to rest."

"Are we going to have to pay a reward?" asked Cohenstein with a smile.

Lohman pretended that he did not know Cohenstein was being sarcastic. "Not that I know of," he said. He added his own jest. "Do you mean to the person who fingers the killer or to the person who did it?"

"Both would deserve it," said Cohenstein.

"So," asked Lohman, "what do you know about it? We have a problem with Graybourne. Pansy says he was due to see Ellis that night up there. He won't say where he was. Today I noticed Ellis's letter opener on Greybourne's desk. He wouldn't tell me how he got it. So he was supposed to be there and has Ellis's letter opener which was probably there with Ellis and he won't tell anyone where he was. You can see the problem if this gets out."

"So, didn't I tell you he was with me," stated Cohenstein.

"No," said Lohman.

The Dead Man Says

"Well, that's where he was. And we were not in the Lake County office," said Cohenstein.

"And where were you? Who else was there?" asked Lohman.

"None of your business. Like Grabby says," said Cohenstein.

Lohman said, "That doesn't help. Now if the press hears of this we have to explain about two people. I think you can see the difficulty."

"Not really," said Cohenstein. "Pricknoodle and that Mic dick both went over this with Grabby and me and they can see he isn't a suspect. They understand that someone of his stature wouldn't be involved in this. Me either. And by now they know who gives the Lake County Sheriff nice big campaign contributions. I reminded them. Anyway, we aren't involved so as soon as you nail the creep who is causing all this trouble the better. Then we won't have to explain anything."

"So do you know anything else about anyone who could be involved?" asked Lohman.

"Oh crap!" said Cohenstein. "Just look in front of your nose. That kid Fluffbottom did it."

"Featherbottom," said Lohman.

"Well whatever his name is, I'll bet his bottom feathers get fluffed a lot," said Cohenstein. "He punched himself in. Who else was there? Wrap it up for God's sake."

"I'll see what I can do," said Lohman. He got up and left.

Lohman went back to his office. Tete was hovering over his desk looking for something. "Hi ya Hon," she said when he came in. "Where did you put that letter to Svenson?" Then she found it and picked it up and started looking at it to see if Lohman had made any changes. "Did you see this?" she asked.

"Yes," said Lohman. "Send it." He stood there mute.

"What's with you Hon?" asked Tete. "You act like you got Alzheimer's."

"I'm just thinking," he said. "The Committee wants me to basically find out who killed Ellis and get the police out of here and end the matter. So who is in charge here? Pansy - Lady Fitch-Bennington - says Graybourne was supposed to see Ellis up in Lake County the night he was killed. So I ask him about it and he says where he was is confidential. On top of that he has Ellis' letter opener now. He won't say when he got it. Zenon says he was with Graybourne, but he won't say where they were either. So why would Graybourne meet Ellis in Lake County anyway. Was he up north of there and coming back to Chicago? Was he going to his Lake Forest house from here? I'll have to ask around and see if anyone saw either of them."

"Why don't you just get the two of them together and put it to 'em. Christ - who can't see that they're going to get it with those stories," said Tete.

"But I just talked to them both. They aren't going to go over this again," he said.

"Just go back to Charlie's office," she said. "They'll both be there by the time you get there."

Lohman just looked at her. How does she do these things? He

didn't ask. He just went. When he got to St. Charles' office they were both there.

"Bumper," said Cohenstein, "I think we realize now that we had better explain about Tuesday night. We see your point now."

Lohman thought what they were seeing was Tete's point and, boy, did he wish he knew what it was. But he didn't ask questions. About that. "So where were you guys?" he asked.

St. Charles looked frozen.

"We were at the Pullman Club," said Cohenstein. "With clients. Till late. We can't remember how late."

"At the Pullman Club," repeated St. Charles.

"It was confidential," said Cohenstein

Lohman asked, "So, Zenon, can you say who was there?"

"Yeah," said Cohenstein. "We were having dinner with Swifty and Biffster."

Lohman asked, "So what is so confidential about that"

St. Charles stirred. "Obviously," he said, "if we told you it would not be confidential."

Lohman sighed. If you asked St. Charles the time of day he would tell you that was confidential too. He looked at Cohenstein. "You guys can't say?"

"No," said Cohenstein. "So look. Now it is shown that we were nowhere near the Lake County office. Period. End of matter. Go nail Flufffy."

Lohman went back to his office and told Tete what happened. She sniffed and said, "They sure eat a lot."

"What do you mean?" he asked.

"Accounting called earlier today," she said. "They got a big one on it." She meant a big bill. The firm had a policy that all food and drink expenses over $1000 for any single event had to be specifically approved by the Management Committee. In practice most of these bills were incurred by members of the Management Committee and Lohman himself approved them and just listed them in a report he gave to the Committee each month.

"How big?" asked Lohman. How big a bill could four people run up?

"It isn't here yet. They are sending it. They told me it was ten dinners and a lot of drinks. The dinners were about $750 and the drink and room tab was about $3500. They were two separate bills. One from the dining room and one from the house service. Like those bills you get when you have a private room for a lunch meeting. Accounting wants to know if the $750 is a separate bill so they can pay it now."

"$3500!" said Lohman. "Four guys drink $3500 of booze?"

"The meal tab is for ten," Tete reminded him. "Who knows how many were doing the boozing."

"Well, go ahead and approve it," said Lohman.

169

The Dead Man Says

Lohman had a quick lunch at his desk and then started reviewing motions that had been prepared by an associate for a case concerning one of his clients. In between he handled a steady stream of calls from clients and from within the firm. Before he went home he called Bungus LaRue and made an appointment to see him the next day.

30 MORE ABOUT BUNGUS AND EGON

Early Friday Lohman walked into LaRue's office. "Bungus. How are you?"

"Fine. Fine," said Bungus. "How are you?"

"Sick and tired of all this continual cloud over us about Ellis. Graybourne and Zenon want me to get it over with."

"Miracles are nice," said LaRue.

"So I have to find out what happened," said Lohman.

"So what could I tell you?" asked LaRue.

Lohman began, "Well, I know you are trying to get a state contract. And I have been told a State type car was outside your house Tuesday night. And I have been told such a car was outside the Lake County office later that night. Now I remember you told me that you didn't see any State car, but I also know that is not to say that it was not there or its occupant was not in your house."

LaRue was not looking happy.

"You can understand that I have to look into everything. The car is outside your house. Then it is at the office. What gives? Someone could say you are implicated."

"Well I'm not," said LaRue. "What if someone was at my house? That doesn't mean I drove the car up and killed Ellis."

The Dead Man Says

"So the other guy could have," said Lohman.

"So?" said LaRue.

"So who was he?" asked Lohman. "Tell me and maybe the both of you can alibi the other."

"I'll try to remember if anyone was there," said LaRue.

Lohman did not push it. He had planted the seed. "I keep asking people things about inconsistencies like this that need explaining. I explain the inconsistency. I explain how this is all going to come out in the wash. I get nowhere. For instance yesterday I asked Graybourne and Zenon where they were and first they told me none of my business and then they tell me they were with two people at the Pullman Club.   It would seem simpler just to tell me the facts to begin with. This is like pulling teeth. After all, what is so confidential about being at the Pullman Club with clients?"

Bungus said, "You don't want to know."

"Oh shit!" said Lohman. "More problems. Look, I don't know. I got to go." He left.

Lohman went back to his office and tried to catch up on his own paperwork. Later that day he had to be in court on a fairly minor matter and he had to review the papers to prepare for it.

That evening he had arranged to see Egon who invited him over for dinner. Egon let Lohman in. Lohman was led to the living room where he and Egon and his wife chatted for a while. His wife, Feelia, was a bit lit. She usually was. Feelia's maiden name was Goodbody and she had a good body. There was little else of merit about her.

The Dead Man Says

Drinks were served by a maid and Lohman explained why he was there and that he was supposed to make the whole thing go away so he was going to try to find out who killed Ellis.

"So," said Lohman. "You two were at the opera the night Ellis was killed."

"Oh yes," said Egon. "And what an opera it was. It was The Lady In Arrears by Gobini. Melba was superb!"

"Who?" asked Lohman.

"Gloria Melba. The Lady in Arrears," said Egon.

Lohman did not know zits about opera. He did know that aficionados of opera or any other high art took secret pride in their ability to bull shit about any artistic subject. Once upon a time he became curious about the art talk amongst certain partners in the office who talked about art gallery openings, art showings, the art in the waiting room and other art matters all the time. Lohman could not understand them. They used words, but he could not tell what they meant. It sounded like a lot of adjectival and adverbial bull poo poo to him. But maybe there were some decipherable principles in art appreciation so he subscribed to a lot of art magazines and read them and some books on the subject as well. Eventually he concluded that, as he thought, the art talk was complete bullshit. However, it took talent to do it. It is hard to talk for half an hour and say nothing.

Feelia said, "Sure. Magnificent!" Then she said, "I thought we were going to take that chest we got at the antique fair to Michigan Tuesday night."

"No dear," said Egon. "You will remember we left the van in

Michigan the week before and we drove back in your car. If the van had been here I would have used it. You remember my car was in the shop and I had to use my parents' car. Thank God I got someone to drive it so I could tell Phil it was hers."

Feelia looked like she had just had a revelation and said, "Oh yes, I remember."

"Was that Tambola?" asked Lohman.

"Yes," said Egon. He sniffed. "She was all I could find on such short notice."

Lohman could have explicitly asked Egon why he needed to lie about the car, but he knew perfectly well that a snob does not want to be associated with a Mercury. He couldn't resist anyway. "Well it was a Grand Marquis I understand."

Egon just gave him an annoyed look.

"Is that what you took to the opera?" asked Lohman.

"Don't be silly," said Egon. "I sent a livery service for the Fengers and the limousine picked us up too." The firm regularly used a livery service that provided limousines, even to take one person to the airport.

They then moved into the dining room and had dinner. It was coq au vin with the usual show by Egon of superior knowledge of wine. He made quite sure that Bumper knew the quality of the wine that was being served. Egon was a snob about everything else. Why shouldn't he be a wine snob?

For Feelia dinner was more vin that coq. Coq she'd get later.

The Dead Man Says

During dinner Egon started talking about the opera again and how the Fengers were enthusiastic about it too. "What opera?" she asked with a slurred voice.

"The Lady. On Tuesday. Two weeks ago," said Egon.

"We went to the opera?" she asked.

"Yes. You remember," said Egon.

"Oh yes!" she said. "Now I remember."

Lohman reflected that whenever he was in the presence of both of them Egon was always telling her what she remembered.

After dinner Feelia suggested Bumper stay for after dinner cordials, but he took his leave.

31 SATURDAY AT THE COLLEGE CLUB

Saturday Lohman spent the morning in his office going through client files and talking to a few other lawyers about work they were doing on the files. He still had a lot to do. He always did. But he did not have anything that had to be done right then so he decided to walk over to the College Club and have a good lunch and walk home.

As he was walking into the dining room he saw Swifty and Biffster at a table. They waived to him to come over and he did. They greeted each other and then Swifty asked Bumper to join them if he had no other plans.

Lohman had thought he was done with work for the day. Eating lunch with these two was work. Damn! And what were they doing here? They were members of a lot of clubs, but they were ordinarily Pullman Club denizens. He told them how extremely lucky he was to run across them and how ecstatic he was about joining them and sat down.

"So Bumper," said Swifty, "what's new?"

"Not a hell of a lot," said Lohman. "When I get home Glor will tell me."

They all laughed.

A waiter came and handed a menu to Lohman. Swifty and the Biffster already had theirs.

They all started examining the menus.

The Dead Man Says

"So what's good?" asked Swifty. "I don't eat here that much."

"Try the pasta with the curried cream sauce short rib meat balls," suggested the Biffster.

"I'm on a diet," said Swifty.

"Then do the fish of the day," said the Biffster. "It's usually good. And the house salad. It's usually good too. And ask me about the wine."

Swifty and Lohman both knew the Biffster was proud of his oneophilistic abilities. But neither asked. They both knew he was a bore about it too.

"I'll pass," said Swifty.

"Any news on Ellis?" asked Biffster.

"Not really," said Lohman, "Except now Graybourne and Zenon think I'm a detective. They want me to find out who did it so we can get over it. It's not nice. I have to ask people all sorts of nosy questions, like the police in the movies. I'd just like to ignore them, but the police do seem to be stuck in the mud."

"So what's the problem?" asked Biffster. "Just ask me if I did it."

"Well it's not that simple. I would have to ask some more detailed questions. I'm not the police. I do work for you guys. We're friends. We pal around together. You want me asking you where you were when Ellis was killed? And then following that up by asking other people where you were?"

At this point the waiter came and took their orders. Whenever you start to get into a topic at a restaurant, the waiter comes and interrupts for something. Guaranteed.

After the waiter left Swifty said, "So where were we?"

"I was telling you I would have to ask a lot of questions about you," said Lohman. "You might be offended by the intrusiveness."

"Oh, how could it hurt?" Biffster asked.

"Yes. How?" asked Swifty. "Just ask us. We'll tell you."

This was a delicate matter. How do you avoid pissing off some of your biggest clients, even though they asked for it? Especially since he did have some pertinent questions to ask them that they really might object to. Since there were a few things he had to know, Lohman decided to try it.

"We can start with where you were that Tuesday night," said Lohman. "Where?"

Swifty looked like he hadn't heard anything. Biffster looked like a deer in the headlights.

"Where?" asked Swifty.

"I'm asking you," said Lohman.

"You're asking me?" said Swifty.

"Yes," said Lohman.

"Why would you ask me that?" asked Swifty.

"You said I could ask," said Lohman.

"Yes, but that was hypothetical," said Swifty. "Now you are really asking."

It is sometimes hard to have an intelligent conversation with an idiot. On the other hand that is one of their methods of coping. Playing dumb has saved many a face. Lohman knew he was in the game. He could go a little further with it, but he knew now he could not force the issue and get a specific answer.

"Do you really think I did it!" said Swifty rather forcefully. "Why are you asking this!"

"No. No. I don't think you did it," said Lohman. "You know how these things go. You have to rule everyone out. So we find out where you were and then ask other people about it and confirm that what you say is so and that lets you out. Or I could be asking you to check up on someone else who maybe said you alibi them."

"Well I don't remember where I was," said Swifty.

Biffster came to life. "I don't remember either," he said.

"Weren't you at the club?" asked Lohman.

"Club?" squeaked Biffster.

"Here. The College Club," said Lohman

"No. I don't remember," said Biffster. "What would I be doing there?"

"The wine tasting committee," said Lohman.

"God yes!" exclaimed Biffster with a show of relief.

179

The Dead Man Says

"You were?" asked Swifty.

"Yes," said Biffster smugly. "Where were you?"

Swifty just gave him an annoyed look.

Lohman sensed he had come to the end of game. Either he went on to try to pin them down or he laid off. He was not going to get any further. At least one thing made sense. Some time ago the Biffster told him he had missed Kirkland at the wine tasting committee the night he was murdered. And one thing did not make sense. St. Charles had said the Biffster was with him at the Pullman Club. Not the College Club where the wine tasting committee met. And Swifty too was at the Pullman Club according to St. Charles. Neither was going to admit to it. Lohman gave up. At least, he thought to himself, neither one seemed to have had a motive to dispose of Kirkland.

Lohman started telling a joke to defuse things. As he was about to deliver the punch line the waiter brought their food and stepped on the line. Swifty and Biffster thought Lohman was just making some inane comment. They ignored it and started talking about golf and the Cubs for the rest of the meal. Lohman mostly nodded his way through this.

32 LOHMAN TALKS TO WINKLEMAN

Monday morning Lohman had made an appointment to see Gordon Winkleman. Ordinarily Winkleman would not see someone he did not know or, in the words of a storied Chicago politician of the past, "I ain't gonna see no one no one sent." However, Fenton, Pettigrew had made substantial campaign contributions to Winkleman's sponsor and Lohman had told Winkleman's secretary that he was the Managing Partner of F, P & C. That often got him through the door, at least with people who knew it was a large law firm. Apart from the fact that Lohman was connected with the firm, Winkleman would have no reason to see him - unless he was dealing with LaRue.

A sponsor in Chicago is someone with clout who sees that someone gets a government job. Lohman had once had a summer job as a court clerk while he was going to law school. He grew up next to the family of someone with clout and that person got him the job, even though he was not active in politics (as in being a precinct worker getting out the vote.) The neighbor had risen to being Chief Justice of the Municipal Court, which was a very clout heavy position since it was the largest of the courts with the most jobs available. It was not an election year and Lohman got the job because the guy liked him. He soon learned that even though only he and one other person showed up every day, there were eight people assigned to the unit. The other people would show up, miraculously, only just before some lackey from the business office came through looking to see if everyone was working.

One day after the guy from the business office had come through one of the other workers was still there and was talking to Lohman. He

The Dead Man Says

asked Lohman, "Who's your clout?"

Lohman was a political innocent. "What?" he asked.

"Your Chinaman," said the co-worker.

"What?" said Lohman.

"Your sponsor," said the co-worker.

"What's that?" asked Lohman.

"Oh, for Christ's sake!" said the co-worker, "How did you get the job?"

Now Lohman understood. "Oh, I see. It was Judge Benton. He got me the job."

"Judge Benton!" exclaimed the co-worker. "Then why do you bother showing up. We don't work here, we just get paid here."

After that everyone seemed to think he was a spy and no one confided in him about anything. He did find out, though, that there was a sheet where everyone was supposed to sign in and sign out. No one had ever told him about this, but when he looked at the sheet he had been signed in at starting time and signed out after quitting time every day.

Anyhow, by now Lohman realized that to Winkleman he was someone who someone sent, but not a big enough deal to be on time for.

Winkleman's office was in a large building from the 1980s which occupied a whole block. It was called the State of Illinois Center. It was about ten stories high and looked like it contained a lot of space. However, the center of the building was a large ten story atrium that consumed much of the space. As a result, the State had to locate many of its offices elsewhere.

The approach to Winkleman's department was the usual government office building approach leading to a department. Within the departmental offices there was a small waiting area that was separated by a counter from a pool of clerks and secretaries. Lohman checked in at the counter and then waited. He was about five minutes early, but he waited for forty- five minutes until the clerk behind the counter told him that Winkleman had been delayed and would be in soon. Thirty minutes later he was told that Winkleman would see him and he was directed to a door at the rear of the clerical pool. Lohman went there and entered a small secretarial office with several chairs.

The secretary looked up and said, "Mr. Lohman?"

"That's me," he said.

"Have a seat," she said. So he did. For about twenty minutes. During this time the secretary did absolutely nothing that Lohman could discern.

Then the secretary said, "You can go in now." Lohman had not noticed any sound or noticed the secretary receiving any other form of communication. He wondered if they just had a set waiting time.

He opened the door to Winkleman's office and let himself in. All of a sudden the decor changed from State utilitarian to Rooms of State. Grandeur.

Winkleman greeted Lohman like a long lost friend. Lohman told him how nice it was to meet him.

The Dead Man Says

They chatted. Along the way Lohman said, "I suppose you know some of our partners."

"Who?" asked Winkleman.

"I thought you knew Bungus," said Lohman.

"No," said Winkleman curtly.

"Well in any event," said Lohman, "I suppose you are wondering why I am here. You have probably heard about out partner Ellis Kirkland. Have you?"

"That guy who got killed?" asked Winkleman.

"Right," said Lohman. "We are trying to assist the police in resolving the matter. You know how it is. It's in our best interests to get it over with as soon as possible."

"Get what over with?" asked Winkleman.

"Find out who did it," said Lohman. "Our Management Committee has directed me to head our efforts in this regard." Lohman was proud of how he was doing. He could have just said, "I'm supposed to find out who did it," but that would just put the wind up Winkleman and he would probably just ask if Lohman thought he did it.

Which he did anyway. "You think I did it?"

"No. No," Said Lohman.

"So what are you here for?" asked Winkleman.

"Just to clear up a few points," said Lohman. He knew there was no soft way of doing it so he decided to get straight to the point. "For instance, where were you the night Kirkland was murdered?"

"Where was I?" Winkleman asked. "I thought you said you didn't think I did it. I didn't even know the guy. What business is it of yours?"

"No. We don't think you did it," said Lohman. "I know it sounds like we are getting into your private affairs, but someone involved has said you were at a certain place at a certain time that night and it is that person whose activities we are looking into."

"Who?" asked Winkleman.

"If I told you, I would be giving hints," said Lohman. "We want to get your information without any hints. You can understand."

"So when was this?" asked Winkleman.

"The night Ellis was killed," said Lohman. "Oh, I'm sorry, it was Tuesday, June 7th. Just about three weeks ago.

"Oh, all right," said Winkleman. He reached for a calendar on his desk which was near Lohman and opened it and started looking at the entries. All of a sudden he closed it and put it down at the end of his desk opposite Lohman. "I was eating," he said.

"Eating?" said Lohman. "Where?"

"At a restaurant," said Winkleman.

"Which one?" asked Lohman.

"Where I always eat," said Winkleman.

The Dead Man Says

"Which is–?" asked Lohman.

"The Courtland Inn," said Winkleman. "I was there till about 10 and then I drove home. Me and my wife were there." He paused and then said, "No one else."

The Courtland Inn was a restaurant at Armitage and Damen in a gentrified part of the city called Bucktown. It was about three miles northwest of the center of town. It was a well-known resort of politicians and had been for years. Since well before the neighborhood had become gentrified.

"So you went home after that?" asked Lohman. "To where? Where do you live? How long did it take to get there? Did you drive yourself? I hate to be so nosy, but we might as well get it over with."

"I live east of there in the Lincoln Park area. In the Belden Stafford near the zoo. Yes, I drove myself. I'm not the Governor or anything. They give me a car, but I don't get a driver anymore. Used to, but the budget was cut. Got home about 10:30. Went to bed. You sure sound like you think I did something. But I'll tell you, I have nothing to hide. I'm fully open about everything."

Lohman thought he was not being fully open about being at LaRue's house, but then again standards of openness for a State Purchasing Director are flexible. "So you get a car from the State," he asked.

"Yeah."

"What kind? One of those Fords?" asked Lohman.

"Yeah," said Winkleman. "Old one. One of those Crown

Victorias. They don't even make 'em anymore. Pretty soon I'll get a new one. They're arguing about which ones we're gonna get. Naturally, I know already," he chuckled. "In the meantime I drive around in this old black thing and everyone thinks I'm a cop. That's kind of handy sometimes. So what else do you want to know?"

"So you don't know our partner Bungus?"

"No," said Winkleman.

"Bungus LaRue," said Lohman. "It's kind of a distinctive name. He's down in Springfield a lot. At the State offices here in Chicago too. He's our governmental affairs partner. Used to be a Congressman."

"Oh him!" said Winkleman. "I've heard of him. I think I even met him once down in Springfield. I never had any business with him though. Is he the one you're checking up on? What did he say about me?"

"Oh, I think you can understand that these things are confidential," said Lohman.

Lohman and Winkleman talked some more and eventually Lohman took his leave and went back to the office.

33 LOOK INTO THIS WILL YOU WIGGY - WHAT DID YOU SAY GILBERT? - LOOK AT THIS BILL!

Lohman was not a detective. But Fenton, Pettigrew had investigators. Private eyes as it were, although their work was often confined to tracking people down and finding out things about their assets. Most of this was done by checking records on computers. They sometimes did other interesting things as well, which included actually talking to people and getting documents and other things and examining them. Lohman called one of them who he usually worked with and asked the guy to come to his office, which he did.

The investigator was Wiggy Rodriguez. He was a short, fat, almost round guy who was born in Mexico. He spoke English well enough, but with a heavy accent. Nobody took him seriously and as a result he could find out a lot of things. Wiggy was not his real name, but he was bald and wore a rather obvious wig so he got the nickname of Wiggy. Since he was proud of his wig, people just called him Wiggy to his face.

"Hi Wiggy," said Lohman. "I've got business for you."

"Hello Mr. Lohman," said Wiggy.

"I keep asking you to call me Bumper," reminded Lohman.

"Yes Sir," said Wiggy.

Lohman sighed. "Here's the deal. There is a Purchasing Director for the State of Illinois. His name is Gordon Winkleman. His office is in the State of Illinois building. He drives a black Ford Crown Victoria. It's a State car. He lives in the Lincoln Park area."

188

The Dead Man Says

Wiggy was writing all this down in a small notebook he had brought with him so Lohman paused a while. "I want to find out what he was doing and when the night Ellis died. That was June 7th. Winkleman says he and his wife, and no one else, were eating dinner at the Courtland Inn and then he drove home in the car. He says he got home about 10:30. I want you to find out if he was there, who saw him, when he got home, what happened to the car, who was with him, what was he talking about. That sort of thing. I have information that he was somewhere else during that time. I want to resolve the conflict."

"Where?" asked Wiggy.

"Not telling," said Lohman.

With his head down towards his note pad, Wiggy lifted his eyes to look at Lohman. "Confidential?" he asked

"Yes," sighed Lohman. And he thought to himself, "Everything involving the Devil is confidential."

"And one more thing," said Lohman. "You know Sean Featherbottom?"

"No," said Wiggy.

"He's one of our associates," said Lohman. "He was up there the night Ellis was killed. He left and then later his code was used to get in. You know Tambola Cook?"

"No," said Wiggy.

"She's another associate. She seems to have a crush on Sean. She says she saw Sean on Halsted Street later that night going into a gay bar

The Dead Man Says

with Jason Kunz."

"Him I know," said Wiggy. "Mr. Fitzhubery had me investigate him. So he could write up a report to get him fired he said."

"For what?" asked Lohman.

"He's a maricon - fruit."

"We don't fire anybody for that," said Lohman.

"He wanted me to dig up some dirt," said Wiggy.

"Did you?" asked Lohman.

"Nah," said Wiggy. "Just what straight people do. Different hole. Sometimes. I even went and talked to him. Nice kid. But queer."

"So anyway," said Lohman, "Sean and Jason both deny that Sean was there. Sean says he was at home. The bar was called 'Drinkers'. See what you can find out about whether or not Sean was there that night."

"Right," said Wiggy. "And what else?"

"So what else," mused Lohman. "Yes. I don't understand about all these cars. That night Egon, Mr. Fitzhubery, was at the opera with the Fengers and earlier that day he was driving around in his parents' car because his was in the shop. But his wife thinks maybe they were doing something with their van, but Egon says it was in Michigan. Anyway, they took the Fengers, Clay Fenger and his wife, they're clients, to the opera in a limo. Our regular service. No. I take that back. I'm assuming that. Try to find out who is driving what to where. Miss Cook says Egon picked her up that morning in a Mercury and had her drive it and they went to see a client and Egon told the client it was her car. Probably because he was ashamed to have the client think it was his. So see what you can find out about all the cars too. I think that's about all for now."

"Right," said Wiggy. "I'll get on it." He got up and left.

When Wiggy left Lohman went out with him to his waiting area and Gilbert Crane was there. Lohman had earlier asked him to come by. "Good morning Gilbert," Lohman said. Once again he was proud of himself for being able to use the correct name. He was not good at names and with hundreds of people around with a constant turnover it was a hard thing to do anyway. At the end of each day he wrote down the names of everyone he planned to deal with the next day on a pad on his desk. He read it first thing every morning. He had read Gilbert's name this morning.

Lohman wanted to know more about the car. After some small talk he asked, "So Gilbert, tell me more about this car you saw outside LaRue's place."

"Well," said Crane, "There isn't much more I can add. I remembered some of the license plate. Did the cops tell you that? I told them."

"Yes," said Lohman. "They told me."

"Did they track it down?" asked Crane.

"They did partially. They said it was a Ford Crown Victoria and they got a list of names of people who had cars assigned with those parts of the license number. I didn't know any of them. I had heard of one, a Gordon Winkleman. Did you ever meet him or hear of him?"

"No. Never," said Crane.

191

The Dead Man Says

"Did you see anyone there?" asked Lohman.

"No. Only Mrs. LaRue," Crane said.

"So tell me about the car. Was it a Ford Crown Victoria? First, was it a Ford? How sure are you of that?"

Crane said, "I saw the Ford name, the oval sign, in the grill. What's a Crown Victoria?"

"They don't make them anymore," said Lohman. "But that's the most common kind of taxi you see. Most are used police cars. A lot of the police cars are still that model too, but they're called Police Interceptors. You see a lot of them with the Crown Victoria name parked illegally outside State and City offices. And then there are a lot of them still used by detectives. They don't have the police markings, but they have the Police Interceptor name plate."

"Yeah. That's what I saw," said Crane.

"Anything else you can tell me?" asked Lohman. "What color was it? Any markings? Anything you noticed inside the car?"

Crane said, "I wasn't paying a lot of attention to it. I didn't notice anything. Just a car. It was black, I think."

"You think?" asked Lohman. "You aren't sure?"

"Well it sure looked black," said Crane, "but it was dark."

So Lohman thanked Crane and they took their leave.

Lohman was due at a Marketing Committee lunch meeting in one of the conference rooms soon, but he had about twenty minutes free. He called the Pullman Club and asked for the manager. Lohman was not a member of the club, but he was there often as a guest and had meet the manager at various times. The guy was an officious little snob polisher and lackey to the highly placed extraordinaire. Creighton Wurble was his name. Ordinarily he would not have given Lohman the time of day, but he knew how Lohman was placed and that it would be a good idea to court him. Lohman knew all he wanted to about Wurble. Ordinarily he wouldn't have talked to him at all.

Wurble came on the line. "Mr. Lohman. How nice to talk to you. How can I help you today?"

"Hello Creighton," said Lohman. "Hello. How are you?"

"Great!" said Wurble. "And you?"

"Fine," said Lohman. He thought to himself, "So that means I'm not as good as you, but you think that's the case anyway."

Lohman continued, "So we have this problem here. Our Business Manager gives me bills for June 7th. That was a Tuesday night. Mr. St. Charles and Mr. Cohenstein say they were there with two other people for dinner. But we have a bill for ten people for dinner and then later about $3500 for drinks. This doesn't make sense. Could we find out what happened here? Who was receiving all this food and drink?"

"Of course, of course Mr. Lohman. I'll find out and get back to you," said Wurble. "There is probably just some bookkeeping error. Wait. You said Tuesday they were here. About three weeks ago?" All of a sudden his tone of voice changed. From lackey condescending to lackey guarded and not so friendly. "Of course we cannot say who was there or what they were doing. We do not keep those kinds of records, nor would we release that information if we did." Now Lohman could hear the sneer in Wurble's voice. "And as you well know, you are not a member and we certainly cannot release confidential information about members to you or anyone else. At any rate, I'm sure it is just some technical error. The bill is correct."

Lohman did not want to burn the bridge so he thanked Wurble profusely for his attention to the matter. He got up and headed for the conference room for the marketing meeting. The main subject of the meeting was how much the firm should spend on advertising in publications that purported to list the best lawyers.

34 THE TEA CUP

After the meeting Lohman headed back to his office. Along the way he was passing the area where Sean Featherbottom's office was located so he decided to drop by to see if Sean was in. He was. The door was open and Lohman knocked on it and stuck his head in the office.

"Oh hi Mr. Lohman," said Sean.

"Have you got a moment?" asked Lohman. Why would the big boss ask? Because Sean had other big bosses too, many of whom operated only on a last minute emergency basis and he might have been engaged on one of those matters.

"Sure," said Sean.

Lohman came in and looked around. He had been in Sean's office before since he often went to see people in their offices instead of having them come to his office. For one thing, it got him around the firm so he could see things and talk to people. He had never paid much attention to Sean's office before, though. Every surface had files piled on it, except for a small work area in front of Sean on his desk. There were shelves along the walls, all filled with files. A typical associate office, except for one area on the shelves. It contained an assemblage of china. Dishes, cups, saucers. Mostly small pieces. There were little bells, little spoons and other accessories. Lohman didn't know anything about China, but he did know it didn't look like it came from Target.

Lohman came in. There was a guest chair with files on it. Lohman picked up the files and put them on the floor. He sat down. "So how are things going?"

Sean looked uncomfortable. "Fine. Fine. Except for Mr. Kirkland. And that stuff."

Lohman reasonably asked, "What stuff?"

"The cops act like I did it," said Sean.

"You did?" asked Lohman.

"God no! You don't think so, do you?" Sean was obviously distressed.

"Well your code was used to get in," said Lohman. "What is everyone supposed to think? All you can say is that you weren't there. You went home. But no alibi. Ms. Cook says she saw you, but you say you weren't where she says she saw you. She says you were with Jason. Both you and Jason deny it. But you offer nothing else to explain your whereabouts."

Sean looked very distressed. "But I didn't do it. I wasn't there. Do you think I did it?"

"Frankly," said Lohman, "I never thought you were the type. And you do good work and I want to keep you here. And I like you. But you aren't much help. Look, tell me more about what you did. How did you get home? Maybe someone saw you."

"My bike," said Sean.

"From up there?" Lohman was a little incredulous. "That's - how many miles?"

The Dead Man Says

"About twenty two to my place. It depends on which way I go. There are bike trails a lot of the way."

"How long does that take?" asked Lohman.

"Hour or so. Hour and a half if I don't hurry. Hour if I hurry. I've got a Schwinoped 980," said Sean.

"What's that?" asked Lohman.

"My bike. A lot of the racers use it," said Sean. Like Lohman should know.

Lohman got up and looked around and went over to the China and started examining it idly. "So did you stop anywhere or talk to anyone? When did you get home? Did anyone see you there? Any phone calls?"

"No. No one. I got home about 10 and I just watched a Hulu show and went to bed," said Sean.

"What's Hulu?" asked Lohman.

"A site," said Sean. "An internet site. You can see TV shows on it. I just turned something on. I don't even remember what it was."

Lohman's eyes focused on a tea cup. It looked like one he had seen on Kirkland's desk. It had the initials "EK" on it. He didn't know anything about finger prints so he did not touch it. He pointed to it and said to Sean, "What's this?"

Sean looked. "That? Where did you get that?"

Lohman said, "I didn't get it. It was here."

The Dead Man Says

"It's not mine," said Sean.

"But it's here," said Lohman. "It looks like one of Ellis'. How do you explain it's being here? You apparently know China. Is this Ellis'?"

Sean got up and came over to the shelf and looked at the cup. Fingerprints be damned, he picked it up and looked at the bottom. "Yeah. That's his. I saw it often. He let me pick it up and see who made it and all that stuff. He didn't let me use it though."

"So your code was used to get in, you have no alibi and you have one of his cherished tea cups. How did you get it?" asked Lohman.

"I didn't," said Sean.

"But it's here," said Lohman.

"I mean I don't know how it got here," said Sean.

"Do you know when it got here?" asked Lohman.

Sean said, "No. This is the first time I saw it. I don't know. I was dusting the pieces last week and I don't think it was here then. I would have noticed a new piece. That's weird."

Lohman pulled a handkerchief out of his pocket and picked up the cup. He didn't know if that was the correct way to protect any fingerprints. He suspected it was just going to mess up any prints. But he wanted to get the cup away from Sean. "I'll just take this for safe-keeping."

"Are you going to tell the cops?" Sean asked. "I didn't do it!"

"Look," said Lohman. "In times of turmoil some people run in circles and scream and shout. Try not to do that. What works better is to just concentrate on your work and do the next thing that needs doing. What are you working on now?"

"Mr. Fitzhubery just gave me this." Sean pointed to a pile of files on his desk. "It's a motion to dismiss."

"For who? Who's the client? Are we making the motion or opposing it?" asked Lohman.

"It's for Western Electronics. They are moving to dismiss a patent infringement claim. Mr. Fitzhubery says it's priority. It's due in two days."

"So you're almost done with it?" asked Lohman.

"No," said Sean. "He just gave it to me day before yesterday. Big emergency he says. I think he forgot about it. Anyway, I was coming back from the john and he was in my office looking for me. He was angry because I wasn't here. He says I can't leave without checking with him. You know how it is. Big emergency stuff."

"He came to your office?" asked Lohman incredulously. "He didn't get you up to his office?" Egon did not usually condescend to go to the offices of inferiors.

"Yes," said Sean. "He came here."

"So do that," said Lohman. "I'm sure it will occupy you. What else are you working on?"

"Well," said Sean, "When Mr. Fitzhubery told me to get on the Western file I was working on the Weinstein file. He had told me to get on that as number one priority. He told me Mr. Weinstein had approved it

199

and we had to produce quick."

"How long were you on that? When did he tell you to go ahead?" asked Lohman.

"Day after Mr. Kirkland died," said Sean.

Lohman thought. "So that was Weinstein. The day after Ellis died? You've been on it since then?"

"Yes," said Sean.

"But you just gave me a memo on that shareholder fight," said Lohman.

"Well, mostly it's Weinstein," said Sean. "You know I have other things to do."

Lohman did. Most of the associates were working on numerous matters, all of which were a priority to someone. Then he added, "Look, I'll do what I can with the police. But for God's sake, give me something to work with. If you think of anything, let me know right away."

Lohman then went back to his office and gave the cup to Tete. He told her the circumstances of how he got it and told her to call the police and see if they wanted the cup.

"So what could they find out?" she asked. "That Sean touched it? He just did."

"Well, what do I know about fingerprints?" said Lohman.

35 SWEENEY'S NEW CLIENT

Just then Sweeney came into Lohman's suite. "Yo, Dude-boss! I got a new client! This'll be soooo huge. Can I get cleared?"

Lohman sighed. "Come into my office," he said.

No one in the firm was authorized to take on a new client or do any work for any client until the firm had checked to see if work for that client would conflict with any other client. The firm also did certain other checks, like a credit check, and a snob check where the client was supposed to be checked for suitability.

They went into Lohman's office and sat down. Sweeney said, "I got an in with several Bulls players who want a new agent. They have an agent now they don't like. He's shittin' on em' man. It's like he's nickel and dimeing em' with thousands of charges for things he isn't doing. It's like sooo bad. And we got him red handed. He's also taking kickbacks form the team owners. He represents like 25 players in the NBA and about 15 football players. As soon as the other guys he represents hear of it they're gone. We can break his contracts with them because of fraud or breach of fiduciary duty or something. Then we can refer the players to an agent I represent. Smiley Gobean. You know him?"

"Not really," said Lohman, "but I've seen some of the bills. Who does the legal work for these players?"

"This agent guy, Man. That's what makes it so totally huge. Smiley doesn't do the legal work. He has me do it all. So I get these guys out of their deal with the badass and I get em' over to Smiley and he sends the legal stuff to me. And they will tip the other players this guy represents and I maybe can get a lot of them to Smiley too. Smiley does some NBA guys and he has a good reputation."

"So the sooner you fill out the forms the sooner we can do the check," said Lohman. "You know that."

"Can't we hurry it up? I gotta move," said Sweeney. "I have the only contact with them now, but they are just sitting out there waiting to be plucked. They told me about it and sooner or later they'll tell someone else."

"Just get me the specific names and the specific matters and a prior legal history on them and I'll see what I can do. You know. Who do they have contracts with, who have they been in litigation with? What other names and connections do these other people have? That stuff. Then we can work on it. Since we aren't going to be their lawyers to begin with, you can go ahead. You better tell them we represent Smiley though. Remember, if they are going to contract with Smiley as their agent, we represent him and we can't represent them in that deal. So don't tell them we represent them. Tell them about Smiley and make sure they understand that you are just referring them to Smiley and that we represent Smiley. But be careful of what you talk about with them until I get back to you. I'm pretty sure we don't represent any teams or owners or other agents, except Smiley. We do represent some ad agencies and companies that use celebrity and sports figures in their ads, so be sure to find out what ad and publicity contracts these guys have and who they are talking to about advertising. Who are these guys?"

"Dwante Bogasn and Shawnley Gibson," said Sweeney. "The Bulls' biggest names."

The Dead Man Says

"They are?" remarked Lohman. "Oh. I guess I've heard about them on the news. You have to listen to 10 minutes of sports news these days to get 5 minutes of real news. How did you dig these guys up? You're only tall enough to talk to their knees." Lohman smiled.

"Chest Man," said Sweeney. "I've been after them since I met them at one of the clubs. We were hangin' and chillin' the other night at a rave after one of the orgs and while we were talking this spilled."

"So what did you just say?" asked Lohman.

"So, like," said Sweeney, "we were at a rave. High class. It was in a rented truck garage. Had air conditioning and toilets and everything."

"What's a rave?" asked Lohman.

"Party, Dude."

"What's an org or orgs?" asked Lohman. "Some kind of organization?"

"No Man. It's like an orgy. A swizzle stick dip."

"You were at an orgy?" asked Lohman incredulously.

"Sure Man," said Sweeney. "How do you think I get a lot of my business? You get someone high. You get 'em laid. You get 'em off in a new way. You get a client."

Lohman asked, just to make sure, "You don't organize these things do you?"

"No Pops. There are so many in the music scene you just pick and choose." To Sweeney this was all a simple matter.

The Dead Man Says

Lohman was thinking of what St. Charles would say if it came out in public that firm members went to orgies. "You know, Graybourne would have a fit if he knew about this. And if it ever got into the papers we would have a problem. What would the conservative clients think?"

"Hey Man," said Sweeney. "At this level it's protected. These are celebrity and rich guy and big mover events. They are held in only a few police districts and the commanders are paid off. And nobody who attends is going to go around screaming about all the dope they are doing."

"You're doing dope?" asked Lohman.

"Nah," said Sweeney. "And before you ask, I ain't dealin' either."

"So what are you doing in these places?" asked Lohman.

Lohman knew the answer the minute he asked the question. "Gettin' clients and keepin' clients," said Sweeney.

Lohman looked like he was thinking the whole thing over. "Look," said Sweeney. "It's not like I'm the only one. You ask what St. Charles would think. What about his stuff over at the Pullman Club?"

"What stuff?" asked Lohman.

"The gambling," said Sweeney. "He and his high class pals have gambling nights over there. I've heard about stakes in the hundreds of thousands."

"What?" said Lohman incredulously.

"Yeah, Man," said Sweeney. "They go over there and have dinner and then join a big group gambling. Usually poker. High stakes. Real high.

And all the social register high rollers in town go there. They're proud of it among themselves. They think it's a secret, but a lot of the people in my world know about it. We got our gambling too. And the club world has a lot of people hanging around who work in places like the Pullman Club and see what is going on there. That's how I know about it. I know a waiter at the Pullman Club who works some of those nights. You'd be surprised to hear the names of some of the people who go there. Like some of our big guys and some of the clients."

"Like who?" asked Lohman.

"I can't remember," said Sweeney.

"Mr. Swifton?" asked Lohman.

"I can't remember," repeated Sweeney. "Wait. I can remember one. The name is a hoot. Biffster. You know him? I heard he was talking legal to St. Charles one night and St. Charles referred to him as client."

Lohman was shocked. "St. Charles? He was there?"

"Yeah Dude," said Sweeney.

"Gambling!" said Lohman. He paused. Then he said, "Biffster, I know him. He's a client. Do you think you can ask your contact if they had one of these events and who might have been there the night Ellis was killed? And if this gambling was going on?"

"I'll try. You get me going on the ball players and I'll find out who was there? Deal?"

"Done," said Lohman. "So, what else do you know about that night?"

The Dead Man Says

"And Kirkland," said Sweeney. "I heard he went there.   He thought he was a high roller I hear. But he was a big looser. Squares don't roll Man."

"Are they using that term these days?" asked Lohman.

"What term?" asked Sweeney.

"Square."

"I don't know, Man," said Sweeney. "He was square as a gift box."

"Well, apparently he wasn't there that night," said Lohman. "But when you are checking out who was there ask what they know about him just in case."

"Ok," said Sweeney. "Will do. What a jerk he was anyway. Like something you'd find floating in the toilet. Why don't we just forget about him and get on with life?"

But Sweeney was not done. "Why do assholes become lawyers Man? I'll tell you. Where else can you fight with people all day long and get paid for it? We should give everyone here a roll of TP to put out on their desk so if anyone claims we are assholes, at least we can say we are clean ones."

"Maybe forgetting about Ellis would be a good idea for some of us," said Lohman dryly, "but the cops are going to nail it on someone and until we clear things up there is going to be a lot of bad talk about the firm. The sooner it is wrapped up the better. By the way, where were you that night?"

"I'd have to check," said Sweeney. Then, "Oh yeah. I remember. I came in here a little late the next day and then heard about him. I was shacked up with Lottie the night before."

"She's your secretary," Lohman said unbelievingly.

"Yeah Man," said Sweeney.

How long has this been going on?" asked Lohman. "I just had Tete assign her to you after you asked for her. You know we don't allow superior/inferior sex." Lohman knew he shouldn't have said this as soon as he said it.

"We didn't do that position, Dude." said Sweeney. "I was just trying her out."

"God!" said Lohman. "I'm going to get her out of there right away. You better use the pool until we get you someone else. I'm going to get you an ugly old one. Keep your hands off her."

Sweeney could not resist. "Dick too?"

"Oh Christ!" Lohman said with exasperation.

Now you may think that this is something out of a bad book like this one, but I am telling you this actually happened.

36 LOHFAHRT'S THREAT

Sweeney left and Lohman's thoughts turned to Lohfahrt. Did he loan the money to Ellis for gambling debts? And what was going to happen about the money? Lohfahrt wasn't going to just forget about it. Lohman had already been talking to Management Committee members about it. Lohfahrt was talking about getting a new lawyer and proceeding to collect. Under the rules of ethics lawyers are not supposed to have business dealings with their clients. Especially where they get money from the clients for anything except fees. The firm might be placed in the position of having to pay the money back itself if Lohfahrt could not get it from Kirkland's estate or the trust he had set up to take effect on his death. Since Kirkland had had to borrow the money, maybe he did not have enough to pay it back. No one knew yet. So Lohfahrt had to be dealt with kindly. Lohman had already told him that the firm was looking into helping him get repaid. Lohman called him. He answered.

"Hello Qwen," said Lohman. "How are you?"

"Lohman?" asked Lohfahrt.

"Yes," said Lohman. "Qwen, we're still looking into your repayment. We don't know about Ellis's financial affairs yet, but we should know soon. In the meantime I have a few questions. We're still trying to find out what happened. For instance we found some of Ellis' notes. Now I really don't want to get into this at all, but we have to. I think that under the circumstances you will understand."

"Understand what?" asked Lohfahrt.

The Dead Man Says

"The notes say you wanted to come in and you threatened him. Did anything like that happen?"

"Well, it depends on what threatened means," said Lohfahrt. "I did tell him I wanted my money and that I was going to do something about it if I didn't get it soon. He said I would get it soon and I kept asking when and he kept dodging me. So I told him I was coming in to talk to him. That night when he died. On the phone. He told me no and we made an appointment for me to come downtown and see him there later in the week."

"I see," said Lohman. "Where were you that night? When did you call? That morning?"

"Yes. We talked on the phone in the morning. That's when we set the meet for Wednesday. That night, Tuesday, I was having dinner with my accountant." said Lohfahrt.

"Who was that?" asked Lohman.

Just as Lohman was remembering the accountant's name from the file Lohfahrt said, "Gunnar Pekka." Pekka's firm represented some of the biggest tax cheats in town. So did Fenton, Pettigrew. Lohman knew Pekka.

"Ah yes," said Lohman. "Gunnar."

"Yeah. Well, I know what you're thinking," said Lohfahrt. "Just ask him. And I have a receipt from the restaurant. I keep 'em all. For IRS."

"I'm sure you do," said Lohman. "Well, I just had to check it out. Thanks."

The Dead Man Says

They hung up and Lohman called Pekka. Pekka was a big shot in a big firm and he was not available. Lohman left a message. Pekka might call back. Pekka might not. Lohman made a note in his diary to follow up.

Then Lohman called Pigman in tech support and asked him if he could find any record of a call between Lohfahrt and Kirkland Tuesday morning. Pigman put Lohman on hold. And hold. Then Pigman came back on the line and asked for Lohfahrt's phone number. Lohman told him to look in the client database. Pigman put him on hold again. Lohman reflected on how much of modern life consists of hold. Pigman finally came back on the line and confirmed that there was a call between Kirkland's office in Chicago and Lohfahrt that morning.

Lohman then called Bigman Wallace, a friend of his who was a member of the wine tasting committee at the College Club. Bigman was his name, but he was a shrimp. "Hi Biggy," said Lohman when Bigman answered. "It's Bumper."

"Hi Bumper," said Bigman. "What's up? I don't have much time right now. I'm on my way to a meeting."

"Not much," said Lohman. He knew Biggy well enough that he didn't have to beat around the bush with him. "Do you remember the night Ellis was killed? Or maybe I'm even assuming that you have even heard of it."

"Yeah," said Biggy. "Who didn't hear about it? Yeah, I remember. Wine tasting committee. He wasn't there."

"Right," said Lohman. "He wasn't there. Biffster told me."

"Who?" asked Biggy.

The Dead Man Says

"Biff McCain," said Lohman. He wished Biggy would listen better.

"Oh him," said Biggy. "Yeah. Ellis wasn't there."

"Was Biffster there?" asked Lohman.

"Him? No. I don't think he could keep an appointment with God. Half the time we have to go get him. Why?" asked Biggy.

"So how could he tell me Ellis wasn't there?" asked Lohman. "He told me Ellis wasn't there."

Biggy said, "Probably because I told him Ellis wasn't there when I called him the next day to fill him in on a new wine we liked and wanted him to try."

"Did he say where he had been?" asked Lohman.

"Not that I remember," said Biggy. "Who cares? I gotta go."

"Just one more thing. Did you call Ellis about the wine?"

"Yeah. Left a message. He didn't call back. I don't think they have phones where he went."

"OK," said Lohman, "I know what you mean. I'll talk to you later."

While all this had been going on Lohman had had Tete make arrangements for him to visit the Fengers the day after next. Until then he intended to devote time to his own clients' matters, which he did.

37 TO KENILWORTH AND DINNER IN HINSDALE

Wednesday Lohman drove out to see the Fengers in Kenilworth. He pulled up in their driveway about 10 a.m. and parked his car off to the side. He got out and walked towards the house and up the front steps. It was a very large house, built in the 1920's. As he went up the steps he paused and looked back. He looked down the long divided driveway that led to the street. In the center was a flower and ornamental tree garden and several gardeners were trimming the trees. He thought to himself how much trouble it must be to care for a place this size. But then the Fengers had someone to do that for them. He turned and went up a few more steps and reached for the doorbell, but before he could touch it the butler opened the door.

"Good morning Mr. Lohman", he said. "We are expecting you." He motioned to Lohman to come in and stood aside. Lohman thought that, since he made an appointment, it would be odd if they were not expecting him, but he was well aware of the way those who thought they were among the upper classes on the North Shore had their servants talk. Also, he considered that the Fengers' condition made it a miracle that they remembered he was coming,

"Thank you," said Lohman. The butler led him through the entrance foyer and through a vast central hall to a library type of room and held the door open for him. The Fengers were seated in two chairs on either end of a tea table. There was a couch along one side of the table and two more chairs on the other side. The butler announced Lohman to the Fengers.

Clayton got up and greeted Lohman. Lohman greeted Joan while she was still sitting. Then Clayton asked him to sit down and Joan rang a little bell on the table. They all continued with little pleasantries and soon several maids came in with trays and set up a tea service on the tea table. First time ever Lohman saw tea on a tea table. Anyway, that's what tea tables are supposedly for.

Joan asked what everyone wanted and the maids served them. Then Joan dismissed the maids who left. Lohman said, "I suppose you wonder why I'm here today."

Joan and Clay looked at each other. "No," said Clayton. "Would you like a tea cake?"

"Oh thank you," said Lohman, "but I'm on a diet." He didn't want any tea cakes. So if they didn't care why he was there he would just get on with it. "I'd just like to ask you about the opera," he said.

That got them. They loved opera. "Oh yes," said Joan. "We love opera. Show him our collection Clay," she said.

By this time Clayton had already got up and was headed to a cabinet along the wall. It had glass doors. In it were papers and brochures in piles. He opened the doors and motioned to the papers. "We keep the program for every opera we attended here. Come on over and see."

Lohman got up and walked over. Clayton picked up some of the programs and showed them to Lohman. Lohman did not know much about opera, but he had heard some of the opera's names and he recognized some of the names of the more prominent singers.

"And we have all the recordings," said Clayton. "If there is an opera recording that exists, we probably have it. In the music room. Want to come and hear some?"

The Dead Man Says

"Not just yet," said Lohman. "A little later."

"So here," said Clayton. "Here's the last one we saw. We can tell because it's on the top." He handed a program to Lohman. It was for Rossini's Barber of Seville which even Lohman had heard of. "And here's the one before that," said Clayton. He looked at Joan and said, "Shirley honey, is this the one we went to with Egon?"

"I think it's Joan," she said.

"Oh yes," said Clayton.

"One of them," said Joan. "I think it was the one before."

"Yes," said Clayton. "Look here," he said as he was showing the brochure to Lohman. "I write down things about the opera. Here. See. I wrote Egon's name on the cover and his wife. We went with them." He handed the program to Lohman.

Lohman took it and examined it. It was for The Lady In Arrears by Gobini. The brochure was full of ads and listings of people on boards of various kinds with the opera house. Towards the back Lohman found the listing of the singers and other people involved in the performance, including each member of the orchestra. Included was a list of the stars and the roles they played. Lohman had even heard of one, the lead tenor. He handed the program back to Clayton and as he was doing so he noted another name written on the cover. "Who's that?" he asked while he pointed out the name to Clayton.

"Nellie Plochova," said Clayton as he read the name. "Who's that?"

Lohman was patient. "Yes. Who?" he said.

The Dead Man Says

Joan piped up. "The Lady."

"Oh yes!" said Clayton. "I often write the name of outstanding performers on the cover. She was magnificent." And he whispered sotto voce to Lohman, "Big boobs too."

"She was the Lady in Arrears," said Joan.

Lohman took back the program and looked at the playbill again. The Lady in Arrears was listed as being sung by Gloria Melba. Joan was going on about how wonderful Plochova was.

Lohman also noticed that the program gave numerous dates for the performances. The same program was no doubt used for all the performances. "So when was this?" he asked.

The Fengers looked at each other. Then Joan rang for the butler. He opened the doors almost immediately. "You rang Madame?"

"James," she said imperiously, "Tell Mr. Lohman when we went to the opera."

"Of course Madame," he said. "Which opera?"

"That one," she motioned to Lohman who was still holding the brochure.

Lohman said, "The Lady in Arrears. Do you know when they went?"

The butler went over to a desk behind the couch and opened the center drawer and brought out a leather bound calendar. He handed it to Mr. Fenger. Fenger just looked blank. The butler then opened the calendar and then pointed to certain entries. "Here is the last one sir. And

215

then the one before that. The one where you went with Mr. Fitzhubery. See. There is his name."

"That must be the one," said Clayton. "It's Tuesday, June 7th. See." He handed the calendar to Lohman.

Lohman looked. Most of the entries in the calendar were printed in a rather distinctive hand. Some were in a different print or script. The entry for that Tuesday was one in the different print. "Who makes these entries?" he asked.

"I make most of them Sir," said the butler.

"Who made this one?" asked Lohman as he showed the Tuesday entry to the butler.

The butler looked. "That one. That one was done by Mr. Fitzhubery. He was here the Saturday before and he wanted to remind us that we had to go to the opera on Tuesday with him."

Lohman thought, "Who is us?" But he could figure it out. He just wanted to ask it out loud to point out that he didn't buy the high class crap. But he didn't. "So Mr. Fitzhubery was here on the Saturday before? What for?"

Clayton took the calendar. "He was? James, was he here then?"

The butler looked in the calendar and pointed to a Saturday entry. "Yes sir. You can see here. I remember making this entry. You remember he and his wife came to take us to the debut party for the Hendersons' daughter. That's what he said. I remember he brought us home at about midnight. In his BMW I think it was. I remember opening the car door for us."

The Dead Man Says

Lohman asked the butler, "So he was up here twice that week? Did he pick them up on Tuesday?"

The butler said, "Yes, as I remember, he did. But Tuesday it was one of those livery limousines. On second thought, he was in it when it arrived to pick us up, but we came home alone."

Lohman had no further questions for the butler and he was dismissed. The Fengers and Lohman talked opera for a while, or at least the Fengers talked about it, and then he told them he had to leave. They were disappointed, but he did. Lohman felt they would soon get over their disappointment because he suspected they would soon forget he had ever been there. Or on what day.

After he had got in his car in the driveway he called the office and told Tete to get ahold of Egon and get him in to see Lohman that afternoon, if possible. She indicated she would do it and told Lohman that Gunnar Pekka had called and said he would be in for a while. She gave Lohman the number and he called Gunnar. Luckily Gunnar was off the phone between calls so Lohman got him.

"Gunnar you old prick," said Lohman. "How are you? Did you tell any fibs to the IRS lately?"

"You should talk," said Gunnar. "You know perfectly well it is our clients who are challenged with ascertaining the truth."

"Yea, I know," said Lohman. "So I'm calling because everyone here says I gotta find out who killed Ellis. So far no luck. But I am going through the process of finding out where everyone who dealt with him was. Where they were when Ellis was killed."

"So you want to know where I was? I didn't kill him," said Pekka.

217

"Yes, I know," said Lohman. "I'm not checking you out. But I do want to know where you were because I'm checking someone else out."

"So you think he killed him?" asked Pekka in disbelief. "He was with me. He couldn't have."

"Who?" asked Lohman.

"Qwen," said Pekka. "We were having dinner out by his house. Out in Hinsdale." Hinsdale was about 20 miles west of downtown Chicago. It was one of the western high toned suburbs. They had horses there.

"Yeah. It's him I'm checking on," said Lohman, "But I don't think he did it. It's just pro forma."

"Well, we were at the restaurant until 10:30 going over some of his business," said Pekka. "I drove him home and dropped him off after that, about eleven."

"OK. Thanks," said Lohman. "That's all I wanted to know. Do we have anything going right now?"

"Not really I don't think," said Pekka. "I'll probably be talking to you soon about this offshore stuff he's interested in, but it's not ready yet."

They bid each other good bye and Lohman started his car and proceeded down the drive way. On the way, several of the gardeners waved at him. He felt like some kind of English lord. Until he remembered that he was doing the driving. Then he felt like the lord's chauffeur.

The Dead Man Says

Lohman stopped at the end of the driveway and pulled over. He called Gloria and got her on her cell phone. "It's me Glor," he said.

"What's up?" she said.

"I'm up in Kenilworth. I'm just leaving the Fengers' place. Dementia heaven. Anyone else without so much money and so many servants would be in nursing homes."

"Right," said Gloria. "But they're nice."

"Yeah," said Lohman. "I'm going to drop the car off and get something to eat at home. You there?"

"I am now," she said, "But when you get here I'll be gone. I'll make you something and leave it in the fridge. What do you want?"

"Oh, I don't know. Just do me something. I always like what you give me," said Lohman.

"Ok," she said. "You want one of those salads with shrimp? I'll leave one in the fridge."

"Thanks," he said. "See you tonight."

She made a kissing sound and they hung up. Lohman took off and soon was driving into the alley behind his house and putting his car in the garage. He went into the house, ate, cleaned the dishes and went out again to catch a cab down to the office.

38 MORE FROM EGON AND WIGGY

When he got to the office he asked Tete to get Egon on the phone for him. He went into his office and began looking over the mail which Tete had opened and put on his desk. As he was doing so the phone rang. Lohman picked it up. It was Egon.

"Where are you?" asked Lohman.

"Here," said Egon. "In my office."

"You got a minute?" asked Lohman. "I want to talk to you"

"I have a little time," said Egon. "I could fit you in. If it's brief."

"Yeah. It won't take too long," said Lohman. Lohman did not say, "Your lordship."

"Fine," said Fitzhubery. "I'll see you soon." He assumed Lohman would come to his office.

Shortly thereafter Lohman arrived at Egon's office. The door was closed and Lohman knocked. "Who is it?" he heard behind the door.

"It's me. Bumper," he said.

"Enter," Egon commanded.

So Lohman did. He came in and greeted Egon while he was sitting down. Egon responded, "And Hello to you. It is a busy day. I hope you understand... ."

Lohman was not going to help him out. Lohman just looked at him.

"I am quite pressed for time today. I hope you understand... ," he said.

"Yes, yes," said Lohman. So he got to the point. "You know what I have to do. I'm supposed to be Mr. Detective and find out who did it to Ellis so we can get out of this mess. So I have to follow up on some things with you. Everyone else too, not just you."

"I see," said Egon. "Who else are you investigating? Do you not know who did it by now?

"No. I don't really know who did it," said Lohman. "I'm still checking everything out. There is no particular emphasis on you or anyone else."

Egon said, "Well I should think it is obvious where you should be concentrating your inquiries. Graybee, even Zenon, thinks you should just have Sean Featherbottom arrested and put an end to this. There are even those who have suggested to them that this matter should be taken out of your hands since you do not seem to see the obvious." He sniffed.

Lohman gave Egon a hopeless look. "Take it. Please. Maybe you could take the job over."

Egon wasn't going to reply to that. That was like a peasant telling the king to do the job himself if he did not like the way the peasant was doing it. "So what is it you want to know?"

"Well," said Lohman. "You were at the opera with the Fengers when Ellis was killed, is that right?"

The Dead Man Says

"I certainly have already told you that," said Egon.

"So what opera was it?" asked Lohman.

"The one at the Lyric," said Egon.

"What one was playing at the Lyric?" asked Lohman.

Egon did not know much about opera, or even like it. He only understood that the better class of people attended. He paused while he tried to think. Tried, because actual thought occurred to him infrequently. But he was in luck. After a while he said triumphantly, "The Lady Behind or something like that. Arrears. That was it. The Lady In Arrears."

Lohman asked, "Who was the singer?"

"There were a lot of singers, as you put it," said Egon. "Do you mean the lead?"

"Yes," said Lohman.

"Oh I don't know," said Egon with obvious indifference.

"What did she look like?" asked Lohman.

"Oh good heavens," said Egon. "Just like any other woman" Then he said, "Gloria Melba. That is who it was. Feelia said there was a piece about her and the opera on the news last night."

"So," asked Lohman, "How did you and the Fengers get there. Did you meet there?"

"Oh no," said Egon. "I picked them up with one of the limousines. You know the livery service."

The Dead Man Says

"The one we have on contract?" asked Lohman.

"On no. Certainly not," said Egon. "Not for a personal expenditure."

Lohman found that hard to believe. Egon would charge everything to the firm if he could. Certainly going to the opera with clients was one thing that would pass the accounting department. "So you used what service? And you are going to pay for it? You know the firm will pay for that."

"No. Our service was booked. I got another one," said Egon.

"Which one?" asked Lohman.

Egon had another wait to think moment. Then, "Midwest Limo Service," he said. "The car picked me up at a client's office up in Highwood and drove me over to the Fengers and picked them up and then we picked up Feelia and went on to the Lyric. After the opera it dropped us off and then took the Fengers home."

"So that was Midwest," said Lohman. "I've heard of them. What about the Saturday night before? I hear you were at the Fengers then too."

"Of course," said Egon. "We went to the party for the Henderson's daughter."

"Where was that," asked Lohman.

"At Olgosia of course," said Egon.

"You used the service then?" asked Lohman.

Egon replied, "No. My car. And I drove them home and went back to the party later. They can't stay out too late. Their age, you know."

"So when did they leave? When did you leave?" asked Lohman.

Egon's attitude indicated that this was all beneath him. "Oh Heavens! I don't know. We were enjoying ourselves. I was not watching the clock. I do not know when they left. I do not know when we left. It was late."

Then Lohman said, "One more thing. Gordon Weinstein gave the go ahead on his work didn't he?"

"Yes," said Egon.

Lohman continued. "So Sean Featherbottom tells me you were yanking him around - do this, no do that."

"He said that?" asked Egon.

"No," said Lohman. "He just told me about his work. I can conclude what is going on. Best to take it easy. By the way, when did you find out about the go ahead?"

Egon replied, "The day after Ellis died. Gordon told me. I told Featherbottom to get right on it."

"All right Egon," said Lohman. "I know you're busy so I'll be going." He got up and left. He didn't say goodbye or anything else. He just left.

Lohman went back to his office. Tete told him Wiggy Rodriguez, the firm's investigator, was looking for him. Lohman went into his office and phoned Wiggy. "Wiggy?' he said. "It's Lohman."

The Dead Man Says

"Oh hello, Mr. Lohman," said Wiggy. "I have a line on Winkleman for you. I went over to that Belden Stafford where he lives. I got the night doorman and I talked to the garage attendant. They're talkers. Not hard. The doorman says he came home about 10:30 that night. There's a garage next door and the attendant on duty that night says he remembers Winkleman driving his car in about that time. He remembers Winkleman because he doesn't tip and he usually comes in when someone else is on duty. A guy on the earlier shift. So what else do you want to find out about this Winkleman guy?"

"I was just trying to find out where he was that night. Did he go out again? Did the car?"

Wiggy said, "The night guy says the car stayed there. He got off at 6 in the morning so I do not know about after that. You sure you don't want more? I already did a credit and background check on the guy. Nothing special so far, but who knows what I can find out."

"Not now," said Lohman. "Maybe later. He seems to be out of the running. And his car too."

"Well, Mr. Lohman, I can always find something on a politician. It's usually fun. So just let me know."

"OK Wiggy," said Lohman. And as an afterthought he added, "Do you know Midwest Limousine Service?"

"I've heard of them," said Wiggy. "Why? What's up?"

Lohman said, "Mr. Fitzhubery was using a Midwest limo on Tuesday night to go to the opera with the Fengers. They're clients of ours. They live in Kenilworth and he says the limo picked him up at a client's place and drove him to the Fengers. After that they picked up his wife and they went to the opera. After the opera the limo took him and his wife home and then dropped off the Fengers later."

"Why Midwest?" asked Wiggy. "Don't we use Central? Doesn't one of the Swiftons own it?"

"Yes," said Lohman. "Why Midwest? Mr. Fitzhubery said he was paying for it himself and Central was fully booked. See what you can find out."

"Right boss," said Wiggy. They hung up.

Lohman leaned back and started to think about all he had learned. So far it was all a lot of miscellaneous facts. Sean's code was used to get in. Why did Lohman resist the idea that he did it? He was already up there. He was the last one there wasn't he? But why would he go out and come back in? For dinner? He couldn't have killed Ellis and then have gone to eat? Would he want to eat then? He wasn't sure the place was empty earlier? "This will take some time," thought Lohman. He did not have the time. He looked at his notes to see what he had to be doing at the moment and it was not trying to piece together what happened to Ellis.

39 EARLY JULY - THE FIRM'S ANNUAL PARTY

Thursday and Friday Lohman had a hellish schedule and he did not have any time for Ellis Kirkland. Nevertheless on Friday afternoon Wiggy called him. "Mr. Lohman," he said.

"Hi Wiggy," said Lohman. "What's up?"

"I checked out Midwest limo," said Wiggy. "They aren't talking. The usual stuff about privacy of their customers. So I found out who the dispatcher was that night and I checked her out. Found out a few useful things, if you know what I mean. Things her boss doesn't know. Talking points, if you know what I mean. They did send a car for the Fengers and Mr. Fitzhubery, but she can't give me details. She doesn't have the records and she can't remember when and where. She remembers the driver, though. I'm still trying to find him. He seems to have quit and I can't get a line on him. The dispatcher says he was there only a few weeks."

"Well, let me know if you find anything," said Lohman. "And find out where the limo went."

"I tried," said Wiggy. "They only keep the requested trip on the order for service. They don't have any records to show where the limo actually went."

Lohman sighed. They hung up.

Lohman was up to his neck in client matters and he ordinarily would have been at it all weekend. The weekend after next though, the firm was having its annual party. All the lawyers. All their family members, and all the clients and other people connected with the firm. Everyone of importance they thought they could convince to attend was invited. So Lohman was straining to arrange it so he could attend without too much disruption in his work.

The party was to be held at the largest hotel in downtown Chicago. The Swifton Palace. Naturally the Swiftons owned a chain of top priced hotels and this was the crown jewel. It was located in the heart of downtown and had the largest ball room in town. It also had numerous smaller ballrooms and meeting rooms in the same area and the firm took them all. Food, drink, music. Five different bands, each playing different types of music. Dancing. Entertainers. And a presentation where the firm gave its members awards and let those in attendance know how good they were.

Most of the people who attended loved it. It gave them an opportunity to mix and mingle with a lot of the best prospects. Others just liked the party. Some of course did not. The non-people persons. Usually some of the associates. But they were there.

One of the nice features of having so much space was that the firm reserved separate rooms to use as lounges or sitting areas, away from all the activity and noise of the party. Some were reserved for specific groups, like the ladies' lounge. There were separate clients' rooms and a large sitting room reserved for the equity partners. This was the key room. Other people who were select enough could be invited in. The rest could be excluded.

Lohman may have been the Managing Partner, but he did not have authority for the party. Responsibility he had. There were plenty of people who liked to play with parties and big deal shows so the firm had a committee for the annual party with all the would be party planners on it. They planned. They supervised. They had the overall wisdom and experience that made it the party of the year. They had the expertise and grand vision that each year placed F,C & P in the forefront of everyone's mind and lifted the firm to new heights. They fucked everything up and Lohman and the Palace's staff had to sort it all out. Lohman delegated most of the job to the business office, but he still had to deal with numerous problems every year. Most of these he could hand off to Tete. Last year it was dancing girls in a cake that had no air supply. What would the last minute problem be this year?

Friday afternoon Lohman went out and asked Tete. "How is everything? Any problems?" He fully expected the usual last minute big mess. None. Not this year. Not so far. It was the July 4th weekend and he could go play.

Wednesday he was back in the office and concentrating on his clients' affairs. Tete and the Events Committee were handling most of the party preparations. By Friday he had caught up somewhat.

He was going to go home when Wiggy rang him and wanted to come by, which he did soon thereafter. Wiggy came into Lohman's office and sat down. "I've got some of the background you wanted."

"About what," asked Lohman.

"Featherbottom and Cook," said Rodriguez. "Nothing spectacular, but often ruling things out is as important as finding things out."

"So what have you got?" asked Lohman.

Rodriguez said, "Featherbottom. Nothing. Nothing on his credit except he has big student loans. Just like a lot of the other associates around here. Half of them leave after they get the loans paid off. Then you guys seem to get rid of the other half before they make partner," he added as an aside. "So he has clean credit. His job history just shows schools and then here. He lives near Sheridan and Diversey. That's not too far from Halsted Street where Ms. Cook says she saw him. He is a big biker according to people in the office. Pedal bike. Not motorcycle. They also say he collects china. The neighbors don't say anything about him, although I could only contact a few. They don't know him. Not surprising considering the hours you work these guys. He dates a woman named Tammy Fine. She's a lawyer at a small firm. Well anyway, a lot smaller than this one. I didn't talk to her. No law suits. Nothing out of the ordinary. Mr. Fitzhubery says he is gay. So I asked Mr. Goren. You know why. He said it's none of my business."

Wiggy went on. "Ms. Cook. About the same. Less school debt though. She lives not too far away, near Addison and Halsted. No bikes though. From the office rumors she probably has brooms instead. She's called Ms. Leftwitch for some reason. The secretaries say she talks about Featherbottom a lot. She has a thing for him. She told her secretary once that Mr. Kirkland was holding her back in her personal development. She said she was going to do something about it, but she didn't say what. This was just a few months ago." He paused.

"Is that it?" asked Lohman.

"Yes. That's it," said Wiggy.

"So I'll see you tomorrow night at the party," said Lohman. Wiggy got up and left and Lohman went home.

40 SATURDAY MORNING OF THE PARTY

Saturday morning Lohman was back in the office in conferences with various people working on the purchase by one of his clients of a rather large company. The client's company was borrowing money to make the purchase with. The people involved in the conferences were bankers and their lawyers. Various problems involving the loan to be used by Lohman's client to make the purchase were being worked out. It was a large deal, so it was a large loan. Lohman's client was also in very healthy financial condition, unlike most borrowers at the time, so the bankers wanted the loan. Lohman was not like most deal lawyers. Most toady to the money which they see as being the banks and investment bankers. Why? They are dying for referrals from these guys. Also, just because these guys ostensibly have the money. Well, maybe they borrowed it all themselves, but they control it. Lohman paid more attention to his clients. One of the ways he did this was to have his clients talk to more than one potential lender at a time. Verboten in the deal world.

The bankers were busy telling Lohman and his client what their terms were going to be. Most business loans are very complicated and contain a plethora of restrictions on the borrower. If the company does not abide by them, it is in default and the lender can say the entire remaining balance of the loan is due and must be paid off. Some of these things can get pretty onerous and even ridiculous. Once, for instance, a lender told Lohman and his client that the lender wanted the borrower to maintain a ratio of accounts receivable to accounts payable of 5 to 1. The borrower had never had a ratio this high and none of its competitors did either. Lohman pointed this out and added that the borrower would be in default the moment the loan was made. The banker said, "Right. That's what we want. We like to have our borrowers under control."

No banker is going to talk to the biggest companies this way. But most borrowers are not the biggest companies.

Is this a bad way to treat a customer? Before the deal is even made? Not in the deal and loan world. By the time you are nailing down the details with a lender a deal is too far along to do anything else. If you don't get the loan from that lender you don't do the deal. And you have all sorts of costs that you have already incurred. Lohman learned early on to have his clients negotiate with more than one lender concurrently. No one ever heard of this apparently. But it made sense to him. The lenders who heard of it would pretend they would not stand for it, but Lohman soon learned that the lenders who wanted the loan could deal with it. However, they made such a fuss over it he did not let each lender know about the others until it was necessary.

Today it was necessary. The point of contention was the interest rate. Business borrowers did not negotiate the interest rate. They hardly negotiated anything else, either, but never the interest rate. Lohman's client wanted a lower interest rate. This bank was talking about a rate competitive with the other potential lenders, but they wanted it to rise after six months to four percent higher than that. The other lenders were not talking about that.

Lohman had just told the bankers and their lawyers that his client could get it cheaper, so to speak. At first they just told him that that was not so. Then he told them the name of one of the other potential lenders. They told Lohman and his client to stop that and behave - otherwise there would be no loan. Lohman told them, "Not from you at least." They said they were going to break off the negotiations. Lohman told them

The Dead Man Says

that was fine with him. He asked them if they knew the way out.

The bankers decided to stay and go over the other issues.

Lohman got rid of the bankers in midafternoon and then went home to take a nap and get dressed for the party. At his age he needed that nap to make it through the party. Hell, at his age he needed the nap to get out the door on Saturday night. Besides, he had to go to work. For some people parties are work. Which should not be any surprise since that is what this party was designed for. The work of promoting Fenton, Pettigrew.

41 SATURDAY EVENING AT THE HOP- WHERE WE LEARN THE NELLIE WAS NOT MELBA

At seven, Lohman and Gloria got a cab to the hotel. The party did not start until eight, but Lohman wanted to be there early in case he was needed to deal with any last minute snafus. A snafu is a particular type of problem that often arose in the last century. They still do. But this night, none did.

Lohman and Gloria mingled with the early arrivals and gradually the place filled up and became livelier. He and Gloria had a habit of splitting up and going their own way at these parties. That way each could talk to the people they wanted to without boring the other stiff. It unnerved a lot of people who expected everyone to be en couple, to use a Franco-American phrase. Lohman often wondered if everyone felt that since they were stuck with their spouse, everyone else should be stuck with theirs too.

Lohman moved about, greeting this person and that person. Stopping to talk to some. Short talks. Longer talks. The longer talks were invariably with people who he didn't want to talk to at all. But there were a lot of people he liked present. One was Bunny Goldberg. Lohman was going out of the large ballroom when she came walking in with Brad Zane, Lohman's college friend who was an editor at the Chicago Tribune. Bunny worked at the Tribune too. Now that the old rag was operating in bankruptcy and all sorts of people had been let go, she was doing dual duty as the society editor and music critic. The old Tribune would not have employed someone named Goldberg, much less as society editor, but times had changed. Bunny and Brad were both married, but not to each other. They often went to events that could produce news together and worked the crowd.

They greeted each other and moved out of the way of the traffic. "So what is going on?" asked Lohman.

"It's your party," said Brad.

"Yeah," said Lohman, "But you get the news. I never hear anything. Except problems and fights."

"That's where we get the news," said Brad.

"I don't Brad," said Bunny. "I make it up."

They both looked at her.

"Well, if I wrote what I think about all these most outstanding in the world divas and maestros I'd get the sack," she said. "Thank God I've reviewed everything that's playing tonight."

Brad laughed. "Yes, well you got the long hair set. You got the long hair too. I couldn't stand that crap. Nothing's been good since Frank Sinatra."

Lohman cringed inwardly at the mention of the name. Bunny laughed and quipped, "Good what? Good crap? Good manure? Good poo?" Good thing she didn't write it up this way. "As the one here who possesses true musical understanding, I might say each to his own."

"So what do you really like?" asked Lohman.

"Oh, I do like the classical stuff. I have to say 'repertoire' in my column. But I actually like it. I just don't like some of the big names. And

The Dead Man Says

believe me, some of the biggest names are some of the worst musicians. Just compare the St. Petersburg Philharmonic to the St. Petersburg Symphony Orchestra. The Philharmonic has the big name. The Symphony didn't even have decent clothes until recently. But they are the ones who knew how to play. And take the Lyric. Tonight they are presenting The Lady In Arrears, a Gobini work. It's one of my favorites, but like all big time operas these days it is performed in a house that is way too big for opera. A 1500 seat theater is what opera was designed for. With an open orchestra pit. Now we have 3500 seat theaters and you hear more of the audience than the performance."

"And the performance!" she went on. "For 3500 seats you need loud singers. That is the primary talent of the modern divas. The other singers too. They are not chosen for the beauty of their voices or singing in tune. They are almost all slightly out of tune with the instruments. If you've ever heard an in tune singer, you know what I mean. We're lucky no one can hear the instruments anymore because they are sunk in a closed off pit."

Brad said, "I don't think you wrote that, did you?"

"Of course not," Bunny said. "I write up the nice part of what I think and just don't say the rest. Look at the Gobini. It's one of my favorites, but not this performance. The soprano," here she looked at Brad, "The star you would say. She's Gloria Melba. She's one of the biggest. You wouldn't believe what she gets for one performance. Probably needs it to feed all 280 pounds of her."

Brad made a scratching movement with his fingers in front of Bunny. "Anyway," she continued, "She's one of the worst. She's not only off, but she varies her pitch. She varies her offness."

The Dead Man Says

"So who is who in that opera?" asked Lohman. "You know the Fengers?"

"Of course I do," said Bunny. "They're some of the biggest supporters of the Lyric." She was referring to Chicago's main opera company.

"Well," continued Lohman, "They were telling me they went and they were raving about some other singer. I can't remember her name."

"Plochova?" asked Bunny. "Nellie Plochova. It's funny. She replaced Melba on Saturday night a few weeks ago. Melba was supposedly indisposed. I think she was strung out. Anyhow, Plochova was terrific. She's just a nobody and she had an engagement with the Milwaukee Symphony's summer program and she knew the part. She was available on short notice and just ninety miles away so the Lyric took a chance on her. She was terrific. I was there that night just because I wanted to check out a change they had made in the sets. I had already seen Melba in the part. It's funny. There was a Nellie Melba early in the last century who was one of the most acclaimed opera singers of all. You remember her?"

"Of course not," said Brad rather churlishly.

"Well she was a big star," continued Bunny. "So now we get a Nellie who is not Melba and who is her equal, and a Melba who is not Nellie and never will be."

"Bet you can't print that," said Brad.

"She was singing on Saturday?" asked Lohman. "Saturday the fourth?"

The Dead Man Says

"Yes," said Bunny. "It was only one performance. Why?"

"The Fengers must have been confused," said Lohman. "Their book said Tuesday. But they had both singers in the program. One written in."

Bunny just said, "Well, they're often confused. Nice though. I once went to one of those Wagner borathons with them. Four hours and two tunes. At least the tunes lasted for twenty minutes each. On the other hand that's better than most modern stuff which is devoid of any pleasant tune. Anyway, after the intermission when the second act started Clayton was sitting next to me. The act started with the fat lady singing and Clayton leaned over and whispered in my ear. He wanted to know what happened to the overture."

"Are you sure you're the official opera critic?" asked Lohman. "Do they print your comments about the fat lady?"

"I write differently from the way I talk," she said with a smile.

"I hope so," said Lohman, also with a smile. "Anyhow, I have to get going and get the show started in the main room." He meant the Grand Ballroom. This was filled with tables where dinner was going to be served. The tables surrounded a dance floor which was in front of a raised stage where a band was playing "big band" type of music. This was mostly modern songs played in imitation 1940 swing band style with a lot more blaring brass , a lot more dissonance, and an electric guitar bass. Each instrument had its own microphone and was separately amplified. The microphones were in the instruments, not in front of them. Even the drums had microphones in them.

The band was on a raised podium behind a long table in the front of the stage. On both sides of the band were tables where various dignitaries from the firm and elsewhere were to be seated during the program. In years past the dignitaries ate at these tables too, but none of them could stand the noise from the band so the tables were now used only for the speeches and presentations before the dinner.

Lohman was not part of the show. He was not going to lead the ceremonies or even appear in them. That was up to the stars. St. Charles and Cohenstein together hosted the show. When Lohman said he had to get the show started, he meant he had to see everything was ready to go and then see that the dignitaries were assembled up on the stage and St. Charles and Cohenstein were ready. He also had to see that the supporting people were ready, such as the people running the tele-prompters. He and Tete had assembled a network of firm people to round everyone up and it was working well. Lohman himself and Gloria were sitting at a table in the front row, but at the side. In effect in a corner of the ballroom. This allowed him to see what was going on and to be able to get around the room if necessary.

All the guests were coming into the ballroom and taking their assigned seats and the waiters were beginning the service of the meal. The meal progressed. The food was good. The wine was plentiful. There had been plentiful cocktails beforehand. The band was blaring. Half the room was lit and shouting their witty conversations. The other half was soberly nodding when accosted and waiting for the end of the meal when they would be left alone.

Finally the time came and Lohman's minions herded their bosses and the selected guests up to the stage. So everything was set up. The assembled people could see the program was about to begin, couldn't they? They could see it was time to quiet down and pay attention. When

The Dead Man Says

did you ever see an event where that happened? Even when the band stopped playing, which it did. For this, and other reasons, Lohman had stationed his minions around the room. Each had a smart phone set to vibrate and at the appropriate time the phones had all started vibrating and the minions had received a text message telling them the program was beginning. They needed to be told too. Then they started escorting people to the stage and telling the audience the program was going to begin soon.

The crowd was still noisy so microphones with powerful speakers were needed and someone had to start talking into them. Not St. Charles. Not Cohenstein. They didn't go through the indignity of getting a crowd to quiet down. Someone else. The firm had two partners who were fairly well known outside of legal circles and they did the job. One was once a star quarterback for the Bears, Chicago's football team, and one had been an actress of note in her earlier days. They got up and did their bit and by the time they were done and had introduced St. Charles and Cohenstein, the crowd had quieted down.

The two then proceeded to introduce various people and give awards and hand out compliments. The awards went to both firm lawyers and people outside the firm. For instance, the mayor was there to receive an award from the firm's foundation for advancing the cause of homeless families. Things like this could go on all night, but Lohman, with the aid of some other sane partners, had convinced St. Charles and Cohenstein to keep it down to one hour. And they gave them a thirty minute script - which they took the hour for. The tele-prompters also showed the time remaining and Lohman, if necessary, could tell the persons running them to omit certain things.

42 THE COPS AGAIN

The blah, blah had been going on for about half an hour. The audience had been taking it fairly well, because many of the guests on the podium, like the mayor, were well known. Lohman was constantly looking over the crowd to see how things were going. Suddenly he saw one of the double doors near him open. It was hard to miss since the lights had been dimmed in the Grand Ballroom's audience area and light flooded in when the door was opened. Fricknoodleh and O'Malley were coming in and Lohman could see a large contingent of uniformed Chicago police behind them. He moved his butt and practically tackled the two officers. He put his arms around them and led them back out into the main hall. Tete was behind him and she closed the doors.

"Hello you guys," said Lohman. "What's up? We don't want to upset the crowd."

"We are having a warrant," said Fricknoodleh. "We are taking the Featherbottom in."

"Yeah," said O'Malley. "He did it."

"You need all these police?" asked Lohman.

"We are not being Chicago police officers," said Fricknoodleh. "They are having the authority."

"But you need so many?" asked Lohman. "This will do God knows what to the party!"

"God could give a shit," said O'Malley. "Where is the little kid? He

241

killed Kirkland. We're gonna get him."

Lohman had to think fast. He said, "I'll get him. Just cover the exits so he can't get out. I'll get him and bring him to you." Lohman pointed to a door down the way a bit. "There. That door goes to the service area and you can cover the service doors from there. You can get all the guest doors here in the grand hallway." Then he turned to Tete and said, "Get people into the equity partners' room. Go get Henner Pigman and give him a list of people and tell him to have our table contacts get these people in the partners' room a.s.a.p.! I'll give you the names on the way there. And message Sean now to come here - now!"

Lohman knew Tete carried a note pad and ball point pen in her purse at all times when she was working. And she considered this event work. She had it out and was using it. He turned to O'Malley and said, "Featherbottom didn't do it."

O'Malley said, "So you're his lawyer. So what. This isn't the trial. We're taking him."

"And if he didn't do it? And you made this fuss at a party where the mayor and some other people you truly care about are present and getting awards? And what if these guys learn the person or persons who actually did it got away? Or later it is revealed who they are and that you made a mistake? And that after waiting for weeks without arresting him on no more evidence than you have now, you were suddenly in a big rush to disrupt a party attended by a lot of people with clout?" Lohman added, "One of them is the mayor of Highland Park. We're one of his biggest campaign contributors. Look around. The Governor is here too."

Fricknoodleh said, "So how are you knowing what we are having for evidence?"

The Dead Man Says

Lohman said, "If you have anything more than the fact that his code was used to get in and he has no alibi, I would be surprised. Look guys, let's do it this way. I want to go over the whole thing with you and when we are done with that, if you still think he did it, take him. In the meantime he will be under your guard. I'll get him to consent to that."

O'Malley and Fricknoodleh looked at each other and they went about fifteen feet from Lohman and conferred in tones Lohman could not hear. Then O'Malley said in Lohman's direction, "OK. Get the kid." Then O'Malley and Fricknoodleh went over to the Chicago officers and spoke to their sergeant who gave them instructions to cover the exits.

As the officers were moving towards the exits Lohman asked Tete, "Did you message Sean?'

"Yes Hon," she said.

Then he started giving her names. "Get these people in there. Sean, his girlfriend, Tambola Cook, Jason. They can all bring their dates or wives or husbands. That's OK. St. Charles. Cohenstein. Egon. Patel. Stone. Weinstein. Lohfahrt. Let's see. Swifty and Biffster. Beth Morse. Jean Bean. Sweeney. Better tell him to watch what he says. Tell him it's serious and Sean could get nailed. Is Pekka here? Get him. Get the Fengers. Bunny Goldberg. Get Crane and Lady Fitch-Bennington and whoever - you know whatever boy toy she has. Winkleman and Bungus. Is Biggy here? Wallace? Get him. Who else?"

"Don't look at me Hon," she said.

"Well start with those," said Lohman.

Tete went back in the ballroom. Soon Sean came out. He stuck his head out and saw Lohman and the detectives. He started to pull back in,

The Dead Man Says

but Lohman said, "Over here Sean."

Sean came over to where Lohman and the detectives were standing. He looked queasy.

"Take it easy Sean," said Lohman. "This may be stressful for you, but I think everything will be OK. I have faith in you. The officers came here to arrest you for murdering Ellis."

Sean started.

"Take it easy," said Lohman. "Everything will be Ok. Here's the deal. I don't know who did this, but many things here don't make sense and I don't think the officers know everything I have uncovered lately. You are going to be under guard while we go through it all. If at the end of it all the officers still think you did it, then they will take you. But maybe they will change their mind. I don't know for sure who did it, but many things are going through my mind and it's time I sorted them out anyway."

Sean looked sideways at Lohman. Then he looked sideways at the detectives. He didn't say anything. Lohman put his hand on Sean's shoulder and said, "Let's go to the equity partners' room." He led Sean and the sergeant and the officers followed. O'Malley started asking one of the Chicago officers to round up the others that Lohman had asked Tete to get and assemble them to the partners' room

They all proceeded down the reception hall to the equity partners' room. By now Tammy Fine, Sean's date, had joined them. "What's up Sean?" she asked.

He didn't answer. She didn't push it, because she could tell something was wrong. She just followed along.

The Dead Man Says

Lohman said to her, "Be patient. All will be revealed. Everything will be made clear." Or so he hoped. At least when Charlie Chan said those things they turned out to be so.

The Dead Man Says

43 HOW KIRKLAND WAS KONKED AND WHO KONKED HIM

They continued down the reception hallway to the equity partners' sitting room and went in. It was basically arranged like a very large sitting room with upholstered chairs all around in random patterns with cocktail and end tables interspersed among them. Against the wall farthest from the door was a raised up platform with chairs on it and a podium with a microphone. Lights along a bar on the ceiling shone down on the podium. In one of the easy chairs on the main floor was Monahan O'Reilley. A glass and a bottle of gin with very little left in it was on the table next to him. He was passed out.

Lohman said to the detectives, "I suggest you place officers at the exits to this room. Just in case, if you know what I mean."

O'Malley said, "Yeah. We don't want just anybody in here."

Lohman said, "Or getting out. You see?"

"Yeah," said O'Malley and he asked the sergeant to have some of the officers guard the doors. "No one gets out without I say so."

Lohman then had Sean come in and take a seat to the side of and near the podium. O'Malley and Fricknoodleh each pulled up a chair on either side of him. Fricknoodleh told him "We are having guns." Then he showed his gun to Sean. Sean seemed to turn green. He sunk down in his chair. Tammy stood up behind his chair. O'Malley motioned her to sit down in a nearby chair to the side of him.

The program in the main ballroom had finished and the sound of

246

the various bands could be heard faintly through the closed doors of the room. Waiters had come into the room and were asking the few people there what they wanted to drink.

O'Malley said to a waiter, "No drinks. You guys get out of here." The waiter was speechless.

Lohman said to the waiter, "I'm sorry. These gentlemen are police officers and they are working on a problem here so naturally they aren't here for the social events."

Then he turned to O'Malley and said, "It would probably be a good idea to let the guests order drinks. It will keep them in a good mood. As you can see, the bar is in the room so there won't be any more coming and going."

"OK," said O'Malley grudgingly. He told the waiter, "Go ahead."

By this time the people on Lohman's list were starting to arrive. Lohman took to the podium and started greeting them, and asking them to be seated for what he called the program. Most of them were pleased to have been invited into the inner sanctum and sat and ordered drinks. Some of the equity partners and their invitees who were not on Lohman's list started to come in. Lohman summoned Tete to the podium and told her to arrange it so no more entered and to arrange for another room to divert them too.

Lohman was just noticing that one of the podium lights was askew and was shining down on Sean's chair, sort of placing him in the spotlight. He was just standing there pondering this when Sweeney came up in front of him.

Sweeney was looking up at Lohman. "What's up, Dude?" asked

Sweeney. "Goblat told me to shut up. If I didn't know her better I'd think she was on the rag."

Lohman came over to the edge of the podium and stepped down next to Sweeney. "Discretion is advised. The cops are here to arrest Sean and I got them to hold off while we examine the matter. I can't see him killing Ellis, so don't say anything to get the cops to go after him. I think I can convince them it isn't him, or at least it could have been some others. Look." Here Lohman took a note book out of one of his pockets. "Here. I have been going into the matter and I have been collecting a lot of facts and I think I can put it all together. I was going to go over this later when I had time, but I guess we have to go through it now." Lohman's hand surrounded the notebook. He held it out to Sweeney.

"You got one?" said Sweeney.

"What? I got what?" asked Lohman.

"iPhone Dude," said Sweeney.

Lohman opened his hand and showed Sweeney the notebook.

"What's this?" asked Sweeney, "The Historical Society? You got a horse too?"

"No," said Lohman, "I've got a car."

"What? A Model T Ford?" Sweeney laughed.

Lohman said, "No, but I do have a Model A." He did, in addition to his regular car.

"A model what?" asked Sweeney.

The Dead Man Says

"Model A Ford," said Lohman. "A 1931 Ford."

Sweeney looked at him incredulously and pondered what he had just said. Sweeney asked, "Did you buy it new Man?"

"Look," said Lohman. "Just sit down and shut up. OK?" Then Lohman remembered why he wanted Sweeney there. "Did you find out who was at the Pullman Club on June 7th?"

"Yeah," said Sweeney. "St. Charles. Cohenstein. Biffster. Swifton. They were all there. With a lot of other people too. Gambling. I know a waiter who does those events. I gave him some meth and he told me."

"Meth?" asked Lohman.

"Crystal," said Sweeney.

"What is that?" asked Lohman. "Glassware?"

Sweeney made a face to indicate that Lohman was hopeless. "Crystal meth. Amphetamine, Dude."

"No," said Lohman. "You take that?"

"No Man," said Sweeney. "It's just that a little drug here, a little there - it gets the job done." Sweeney paused. Then he said, "I don't deal or anything like that. I have someone else deliver it too. Can't trace it."

Lohman looked at him with a blank stare for a while. Then he said, "Look. Just keep your mouth shut."

Sweeney went off to the periphery of the room and joined his date.

The Dead Man Says

Most of the requested people were in the room so Lohman went back to the podium and quieted everyone down. Then he began.

"Thank you all for coming. You came for a party and now you are getting something else. You are probably wondering what you are doing here. And with police officers around. Well, I won't waste time. You are here because we want to go into who killed our partner Ellis Kirkland. By now it is no secret that the police think he was murdered. Many of you have been interviewed by the police."

"I will get to the point," he said. "The police came here to arrest our associate Sean Featherbottom." He pointed down to Sean who was still sitting in the spotlight. Sean sunk down further in his chair. "Ellis was killed in our Highland Park office Tuesday night, June seventh. He was killed between eight p.m. and midnight according to the police. You may not know this, but our computer system automatically locks the doors up there at 5 p.m. After that you need a code to get in or someone has to let you in. The doors were locked that night as usual."

Lohman continued. "After 5 people started leaving. From those who were there we know that by 5:30 all the partners and secretaries had left except Ellis. By 7:30 all the associates had left except Sean. Just he and Ellis were there and the cleaning staff. Was Ellis alive? The time of death is not certain. The police give a range that could mean Ellis was dead by this time. But we know he was alive. Sean says he conferred with Ellis about a matter before he left and he says he left between eight thirty and nine. Ellis was waiting to get the go ahead from our client Gordon Weinstein on a certain matter and Sean and Ellis talked about that. Ellis told Sean he had not got the go ahead."

"Furthermore," said Lohman while looking at his notes, "our

computer system tracks all calls. It tells us what number a call is from and what number it went to and it tells the times of the calls. So what does our system tell us? It tells us that at," here Lohman leafed through his notebook, "At 7:34 a call was placed to Sean's desk phone. It came from outside the firm. It was traced to one of the few pay phones left in Chicago. It was in a 7/11 store at Roscoe and Halsted in Chicago. Sean tells me this was a wrong number."

Lohman kept referring to his notes. "After that Sean's billing records have entries until 7:45. He says he left between 8:30 or 9:00 and he got home at 10. He says he rode his bike home. The cleaning people, except for one woman, had all left by 9:00 and the last to leave, Wanda Kazmerski, says only Ellis was there at that time. She says she left around 9:15 and the owner of a nearby convenience store confirms that she came in there shortly after 9:15. So that left Ellis there alone. She says she saw Sean leave earlier. What happened then? Ellis was alive and alone."

Lohman continued. "At 9 the computer records a call from Ellis' phone to our client Hodie Patel. Then at 9:15 the computer recorded a call from Gordon Weinstein's number to Ellis. Gordon confirms he called then and he confirms that he gave the go ahead to Ellis in that call. The authorization to Ellis to go ahead with the matter Ellis was waiting to hear from him on. Now I found some notes on his desk made by Ellis where he put down the date and a time of 9:10 and said Weinstein approved. Since the computer is accurate and the notes would be an approximate time, I think we can take it the notes refer to the 9:15 call. As we all know, computers never lie."

"What happened then is that at 9:30 p.m. a code was used to get into the office. It was Sean's code." Lohman pointed down at Sean again. "There is no evidence that anyone else came in after that until the

The Dead Man Says

employees came in the next morning. Ellis had been hit over the head with a bust and stabbed with a dagger. There were used tea cups on his tea table. No one knew about this until Jean Bean went into his office the next day to get a file and found him dead."

"Now at this point," said Lohman, it looks like Sean did it. Ellis is there alone and Sean's code is used to get in. These codes are confidential for security purposes. Apparently no one else has Sean's code so he did it. Open and shut. The police see it no other way."

"But first," said Lohman, "Sean says he went home. And stayed there. Does he have any witnesses? No. However, our own Tambola Cook says she saw Sean going into a bar at Halsted and Roscoe in Chicago named Drinkers. Remember where the call to Sean came from. A 7/11 at that intersection. She says she saw him go in there around 10:30 p.m. with Jason Kunz, one of our file clerks."

Sean sunk even further down in his chair.

Lohman went on. "Sean denies that he was there. Jason says he did go into Drinkers about this time, but that Sean was not there. So this presents inconsistencies. Sean apparently has an alibi which he denies. So did Tambola actually see him there? One thing I found out is that Tambola had Sean's code. She got it out of him earlier under some ruse. Was she near Halsted Street or was she the one who went in to the Highland Park office using Sean's code?"

Lohman continued. "Now, I looked into this Drinkers place. It apparently is a bar for homosexuals."

Sweeney said in a loud voice from the back, "Gay!"

Lohman said, "I stand corrected. I never know what to say. I just thought I wasn't supposed to say queer. Anyway, this Drinkers is in an area which I found out is called Boystown. Apparently the homo - gay area."

Sean could be heard in a soft voice. "I'm not gay."

"What's that?" asked Lohman. He didn't hear Sean.

Sean said much more loudly, "I'm not gay!"

At this Tammy Fine got up and went up to the platform below Lohman and said in a loud enough voice for everyone to hear, "He's gay. He's sooo gay. Believe me. Toe-totally gay. He probably was there with Jason. Sean and me, we're just friends. We cover for each other at events like this. We aren't intimate. You think I want to let some guy's Richard play with my Kitty?"

"No!" blurted out Sean. "I'm not gay!"

"Oh God Sean," Tammy told him. "Tell the truth. It's OK."

Sean leaned forward with his face in his hands and started sobbing. "I can't help it," he said.

Not good enough for Tammy. "Is that a yes Sean? Tell us all! Christ. I'd like to go to one of these parties where I could put the make on one of the ladies without having to worry about outing you. Tell us!"

"Yes," mumbled Sean.

Jason had jumped up and came over and hugged Sean. He looked up at Lohman and said, "We were there at Drinkers. He was with me. I lied."

The Dead Man Says

Lohman had been following all this and he finally said, "Yes. Well so much for that. If that's true that means Ms. Cook actually did see Sean and you there. Which means that she was there. So who got into the Highland Park office? Or is this merely a show for our benefit?" Lohman thought for a moment and then said, "We have another thing to consider. The whole lot of you could have gone back up there and done it."

Jason jumped up and said, "No! We went to Sean's. We were there all night. I slept there. He was there the whole time."

"What time was this?" asked Lohman. "When did you leave Drinkers?"

"Around 11:30." said Jason.

"So Ms. Cook went with you?" asked Lohman.

Jason made a face. "No. Just me and Sean."

"So," said Lohman, "were there any witnesses?" Then he turned to Ms. Cook and asked, "And is there anyone who can tell us what you did after you saw them around 10:30?"

Tambola just pouted.

Lohman continued. "Well, we know you were angry at Ellis about your personal development. You felt he was holding you back. And I have heard you said you were going to fix him or something like that."

"No!" said Tambola. "Well maybe. But I just meant I was going to go over his head. To you. That's why I talked to you about it."

Lohman continued. "I see. So we have your word and the words of Sean and Jason that you were all down in Chicago when it happened.

254

But no witnesses except yourselves and yourselves - Ha! - you have lied to us before. How many times have I told clients that when you expose a liar and he admits it and then tells you something else and tells you what he says is really the truth this time, well, you are probably getting another lie."

Tambola shook her head. "I didn't lie."

Sean and Jason were looking back and forth at each other and Lohman.

Lohman continued. "Well, at least we have a plausible explanation for the lies. Apparently Sean did not want anyone to know about his being homo- er - gay. But then we have the matter of the tea cup. Sean has one of Ellis's tea cups in his office. He admits it got there after the murder. He has no explanation of how it got there. He collects china. His code. Ellis' tea cup. No witnesses. Except of course Jason and Ms. Cook. Who else says they were together or where they were?"

Lohman then paused. He continued, "Well Sean, you possibly did it, but you possibly didn't. Same for Ms. Cook and Jason. What else do we know? Well, let us look at the other people involved and the other facts. First the car. At about ten our client Vic Stone tells us he was driving by our office and sees Ellis's car and one of those Ford Crown Victorias in the parking lot. So let's us examine this. We have another suspect here. Vic says he was there. So is he the one? How did he get in? Did Ellis let him in.? Probably not. We know Sean's code was used to get in at 9:30. Someone probably was in there already. The person who had the Ford."

Now Lohman had to cover. He had called a client a murder suspect. "Of course, in all this, one thing stands out and that is Vic's integrity and history of solid truthfulness. Ellis thought the world of him and there is no reason in the world he would wish Ellis, or anyone else for that matter, harm." Lohman paused again. He was amazed at his own bullshitfulness. "Is that a word?" he thought. A little voice told him, "Ask a bull."

Additionally we do know that several people planned to see Ellis up in Highland Park that night. One was another of our clients, Qwen Lohfahrt." Here Lohman cleared his throat and looked from side to side. Then he pretended he was examining his notes again. He was in the shit pond again. Not just another client, but could he tell everyone that Kirkland had borrowed big time from him and wasn't paying it back and Lohfahrt had threatened Ellis? No was the answer to that. "Mr. Lohfahrt had talked to Ellis on the phone that morning. There was a matter of some urgency he wanted to discuss with Ellis and he wanted to come in to see him that evening. He says Ellis told him to come in the next day. Did he? Of course he didn't see Ellis the next day, but he did come in and I met with him. What about the evening before. Was he there? In the Lake County office? He says he was having dinner with his accountant in Hinsdale. This is Gunnar Pekka, one of the leading accountants in the Midwest. I know Gunnar well. And Gunnar confirms that he and Qwen were at dinner in Hinsdale till about ten thirty and he dropped Qwen off at his house around eleven. Hinsdale is about 20 miles west of downtown. Highland Park is about 25 miles north. He could have got there by midnight, but it would be a stretch. Anyway, how did he get in?"

"Then we have our own Graybourne St. Charles. Our chairman. Everyone knows him. Why would we even mention his name in connection with this matter?"

Lohman paused and St. Charles could be heard saying, "Hear, hear!"

The Dead Man Says

Lohman started up again. "One has to go over all possibilities and we are told Graybourne was going to see Ellis that night up in Highland Park. Now, of course he didn't, but I had to check this out. In addition, like Sean, he had something that belonged to Ellis. He had an exquisite bejeweled letter opener that belonged to Ellis. Like Sean he could not say where he got it. Or, in his case, even when. Couple this with the fact that his whereabouts and activities on the night in question were confidential and he could not reveal them to me and you can see I had to look into this to make it plain to everyone that he was not involved. Suffice it to say that we have evidence that he was at the Pullman Club that night with clients. At first the clients in question did not want their business revealed either and could not say where they were that night. But," here Lohman motioned towards Swifton and then Biffster, "we have confirmed with witnesses that they too were at the Pullman Club. With Graybourne and Zenon too, I might add."

"It was confidential! Attorney-client," shouted Cohenstein.

"Hear, hear!" said St. Charles.

"Of course it was," said Lohman, "And that's why we can't reveal what all this was about. Suffice it to say that we do have independent witnesses and our receipt from the Club to show you were there. I just want to mention that there will be many people who will be grateful in due course for your charitable fund raising that was involved that night." Lohman thought, "I hope that gets me out of it."

"Who told you what?" said Cohenstein.

"Oh nothing, no one. I just heard you were giving money away that night so I assume it is another of your charitable ventures in the planning stages." Lohman hoped that would do. If he had to admit he knew about the gambling at least it shouldn't come out here in front of everyone. Apparently Cohenstein thought of this too and he dropped the subject. Lohman didn't think St. Charles was a good prospect anyway and he dropped the subject too.

He went on. "Now let's look at the car. There was a car at the office that Vic Stone saw. A Ford. A dark color. Black he said. Is this the car of the murderer? Who had a black Ford? Apparently a Crown Victoria, one of those cars the police use. It is no longer made, but there are still many being used. Public agencies use it too. And detectives." Here he pointed to Fricknoodleh and O'Malley. "So who had one? Someone named Gordon Winkleman. There is not much of a connection here, but he works for the State of Illinois and he was driving such a car that night." Here Lohman realized he was in trouble again. Was he going to mention that anyone who drove a black Ford Crown Victoria was a suspect? Or was he going to mention what Winkleman did and that he was meeting with LaRue that night and that Ellis had tried to get LaRue thrown out of the firm. And that neither LaRue nor Winkleman would talk, which made them more suspicious and that this suspicion could be held in abeyance by the most reasonable explanation, which was that Winkleman and LaRue were up to putting the fix in on State business?

No, he wasn't. He was going to fink out. "This is the only other Ford I could find remotely connected to this case. The connection is of the slightest relevance. Mr. Winkleman had once had some contact with one of our partners and he used this type of car. At any rate, we checked this out and found that Mr. Winkleman was home by 10:30 that night and the car came with him and stayed in the attended garage where it was parked." Lohman considered whether he should say how he knew where the car was before that, say at 10 when Stone saw the Ford in Highland Park, but he did not want to say the car was seen at LaRue's place. So he didn't. Winkleman was not a good candidate either.

"So what else," mused Lohman. He looked at his notes. "Egon. Our partner Egon Fitzhubery. There are some very curious things here. I might say there have been curious things all around since everyone I talk to either has denied being where they were or has claimed that everything is confidential. But what else is new? Lawyers deal in confidences."

"So what about Egon? Egon and his wife Feelia were at the opera that night with the Fengers. He went over to the Fengers' house to pick them up in a rented limousine that night. The Fengers' butler confirms that. And that the limousine later brought them back. The Fitzhuberys tell us they had been dropped off first. Usually when a member of our firm socializes with a client or hires a car for any reason they use Central Limousine Service and the firm pays for it. Egon says he was paying for this himself so he used another service. Midwest Limousine Service. Their records show that the car was hired to go to the opera, but they cannot say where it actually went. The driver quit and we cannot find him."

"The Fengers," here Lohman motioned to the Fengers. "They say they went to the opera with the Fitzhuberys that night. They showed me their calendar to prove it. Mrs. Fitzhubery, when I asked her, thought they were going to take an antique chest to their Michigan house that evening, but Egon reminded her that their minivan was in Michigan."

Lohman paused and looked at his notes. His notes were made in chronological order as he had made them. They were not conveniently arranged by subject. He found what he wanted and continued. "We know that the previous Saturday, June 4th, Egon came over to the Fengers to pick them up in his own car. Ostensibly to go to a debut party for the

259

The Dead Man Says

Henderson's daughter at Olgosia. At that time he wrote the opera date down in the Fengers' calendar. Tuesday when the limo came Egon said his van was in Michigan and his car was in for repairs."

LaRue piped up. "We were there. Me and Trina. I didn't know Egon was there too."

"Where?" asked Lohman.

"At the Henderson's party," said Bungus.

"Did you see them?" asked Lohman.

Bungus looked at Trina. She shook her head. "No," he said. "It was a big party."

Feelia added, "We go to so many parties."

Joan Fenger said. "You mean April Henderson? How could she be coming out? She's just twelve or something like that. It seems just like she just had first communion."

"But we were at the coming out party Shirley," said Clayton.

"When?" she asked.

"When Egon said," is what Clayton had to say.

"When was that?" asked Joan.

Clayton turned towards Egon and asked, "When was that?"

"Saturday," said Egon.

Clayton turned to Joan and said, "Saturday."

The Dead Man Says

Lohman collected his thoughts for a moment and then went on. "Why do I go into all this? The opera was the Lady In Arrears by Gobini. It was at the Lyric Opera over here on Wacker Drive." Lohman motioned in that direction. "The Fengers are great opera buffs and they keep all the programs. They had the program for this one. They wrote on it Egon's and Feelia's names and the name of the lead singer. 'Diva', the opera people say. The name was Nellie Plochova. Yet the singer listed in the program for the part was Gloria Melba. Bunny Goldberg, you all know her," Lohman pointed to her. "She's the music critic for the Tribune. She tells me Nellie Plochova was an emergency fill in for Gloria Melba for only one night and that was Saturday. She did not sing on the night - Tuesday - that Ellis was killed."

"When did they go to the opera? The Fengers are not always clear on their dates and things." Lohman did not have to explain this to those who knew them and the Fengers themselves did not pay much attention to it - or anything else. As for Feelia, what could Lohman say? "Feelia is unclear about the days too. Unfortunately she has a rare medical condition that brings on temporary memory lapse. Egon himself says the singer was Gloria Melba. So maybe that is where he was on Tuesday."

Lohman looked at his notes again. "Well what about motive. Why would Sean kill Ellis? Ellis did not approve of Sean and he was tough on Sean, but we know he held all the associates to high social and work standards. Jason Kunz? I don't know if he had much to do with Ellis. In any case there has been no suggestion of a motive that I've heard of. Egon though. Egon gets all, or most of, Ellis's clients. Of course, lots of people in the firm who are just under the big billers have this motive to kill their superior partners."

The Dead Man Says

"What we do know is that shortly after the killing Egon had a file off of Ellis' desk in his office. The World Systems file. He can't say when he got it. And let's see about things in peoples' offices. The tea cup belonging to Ellis in Sean's office. And his ornamental letter opener in Graybourne's office. Are those people the only people who could have got those things and put the things in their offices? Egon is frequently in Greybourne's office. One of the most frequent visitors. As a matter of fact, almost every time I go there, at least in the early morning visits." Lohman now took pride in the fact that he did not claim Egon's visits were to renew the brown cast to his nose. "And we know that shortly before I found the tea cup in Sean's office Egon was there to give Sean instructions. He hardly ever goes to an associate's office."

"Now about the tea cups in Ellis's office," said Lohman. "It looks like Ellis had tea with someone that night. We in the firm all know that Ellis was quite proud of his social background and rank and he was careful about who he had contact with." That didn't sound too good to Lohman so he added, "As, by necessity, are all people of importance." That didn't sound much better. So he moved on. "As for the tea, it was a ritual with him. He would do it only with people of similar standing. For instance, I am the Managing Partner, but I am of plain background and he not once asked me to tea with him. Would he have tea with Sean? No. Sean was an associate. That alone determined the matter. In addition, Ellis did not approve of Sean's background. Would he have tea with Egon? Yes. I have heard that they did it many times. Who else? Certainly Graybourne. They were 'at tea', as they put it, many times. But since we have no evidence Graybourne was there, this means nothing with respect to him."

"And the car. There was a black Ford Crown Victoria up there. Who was driving a black Ford Crown Victoria that night other that Mr. Winkleman? No one that I know of who is connected to this matter. But

The Dead Man Says

Egon was driving his parents' Mercury Grand Marquis earlier that day. A dark blue Mercury Grand Marquis. This is actually the same car as a Ford Crown Victoria with a different grille and different name plates. At night in a dark lot it will look exactly like the Ford Crown Victoria and the dark blue will be indistinguishable from black."

Lohman continued. "Later, in the evening, he picked up the Fengers in a limousine. This is confirmed. What he did after that is not. The limousine came back with the Fengers and without Egon. Supposedly it dropped him off on the way back from the opera. Of course the Fengers themselves seem to confirm this." Lohman added, "In their own way."

"So," continued Lohman. "Egon is starting to look like a suspect too. But like all the rest except Sean or Ms. Cook, how did he get in? Well I'll tell you how he could have got Sean's code. Our computer system would show if anyone, here I'll use newspeak, if anyone accessed Sean's code since it was assigned. No one did. So Egon couldn't have got it that way and Sean says he never gave it to anyone except Ms. Cook."

Tambola said, "I don't have his code!"

Lohman said, "Sean tells me one evening you called him and asked for his code to get into the Lake County office and told him you forgot your code so you wanted his to get in. Is that so? Did you?"

Tambola just blew out her cheeks and sat mute with her eyes looking from side to side.

"Well," said Lohman, "What about it?"

"I don't remember," she said.

"So," said Lohman, "did you ever give the code to anyone else?"

263

The Dead Man Says

"I don't remember," was her response. "How could I? I didn't even know I had it."

Lohman looked at his notes and then said, "Well, so far as we know then, the code stays with Sean. However, Sean went up to the Highland Park office with Egon not too long before June 7th, the night of the murder. This was after hours and a code was needed to get in. When Sean was entering his code Egon was standing right behind him. Egon spoke to Sean from this position and Sean tells me it was like Egon was speaking right in his ear. Certainly from that position Egon may have been able to see the keys Sean was touching. So - Ms. Cook and Egon. And Sean. Maybe one of them used the code."

44 THE DEAD MAN SAYS

Lohman stopped and looked around. "So that is about what we know. Nothing definite. No hard proof of anything. Except for one thing. Gordon Weinstein gave Ellis the go ahead in a phone call at 9:15. Ellis made a note of it. Everyone else had left the place. No one was there and Ellis did not call anyone after that to tell them. Then he was killed. Who would know that Gordon gave the approval? Someone Gordon told? He told no one until the following Thursday when he told Egon. Yet before that, on Wednesday, Egon told Sean that Gordon had approved and told Sean to get to work on the matter. Gordon did not tell him until the following day. Where did he get the information? The only place that information existed was in Gordon's head and Ellis' head and Ellis' notes. He had to get it from Ellis. Either Ellis told him or he saw Ellis' notes. In this case the dead man says who killed him. The dead man says - Egon, you did it."

Egon got up and shouted at Lohman, "You insolent swine!" and he ran for the door. A kindly Chicago police officer detained him before he could leave the room and Fricknoodleh and O'Malley soon collared him.

Lohman then continued from the podium, thanking everyone for being there and for all their help in resolving the matter. The cops took Egon away and the doors were thrown open and the sound of music could be heard coming from the other rooms. Couple, by couple, the room emptied as people went off to enjoy the rest of the party.

Monica Platt came up to the podium and said, "Great show Bumper! We loved it!"

The Dead Man Says

As Lohman was stepping down from the podium he responded, "Unfortunately this isn't show business where what matters is getting your name mentioned, regardless of what is said about you. All this can't be good PR. What do you think? Could we put out a story that Egon is mentally ill or something?"

As they were walking out Gloria came up and the three walked off towards the music together.

Tete was still seated in the room with her husband and she saw this. To no one in particular she said, "See. Look at that will you!"

The Dead Man Says

DON'T COMPLAIN. YOU WERE WARNED UP FRONT.

The Dead Man Says

For more of the Dead One series

go to:

DONNIESYELLOWBALLBOOKS.COM

Made in the USA
Charleston, SC
22 January 2015